taking place in the world. Therefore, we are very pleased to bring DD readers a new interview with Peter, as well as a new article in which he details his notion of sinister forces.

Also this issue, as evidenced by his handsomely gracing the cover, we have a new interview and a piece of original fiction from author Paul Tremblay, of whom Stephen King recently remarked that Paul "scared the living hell out of me… and I'm pretty hard to scare." JournalStone's own Douglas Wynne conducted the interview for DD again and did an excellent job. Be sure not to miss this one! We also have a new interview with legendary editor Ellen Datlow conducted by Chris Kelso, in which Ellen updates us on her several recent anthologies to hit the market.[1]

The fiction in this issue explores the *Supernaturalism* theme from a variety of approaches. In addition to Paul Tremblay's excellent new piece, we have a visceral new horror story from female Cenobite Barbie Wilde, which is sure to mess with your eyes. Veteran horror author Brian Lumley of the *Necroscope®* series brings us a haunting new Irish ghost story. Weird fictionist Reggie Oliver offers a new strange tale that plays with the multi-perspectivalism of the theme, and rising speculative fiction authors Molly Tanzer and Bracken MacLeod both plunge their readers

into the subtle, uncertain, and atmospheric tones of the supernatural world.

For our nonfiction, besides the interviews, and the new article from Peter Levenda, we have a great special review of the *Fantasia Film Festival* from Nancy Kilpatrick, which is hugely informative in terms of what horror films you need to be watching. Donald Tyson in his column Murmurs in the Dark explores astral travel and dreams. The insightful Laird Baron offers his recurring The Black Barony column, plus there are two horror film feature reviews by Colleen Wanglund. Richard Dansky and Robert Morrish deliver great new columns, including an interview with Kelley Wilde. Unfortunately Mike Davis had to step down from doing his Weird Reflections column to focus on his *Lovecraft eZine* book-line, but to the rescue is JournalStone's Brett Talley, author of *That Which Should Not Be*, who will take over discussing Lovecraft and weird fiction for the Weird Reflections segment until Mike can make his return.

And now, without further ado… on with the show…

—AARON J. FRENCH
EDITOR-IN-CHIEF

---

1   Incidentally, Ellen Datlow's initials are *ED*—I'm just saying, ed. are also the initials for editor! Talk about being born for this stuff…

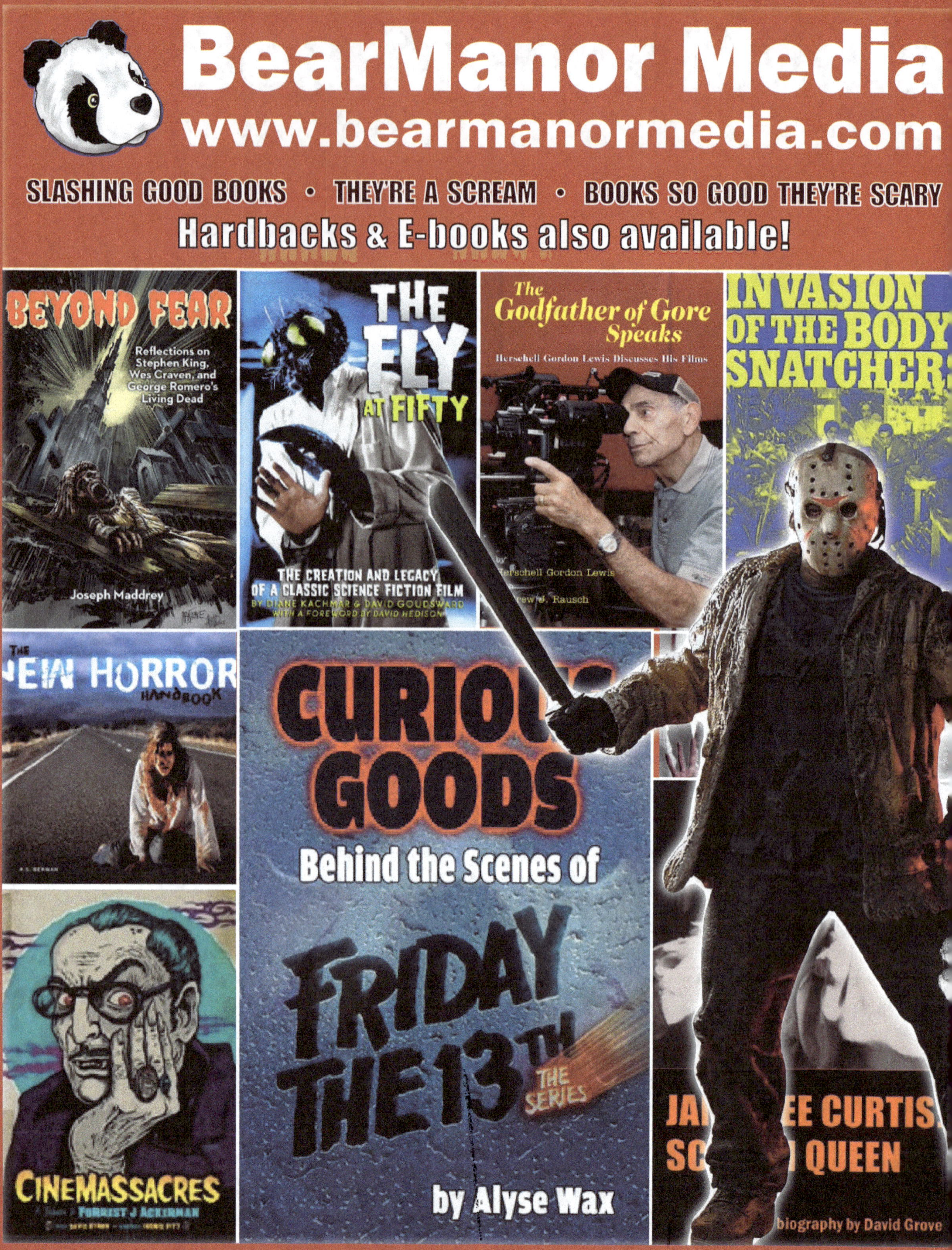
BearManor Media
www.bearmanormedia.com
SLASHING GOOD BOOKS • THEY'RE A SCREAM • BOOKS SO GOOD THEY'RE SCARY
Hardbacks & E-books also available!
BEYOND FEAR
Reflections on Stephen King, Wes Craven, and George Romero's Living Dead
Joseph Maddrey
THE FLY AT FIFTY
THE CREATION AND LEGACY OF A CLASSIC SCIENCE FICTION FILM
The Godfather of Gore Speaks
Herschell Gordon Lewis Discusses His Films
INVASION OF THE BODY
THE NEW HORROR HANDBOOK
CURIOUS GOODS
Behind the Scenes of
FRIDAY THE 13TH THE SERIES
by Alyse Wax
CINEMASSACRES
biography by David Grove

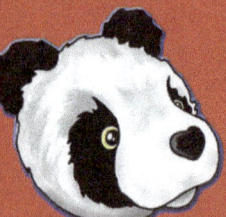

DARK DISCOVERIES

Winter 2017, Issue Number 37, www.DarkDiscoveries.com

Publisher
JournalStone Publishing, LLC

Editor-in-Chief and Art Director
Aaron J. French

Assistant Editors
Russ Thompson (Senior Submissions Editor)
Stuart Conover (Assistant Reviews Editor)

Layout and Design
Paul Fry

Contributors

Aaron J. French
Peter Levenda
Paul Tremblay
Douglas Wynne
Reggie Oliver
Brian Lumley
Bracken MacLeod
Barbie Wilde
Molly Tanzer
Chris Kelso

Ellen Datlow
Nancy Kilpatrick
Laird Barron
Colleen Wanglund
Kelley Wilde
Donald Tyson
Robert Morrish
Brett Talley
Richard Dansky

Founding Publisher and Editor
James R. Beach

Special Thanks

Peter Levenda
Paul Tremblay
Douglas Wynne
Jen Salt

Kelley Wilde
Nancy Kilpatrick
The Lumleys
K. H. Vaughan

Contributing Artists/Photographers
Jen Salt (front cover and interior photographer)
Jen Salt (cover art)
Greg Chapman (pg 49 & 67)
Steve Santiago (pg 13 & 77)
Luke Spooner (pg 27 & 91)

DARK DISCOVERIES
(ISSN 1548-6842) is published (Qtrly) by
JournalStone Publications
3205 Sassafras Trail, Carbondale, IL 62901

Christopher C. Payne
JournalStone Publications
3205 Sassafras Trail, Carbondale, IL 62901, U.S.A.
christophercpayne@journalstone.com.

Please make check or money order payable to:
JournalStone Publishing and send to the address above.
Credit/Debit cards via Paypal at:
christophercpayne@journalstone.com. Advertising
rates available. Discounts for bulk and standing retail
orders.

EDITORIAL

In the modern scientific age, with its iPhones, *Pokémon Go* augmented reality games, quantum computers, and so much more, we have grown accustomed to seeking for the causes of events in material factors. The allure of the physical has become so great that this makes absolute sense. We can mine certain rare minerals in the African Congo and extract a valuable element known as columbite–tantalite, which is used in smartphones, DVD players, video game systems, tablets, and computers. This is truly an astounding feat that boggles the mind. No wonder we have become so deferential toward physical conditions.

In the world of scholarship, this is referred to as materialism, and it has its roots in Marxism and various thinkers of his time. Materialism states that material factors connected to the physical world determine events, not supernatural or metaphysical ones.

If a person exhibits deranged behavior and madness, modern people look to the world of psychiatry to understand what's wrong with the person. Madness is caused by mental illness, not demonic possession. Any rationally thinking human being comes to this conclusion. However, this of course says nothing of the religious fundamentalists, both East and West, so prevalent in the world today who do not draw this conclusion; nor of the remaining indigenous populations. But we are referring here to society in general, which in the modern world prides itself on rationality, so it is acceptable to operate under this assumption.

The literary movement that emerged in response to modernity, materialism, and modern science was referred to as "naturalism," and it mimicked the scientific method in its materialistic portrayal of reality. In these writings, logic and objectivity trumped the imaginative and supernatural, to paint a picture of a world controlled by random, purely material causes, without any recourse to the metaphysical. The movement's founder was Émile Zola, and other notable authors included Thomas Hardy, Stephen Crane, and Frank Norris. In one sense, naturalism could be thought of as the antithesis of magical realism.

The theme of this issue of *Dark Discoveries*—Supernaturalism—could also be thought of as the antithesis of naturalism, however the term expresses something much more specific. What is evoked by the word "Supernaturalism" is the fictional portrayal of a world in which supernatural or supersensible (beyond the five senses) forces play a greater causal role in the unfolding of events than is rationally thought possible. Such a battery of forces are not limited to the realm of religion, but include anything that takes action from beyond the natural realm perceptible by our five sense alone. The junction at which the invisible penetrates and directs the physical is where we can begin to explore this issue's theme.

Peter Levenda's *Sinister Forces* trilogy traces the phenomenon that the theme of this issue centers on; namely, the idea of hidden, immaterial casualties behind events

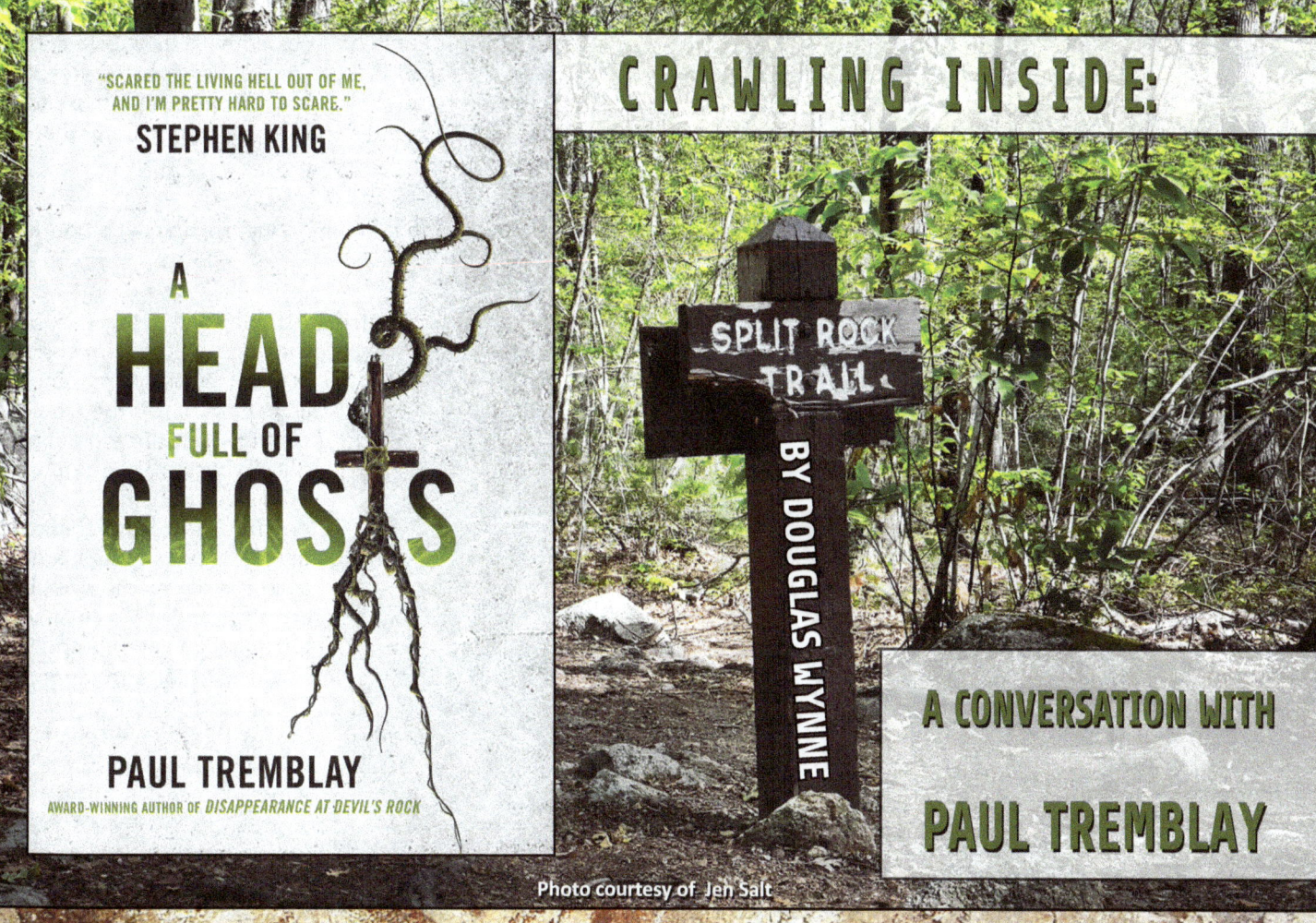

CRAWLING INSIDE:

SPLIT ROCK TRAIL

BY DOUGLAS WYNNE

"SCARED THE LIVING HELL OUT OF ME, AND I'M PRETTY HARD TO SCARE."

STEPHEN KING

A HEAD FULL OF GHOSTS

PAUL TREMBLAY

AWARD-WINNING AUTHOR OF *DISAPPEARANCE AT DEVIL'S ROCK*

A CONVERSATION WITH

PAUL TREMBLAY

Photo courtesy of Jen Salt

Apart from being monstrously talented, Paul Tremblay seems like a perfectly normal guy. He teaches math, plays guitar, and has a lovely family. He's quick with the self-deprecating humor and strikes me as the kind of writer who keeps his demons relegated to the page. None of which keeps me from feeling just a little bit creeped out as I hike with him through Borderland State Park to Split Rock, the location near his home in Massachusetts that inspired his second novel, *Disappearance at Devil's Rock*. It's like stepping into the book; a book I found heartbreaking, disturbing, and infested with unsettling possibilities both natural and supernatural.

The rock itself is a thing to behold, titanic and menacing. Someone has painted a small blue pentacle on the lichen-flecked stone, and the air inside the cleft feels cold and claustrophobic even on this warm September day. After a photo shoot in which no one goes missing, we settle on top of the rock as the declining sun dapples the forest floor below to discuss the author's fast-growing body of work and the current state of horror fiction.

***

Douglas Wynne: Maybe people should read the story before the interview, but can you tell us something about the inspiration behind the story you have in this issue of *Dark Discoveries*?

Paul Tremblay: Yeah, actually, it's funny… You know, sometimes I just start off with a *what if*? You know, a crazy *what if* just occurs to you. I was at a reading in Providence, at the Lovecraft Arts and Sciences. It was a fun reading, it was a great day, and I don't know… horror writers, we just get these dark thoughts sometimes. I think I had just finished my reading and sat down and looked around—everyone was happy, everyone was complementary, and I was like: Jeez, what if I got up there and just pulled out a gun and shot myself? Which, you know, I do not think that way in general about self-harm, but the thought was really like an exercise in wow, what would happen? And how could you play with that as a story? That was the start. I mean, it's not a big secret, because within the first couple paragraphs you realize that somebody is talking about his writer friend who shot himself.

DW: (Laughs) Cool. Speaking of short fiction: how did your short story "The Growing Things" become integrated into *A Head Full of Ghosts*? Were the sisters from that story prototypes for Merry and Marjorie?

PT: I think they were without me realizing it necessarily. And I have sort of cannibalized my own short fiction in the past, at least idea wise. Like my first novel, *The Little Sleep*. There's a scene in a short story called "There's No Light Between Floors" that appeared in my collection, and there's a scene in that book that I essentially just moved over to *The Little Sleep*. Sure, right? Might as well.

DW: Did you know that that story would figure into *A Head Full of Ghosts* when you started writing the book?

PT: I didn't, but I think I definitely had those two sisters in my head. There was certainly something about their relationship, and as soon as I figured out in *A Head Full of Ghosts* that the girls were telling stories to each other, I definitely thought of the "Growing Things" story right away and figured okay, I wanna work that in there, and I was like, Oh, look at that, these sisters are already like a cool mirror image of the two sisters anyway. I think maybe subconsciously it was there, but once I thought Oh, "The Growing Things!" it instantly became a major part of the book.

DW: In the collection you mentioned (*In the Mean Time*, Chizine 2010), there are a lot of apocalyptic short stories, which was interesting to me because apocalyptic fiction is

Photo courtesy of Jen Salt

usually done on the novel scale. You give us a lot of cool glimpses of apocalypse-in-progress where we might not get the full picture but it's intriguing. Do you think you will eventually take on an apocalyptic novel?

PT: Um… actually sort of, yeah. Yes. I think in the novel I've just started now, there is the potential for an apocalypse at the end, like maybe there is, maybe there isn't kind of thing. Yeah, that short story collection… I was definitely kind of obsessed. I think more so than any of the other things I've written, those really represented my fears as opposed to just general ideas. I would say for at least five or six years I was definitely obsessed with the world ending. It was a great fear of mine that I was going to live to see the world end. And live to see my own children's end. And to me, you know, that's the most horrific thing that I could think of.

DW: Of course. Was that tied in to a particular set of world events at the time?

PT: I think, honestly, Katrina actually had a big part in that. I don't know if people remember, but even things economically for the whole country were thrown out of whack because of the port of New Orleans being shut down. I had a lot of friends in the New Orleans area and I was reading their accounts and it was just so terrifying and awful. And it sort of tied in to my larger fears about what's happening with climate change and whatnot, and so for a while—I mean, I still have a great fear of all those things but I feel like I'm in a healthier place with regards to them.

DW: Maybe writing through some of those fears was helpful?

PT: Yeah, maybe. Sure.

DW: So what is your process like for writing a novel, and has it changed much in the course of writing your most recent books? Do you plan a lot, or is it more improvisational?

PT: I've done both. Every book has been different for me. I'd say more times than not, though, I've written like a 10 or 15 page summary first before doing the novel.

DW: Does that include the ending typically?

PT: Yeah. And that's not to say things can't change. For stuff like my mystery novels, I'm not good enough to make up a mystery plot as I go, so I knew that I had to have at least the bare bones of what the mystery would be. And *Devil's Rock*—I felt that it had more of a mystery setup or component to it than *A Head Full of Ghosts*, let's say. So I did do a summary for that as well. But *A Head Full of Ghosts* I sort of made up as I went. You know, I was sort of lucky that I knew almost from the beginning that there would be the two sisters, there would be sort of this three-part structure where it's before the reality show shows up, when the reality show shows up, and after. So I had all of those pieces as sort of big blocks in my head. I didn't know *all* the details.

DW: I saw the notebook that you posted on your blog where some of those early ideas came up. It's cool how much of it is there in the inspiration.

PT: The notebook for *Devil's Rock* is a mess. For *A Head Full of Ghosts*, it's… I don't know… I feel like I got lucky with that story. It's like it's pretty clean, I sort of knew what I wanted.

DW: It presented itself kind of fully formed?

PT: Yeah, whereas *Devil's Rock*, I have just reams of notebook paper, of different ways the plot went and I crossed it out and went into some other stuff.

DW: Do you do a lot of *what ifs* in the process? Maybe this could happen, maybe that?

PT: You know, I just try to think it out and then, maybe that's the one place where the math part comes in… I have to believe that *this* could happen. Even though there's a potential supernatural thing, if I feel like there's any kind of crack or it doesn't make sense, I scrap it and start over. And that was, I think, the hardest part for me for

getting a handle on *Devil's Rock*, that there were a lot more moving parts. I tried to make it somewhat realistic, like this could have really happened, so there was a lot more work to it.

DW: You mentioned cannibalizing things from your short stories for new work. And you mentioned at a reading I attended that you were working on a different book when the idea for *A Head Full of Ghosts* came to you, and it had an awesome title: *Charles Manson Doesn't Answer My Letters*.

PT: (Laughs) Yeah.

DW: Do you think we will see that reincarnated in some form? Will that be cannibalized possibly? I guess it's hard to say…

PT: I would like to go back to something there. I sort of lost where I was going with it a little bit, and I kind of feel like, you know, part of it was going to end up almost like what Nick Mamatas did with *I Am Providence*. So I would feel like I would have to go in a different direction because there was going to be a part that would take place at a Lovecraftian convention.

DW: I thought of Nick's book when you mentioned the idea behind your story with a suicide at a Lovecraftian reading venue.

PT: Yeah.

DW: I always think of Mulder and Scully, their dichotomy, when I'm reading a Paul Tremblay book. And I admire how you sustain the tension over which way the story will break. When facing the unknown in real life—questions about things like Bigfoot, and I've seen you do the Bigfoot walk—are you more of a Mulder or a Scully? What's your predisposition?

PT: I'm definitely more of a Scully, but I wish I was a Mulder.

DW: You want to believe.

PT: During the day, I mean 95% of my life, I feel like I'm a card-carrying rational skeptic. But there is that other 5%. It's usually at night, or if I'm home alone at night, or if I just wake up from a really weird dream, you get that feeling of maybe there *is* something. But you know, the next morning you wake up and it's like, *Eh…* So for those two novels especially, those are the two sides I grappled with. I mean, some of the ambiguity in both books was me trying to satisfy my own neuroses, like: that wouldn't happen. I wouldn't believe that would happen. Or maybe it would, if it was presented in such a way.

DW: So it takes a lot for you to suspend your disbelief as a writer?

PT: It does.

DW: It has to stand up to possibly more than one interpretation.

PT: Absolutely. I also think if I was experiencing something supernatural, I would have a hard time recognizing that it was, in fact, supernatural. I don't think it would be like this big clap of thunder or something. I think it would be really subtle— and unsettling *because* it was so subtle—that you wouldn't be always questioning it. That's how I've approached it with those two books, anyway.

DW: In *Disappearance at Devil's Rock* you do eventually take a side on whether or not there's something supernatural happening, but only after maintaining that delicate balance and ambiguity for almost the whole book. After two novels that have straddled the line between supernatural and psychological horror, do you see yourself going all the way to one side or the other in a future book?

PT: It's funny, my agent and editor sort of joke that I'm Mr. Ambiguous Horror for those two books. I feel like I can't

do that forever. I think people would get tired of it.

DW: But it's interesting territory to explore, and not many people are.

PT: Absolutely. The novel I'm working on now I think would be a nice third book to go with the other two. So there will be some play of *is there something supernatural or not* to that book, but I'm going to approach it in a little bit of a different way. I feel like with *A Head Full of Ghosts* and *Disappearance at Devil's Rock* that in those books what happens in reality is, I think, the most horrific parts of the books. But whether or not it is supernatural is hopefully what lingers with the readers. With this next book I'm going to try to flip that a little bit. You know, what's going to happen in reality is really awful, but I want the potential supernatural ramifications, like if there is in fact something supernatural at play, to be the most horrific thing. So I'm going to try to flip it a little bit in the third book.

DW: Very intriguing. Is there anything about the premise of the book you're working on that you can share with? Is it too early for that?

PT: I'll just say it's going to be sort of my take on a home invasion story. I think it's gonna be a fairly short novel, but hopefully intense, and I'm pretty excited about it. The idea came to me in much the same way the idea for *A Head Full of Ghosts* came to me. But I did write a summary. I sort of had to pitch it to my editor. But yeah, I'm excited about this book.

DW: Do you have a title for it yet?

PT: The book will be called *The Four*. And if all goes well, it will be released the summer of 2018.

DW: Cool. Getting back to *Devil's Rock*: what got you interested in the doppelgänger idea? It seems to me especially resonant when you think about the multiple selves we all seem to have on the Internet and especially for teenagers who are grappling with identity and social media… Were those issues overtly on your mind while writing the book, and did being surrounded by kids in that age group as a teacher have an influence on the book?

PT: Wow, that's a great question. I would say yeah, I mean I think the short answer would be that's why I ultimately

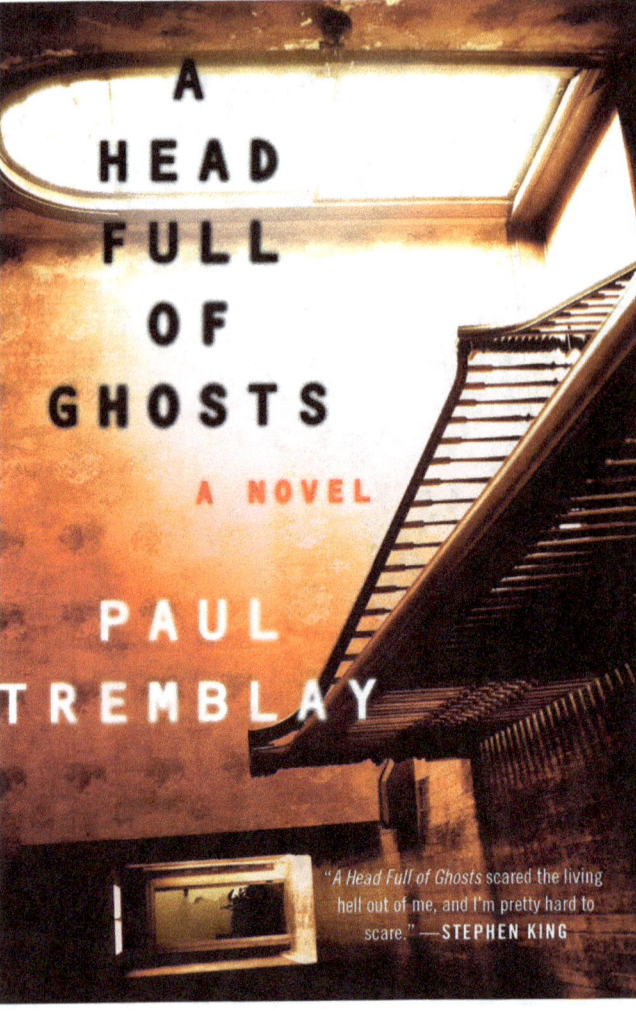

"*A Head Full of Ghosts* scared the living hell out of me, and I'm pretty hard to scare." —STEPHEN KING

ended up going with the doppelgänger. Some of it just started off that I love the movie *Lake Mungo,* and I'm really interested in doppelgänger stories as well. So I think people who have watched the movie *Lake Mungo* will certainly see that there's more than a wink and a nod to that.

DW: As a teacher, you have very well drawn teenaged boys in the story. I know that you're a father of a kid that age, but did you find details working their way into the book through the day job?

PT: Oh yeah, the slang that the boys use was taken from my school. That slang is probably already a couple of years old. I've noticed them using it less and less. And as a teacher, that's sort of the fun part is the voice because, especially a high school teacher, these words will come up every once in a while, and these words tend to mean the same thing the old words might have represented a few years ago. Usually, giving a kid a hard time, at my school, has become a "chirp." I can't remember what it was previously but it was something else and you know, "hardo" used to be like a huge thing, everyone was calling each other a hardo, and I noticed that started to wane a little bit.

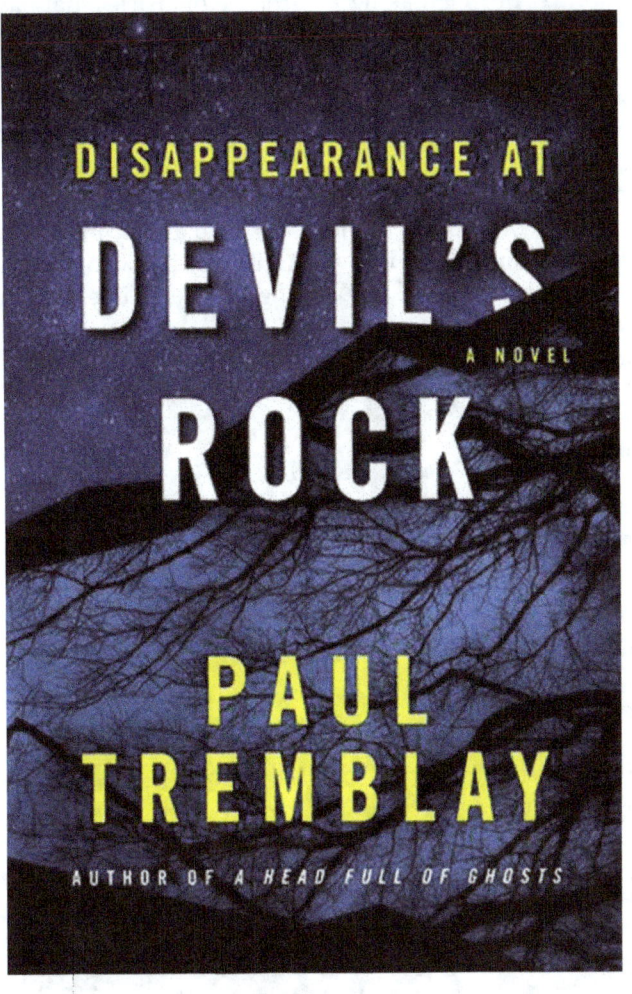

DW: There's a postmodernism influence in your work. Where does that come from? And what attracts you to the use of narrative devices like blog and journal entries and interview transcripts and those kinds of things?

PT: Honestly, some of it just comes from my own interests as a reader and reflects my day-to-day life, like how much I am reading online and reading blogs and Twitter and whatnot.

DW: A fair amount of your reading is nonfiction?

PT: No, I just mean more like the social media hangout aspect of it. Just reading other writers blogs and stuff like that. Especially when I was first writing, I felt like I was reading people's Live Journals a lot. That sort of stuck with me. And the stories that I write… I'm really interested in writing a story that's part of what's happening now. I mean, to me the idea of deathless prose, it makes me roll my eyes a little. I can't imagine worrying about writing a

story that would be considered deathless prose when it's hard enough to write a story that people are interested in reading now.

DW: You want something tuned into the world we're living in and not worrying that some of the references are going to seem dated.

PT: Right. I don't worry if the references will be dated because I feel like if you tell the story well enough, if you're not just putting in those references to be clever, if they are actually part of the story, then people will get it—well, if there are still people around to read these stories 20 or 30 years from now… But if you made, say, Twitter an integral part of the story, they'll figure it out, they'll go *Oh, okay.* And it'll be a part of the setting.

DW: It will be historical fiction. (Laughs)

PT: Sure. It'll mark the story as 2015, and that's okay because the story took place in 2015 and that time was important to the story.

DW: We all geeked out on *Stranger Things* because it had so much of the tangible 80s we remember. And I saw a Facebook conversation recently—I think it was Simon Strantzas—talking about how 70s horror novels have a certain vibe to them and what is it that brings that vibe to it? But I think that's part of the enjoyment of reading something that's of an era.

PT: I totally agree. Someone posted an article, an essay… I'm probably gonna butcher the point but… It wasn't about deathless prose but it sort of came up in it. She brought up *Neuromancer* by William Gibson and the first line: *The sky was the color of television, tuned to a dead channel.* And I obviously instantly know what that is, but if someone like a millennial was reading that now, they might not remember it. But that's okay because within the rest of that novel you're going to figure out what he means because all of the references are such a part of the world that he created.

DW: The past can be presented like fantasy fiction where not all of the terms are explained but you pick it up as you go, the elements of this world you find yourself in.

PT: Exactly.

DW: Let's talk about the state of the horror genre. It's hard for me to know how much of my perception is what Robert Anton Wilson would call my immersion in the "reality tunnel" of horror fiction and horror entertainment, but it seems to me that we are sort of on the cusp of a horror renaissance in fiction and film. I'm curious what you think about that. What's your impression? Is horror making a comeback?

PT: I definitely think so. I mean, some of it is a little bit of ego on our parts because every writer working in their time would like to think they're working in the Golden Age, right? But I do believe there's some truth to that. After the 90s, there was clearly a bust… you could point to the mainstream sales of horror and how it tanked, and how horror really hasn't been a publishing niche or market for a while, at least in terms of the mainstream. But because of the advent of the Internet and how the small press has become so vibrant, there are these groups that are not only keeping horror alive but I think making some of the best horror fiction.

DW: I'm hoping that will make it more viable to larger publishers like yours, that small presses are demonstrating that there's an audience. But around the turn-of-the-century, do you think 9/11 had anything to do with the drop off in interest? I remember reading a comment by Clive Barker where he said basically that when real horror is too close to people, they don't want it as their entertainment.

PT: I've read the opposite: in bad economic times people go there.

DW: So vote for Trump if you want to sell horror books?

PT: Well that was sort of the joke with Bush, we were all like yeah, you know it's bad times, it's gonna be good for horror. I'm sure someone could make the argument that the unbelievable boom in zombie fiction happened right after 9/11. I know there was some before it but… I think there could be arguments either way.

DW: It seems like sometimes a sub-genre of horror will become huge but no one really feels like horror is making a return. Apocalyptic is huge now. Zombies were huge.

PT: Certainly from my experience it does seem like more readers are looking for horror than they were maybe 10 years ago, from what I can remember. And obviously I think it's a great sign that a schlub like me can get a

Photo courtesy of Jen Salt

deal with William Morrow. And they published Stephen Graham Jones…

DW: *Mongrels* is a great book.

PT: It's funny, just in the last few days there have been a couple of articles that have talked about a second wave of horror after the boom of the 80s, and that maybe this isn't the tail end of that boom. This is what would be considered the second wave. People who grew up with the horror of the 80s, these are the people who are now part of a second wave, which is an interesting way of looking at it.

DW: And there are so many creative people working in other media who were so strongly influenced by reading Stephen King growing up. I know movies have influenced a lot of your writing, like independent films such as *Lake Mungo*… I wonder how much the sort of small press equivalent in video—live streaming services such as Hulu and Netflix, even HBO and Showtime, which have the creative freedom to do things now at greater length and in the serial formats that have become so popular, things that you can't do with a two-hour film… I wonder if that's going to spill over into books again and establish more of a horror climate.

PT: I think it already has. The health of the independent horror movie business over the past 5 to 10 years, you know *It Follows*, *The Babadook*, all of these great independent movies that have had buzz and have done well, that's a snapshot hopefully of the health of the genre overall. There's no doubt that video has helped save, or at least helped move the horror fan into getting them to be able to see the movies. I was just watching *The Thing* last night, you know the classic horror movie. When it first came out, it didn't do very well at all. It was video that saved it. It was video where it found its audience. Now we're surrounded by video and DVDs and it's easier to find that horror audience because it is there.

DW: Do you, on the other hand, have any concerns about being typecast as a horror writer when your previous work shows more diversity? You've dabbled in noir detective stories and some science fiction stuff, some things with comedic elements also.

PT: Not right now. I think I would like to write (hopefully) a humorous book again someday. But I'm pretty content to do the new novel I mentioned and maybe one after that as well. But I'd be lying if I said it wasn't frustrating when I tell someone, when they say, "Hey, what do you write?" and I say horror, or if I'm feeling particularly obnoxious, literary horror, and more times than not their eyes sort of glaze over. I have a feeling that attitude is maybe going away but it's still there, you know?

I was at the literary convention in Newport. I hesitate to bring up the story because I had such a wonderful time at the Newport Book Festival. But I was at the dinner and I ended up talking to these writers who I wouldn't ordinarily end up talking to in my everyday life. They're from England, some of them are historical writers. And when people ask me, "What do you write?" and I'm like, literary horror… "Ah, I can't read that stuff. I don't read that stuff." At the time, I'm like yeah, I understand, whatever, I dismiss it. But I woke up in the hotel at like five in the morning thinking about it. What if the woman I'd talked to had said, "I write historical fiction from the 1600s," some very specific time period in England, and how would they have reacted at the table if I'd replied, "Ah, I don't read anything from before 1750." It would seem totally obnoxious. So it's weird how it's still totally okay to pan horror or speculative fiction in general.

DW: It took a long time for even Stephen King to finally have some critical acclaim. I don't know… maybe he'll be the only one who finally attains that, but Peter Straub is certainly respected, and we're starting to see literary horror books garnering good reviews in the New York Times, so maybe there's hope. Even runaway mainstream children's fiction like Harry Potter is deeply influenced by horror. You can't separate the two. So you would hope that people would get over it and accept that they are horror fans, even if they don't call it that.

PT: I do think the attitudes are getting better. It's interesting that you mentioned Harry Potter, and I think people are more willing to accept genre fiction because so many people grew up reading Harry Potter and it wasn't a stigma to read Harry Potter for them.

DW: Right. They were young, so they were granted permission to read genre fiction.

PT: Absolutely. I think a lot of those readers are continuing to read. Even if they have a more literary sort of interests, you can find any kind of genre fiction that has literary interests as well.

DW: What is your definition of literary horror? What sets it apart from other horror fiction? I know you talked a bit about this in the introduction to an anthology you co-edited called *Phantom*, but I wonder if you could sum up your current thinking on what makes a piece of horror fiction literary.

PT: How about horror that doesn't suck? That's not necessarily fair. So… horror that isn't only concerned with gore or attempted scares or the twist, or funhouse horror. Aside from employing well-constructed plots, themes, characters, I would argue that literary horror aims to push beyond the scare or effect and ask of the readers the most difficult and transgressive questions literature or art can ask. Don't get me wrong, I like me some funhouse horror too. But instead of the jump scare that's fun for thirty seconds but easily forgotten, I tend to prefer a story that crawls inside and lingers there, becoming a part of me and changing who I am and will be at the same time.

DW: Two silly questions left. This past summer you exhibited your amazing T-shirt collection on social media. Do you have a favorite? If you could keep only one, which would it be?

PT: Oh boy. If I could keep only one… I have to think about that… I can't just keep only one! Can I admit something embarrassing? I was looking at my T-shirts today and thinking, *I don't have any cool T-shirts to wear.*

DW: Are you kidding? How bad is the laundry?

PT: My current favorite is the new one, the Black Phillip Butter T-shirt. It's new, so I really like that one. But what is my go-to T-shirt? I really like my Creature Double Feature T-shirt. Channel 56. It fits me well, too, makes me look bigger than I am.

DW: And the last thing; you knew it had to come up… You knew I couldn't let you off without asking about pickles. You have a notorious aversion to pickles.

PT: I do. That's all I'll be remembered for.

DW: I gotta know: when was the last time you actually tried one?

PT: …Never.

DW: Never? How do you know you hate them?!

PT: Just the smell and the look and… yeah. I mean, I've had like pickle juice infect a sandwich and it's just awful.

DW: Does this apply to cucumbers too? Does it carry over? Or is it the vinegar?

PT: No, I like cucumbers. It's just pickles.

DW: And what would it take to get you to try one? What's your pickle price?

PT: It's not gonna happen. Nope. No pickle price.

DW: All right. That's all I got.

PT: Nice.

can only tell this in pieces. It's all in pieces. Each piece seems worse than it did the day before or the hour before, as though remembering is a conspiratorial act of further implication, of making *more* worseness.

The last piece arrived today.

***

Nine days ago, I received an envelope in the mail from Peter. It was exactly one month after he killed himself. I'd been in my new apartment for ten weeks. Time is not an arrow. It is a bottomless bag in which we collect and place things that will be forgotten.

The envelope was blue and greeting card sized. A yellow *notify sender of new address* sticker was plastered diagonally over my old address, a PO Box I'd rented during the blurry thirteen months I guest-room surfed with other writers and artists in the Hudson Valley. Peter's name and return address was a scrawled blotch on the envelope's upper left corner, nearly illegible in black ink, the first of many Rorschach tests. I'd seen enough of his handwriting to determine he was careless and rushed through writing his address. Or maybe he wasn't concentrating, writing on autopilot. Or he was ashamed, and the envelope and its contents were a cry for help I wouldn't hear until it was too late. I've become both expert and failure at finding meaning in the meaningless.

More time again: The postage stamp date was six days before he killed himself, four days before I left for Providence. My shitty one room efficiency in a shittier neighborhood and his beautiful, newly constructed house in a suburb of Boston were separated by less than two hundred and twenty-five miles. (And sometimes more). If he'd sent the envelope to my new address, I would've received it before I saw Peter that weekend.

***

The Sunday morning of the reading/book signing, only four hours before he would be dead, I went out to breakfast with Peter, Lauren, and their lovely children (now a teen and a pre-teen) Steph and Maggie. Steph and I traded New York Yankees/Boston Red Sox quips despite neither of us being big baseball fans. Steph was over six feet tall and armored in his new, easy muscles, but he has always carried himself like a smaller child. He was reserved, spoke softly, avoided eye contact, and most of his smiles were fractional with half-lives measured in seconds. I've wondered what kind of father Peter was and if I was better or worse than him, even when I knew the answer was neither. Maggie was flamboyant, manically friendly, an excited electron looking to bounce and charge. When she was younger, she used to draw pictures of me with my beard's length greatly exaggerated and leave the artwork on the floor for me to find when I'd stayed at their house. That morning she had newly pink hair and only wanted to talk to me about what horror movies I thought she was old enough to watch.

Peter paid for my coffee and short stack of pancakes. I tried to give him a ten but he wouldn't take my money.

The gesture was kind and it was humiliating even if he didn't intend it to be.

I was the last to leave the breakfast table. Peter stood and walked away after his kids, then Lauren right behind Peter. She ran a hand up and down Peter's back. He turned around and smiled at Lauren. Did that flash of physical affection make him rethink what he was planning to do? Peter briefly surveyed the small dining area filled with patrons and their over-easy eggs and mugs of coffee, and then he looked back at me, or next to me, as though someone else was there sitting in the empty space to my left.

***

I imagined the first envelope contained a letter, encyclopedic in detail about why he did what he did and then I would have to show it to Lauren and/or someone from the Providence police department.

I carried the unopened envelope to the kitchen table and dropped it there. I cried, briefly, and said, "You asshole," a few times. I knew that wasn't fair. He killed himself because the stew of chemicals in his brain had morphed into a dirty rotten cheat and a liar.

Inside the envelope was not a letter, but a greeting card. Its cover was green with a neon blue cursive *Thank You.* I opened the card and a photo slid out. I assumed the thank you card wasn't meant to be mocking but simply a vessel for the photo, something Peter grabbed in haste. The photo was printed on regular white paper and not glossy photo stock, so it had a grainy look and the amount of ink curled the paper at its margins.

In the photo, Peter was alone. He stood in front of his bathroom mirror, holding his cell phone in one hand, a little star flash obscured the left half of his expressionless face. He wore black boxer briefs and nothing else. Red and purple acne scars dotted his pale skin. His posture was hunched, curved into a cruel kyphosis, like he didn't have the strength to hold up his chest and its vulnerable contents. He was a thin, wiry man, but the exaggerated, chest-caved-in posture made his skin sag and melt into rolls that hung over the waistband of his underwear. It appeared he was attempting to make himself look ugly, haggard, grotesque. Seeing him this way, I wanted to cry again, and I wondered why he would take such a photo of himself. I concluded that in the grips of some dreadful psychological illness this was how he saw himself, how he thought other people saw him. Then I found and read the brief note written inside the thank you card.

"Lower right of the photo. Can you see it? You can't show it to anyone else."

***

Peter and I saw each other two or three weekends a year at various writers' conventions and author readings in the northeast. I stayed at Peter's place for a weekend each February and then we'd drive into Boston for a small science fiction convention that inexplicably invited us horror writers to speak on some panels. We generally talked on the phone once a week. The frequency of calls increased dramatically in the weeks leading up to my divorce as in the weeks after, and during those calls he'd keep me talking and tell me that I would be okay and that the relationship with my son Dominick would evolve and survive. Before my divorce, Peter would visit and stay at my house for a few days, usually during his school's spring break, and Dominick reveled in showing off his new karate moves. Dominick is kind, joyously physical in his expression of enthusiasm and curiosity, and as socially awkward as his father, I'm afraid. I only see Dominick and his very worried face every other weekend now. As long as the ponds and rivers aren't frozen over, I take him fishing so that our barely speaking to each other becomes pragmatic instead of soul crushing.

I have plenty of acquaintances and colleagues, maybe too many. Most of whom are digital—a collection of avatars, likes, retweets, and emails to which I now infrequently respond. Peter and I were friends. I don't say that lightly. He called me his brother less than a minute before he killed himself.

Why didn't he email me the photo or tell me about it on the phone? Why didn't he show me everything when I was right there in his house, or when we were in Providence?

Why hadn't I seen it in the photo for myself (when it is now so clearly *there*) before I read his message in the thank you card?

***

A second envelope, same size as the first, arrived a few mornings ago. I haven't opened it yet. The morning it arrived, I let it sit atop a mass of photos that I printed out, including the pictures I'd started taking of myself. And those photos of me were a layer of ash on top of printed out photos of Peter. Those Peter photos were cut up and spliced and taped together, and somewhere under those was the first photo he mailed to me, and under that was the thank you card and the first envelope, and under that was the kitchen table top, and it all connected and it all infected, and this is the cat that killed the rat that ate the malt that lay in the house….

The new envelope. Its postage stamp date was four days before he killed himself, which was two days after he mailed the first envelope, three days before I left for Providence.

Time is not an arrow. Sometimes it is a deck of cards that you can shuffle. And cut.

***

In a different universe, the one in which I had received the card and photo before leaving for Providence, I might've assumed Peter was scheming some new and odd viral marketing campaign. Peter was much more active and social media savvy than I was. His easy going, friends-to-all persona was naturally geared toward successful online promotion that managed to walk the line between an endearing aw-shucks-isn't-it-cool-that-this-is-happening-to-me and being an annoying spambot.

In his newest novel, only two months old, characters think they see fleeting dark shapes in corners and empty spaces of rooms and peering into their windows. The dark shapes may be portents of doom, or the shadow of a real person and representing the mundanity of evil, or a literal devil, or the echo of guilt and shame, or the avatar of violence following the characters (even the dead ones) into a kind of afterlife, or it's all nothing but the figments of grieved imaginations, or something else entirely, or something that's not there at all.

In the photo, to Peter's right, below the granite bathroom sink counter and toward the corner of the wall and linen closet door is a dark shape. At first glance and second glance, and third, one might have assumed it was the ink jet printer spasming, unable to recreate the photo flash effect in a darkened bathroom. I kept giving the photo more glances, and the dark blotch of ink seemed to refocus and not quite take a recognizable, organic shape, but come maddeningly close so that it blurred and subtly reformed the longer I looked at it. But then if I blinked or turned away it snapped back into whatever form I thought I saw initially.

I turned the photo, flipped it, held it up to the light, thinking I might see a boundary, a line where the darkness began or ended.

***

Upon arriving in Providence on Saturday around 1 pm, I met Peter and Frances at the Trinity Brew Pub, only a block away from the library, one of the venues hosting the Lovecraft Film Festival. Frances was in her early thirties, a decade-plus younger than Peter and I. She was an indie filmmaker adapting one of my short stories into a film. She wanted me to have and take home a large prop made for the movie, a rib bone six feet in length curling from tip to tip. I had no space for it in my apartment, but I toyed with bringing it back to give to Dominick. Maybe I would've brought it back for him if everything that happened on Sunday hadn't happened.

Peter and Frances had already secured a table and were two beers deep. We exchanged greeting hugs, something I'm terribly awkward with, particularly when tired, hungry, and stressed out from a long drive. And, to be honest, my social anxieties were one of the reasons why I had decided to stop frequenting conventions and readings, with finances being another reason—and yet another, the notion that I could prevent the inexorable untethering from my son Dominick if I remained geographically fixed within the Hudson Valley at all times, like an old stone fence in a forgotten stretch of woods.

Peter often made a joke about my awkward greetings, but didn't that afternoon. He said it was great to see me, and he lingered. He lingered there, within arm's length, his large, spidery hands on my shoulders. I shrugged him off and said I'd be more human after food. He asked if I'd received anything from him in the mail.

It's odd now in retrospect that he would ask right then, because depending upon my answer, he would have had to explain to Frances what it was he'd sent, unless he thought he could count on my confusion and/or discretion to not fully detail the contents of what I'd received.

I told Peter there was nothing from him in the mail this week and I asked what he'd sent.

He smirked and side-glanced at me, a mischievous look, or perhaps he wasn't sure if I was telling the truth. He dismissed me to sit in the booth by waving a hand, and then he lied. He said it wasn't a big deal and that it was an extra copy of a new writer's short story collection.

The three of us fell into an easy conversation about movies and books, and Frances told stories about her screenwriting work on prior films. Peter was engaged, content to listen more than he talked until Frances asked him what he was working on. He mentioned a novel that was in the earliest planning stages but didn't give any plot or character details. I don't recall if he was prompted by a follow up question or something one of us said, but Peter went on to say he'd been having trouble coming up with an idea for the next novel; he'd struggled with it all spring and now into summer. He said ideas are fleeting like that sometimes, just out of reach, or seeming to always belong to someone else. He said sometimes an idea felt like it had been there in his head since before he was him, and the idea was patiently waiting, plotting for the right time to show itself. He said sometimes an idea was a bully and would take him over, hold him hostage, and he'd be powerless to do anything else but think and worry at it.

***

I stayed at Frances's and Victoria's house in East Providence for five days, not returning home until after Peter's wake and the funeral. I stayed in their guest room and only came out to eat and use the bathroom and apologize for all the whiskey I was drinking. I spent the rest of the time on the Internet.

Peter's death and the *how* of it caused an online and offline shitstorm. The small horror writing community was shocked, devastated, and confused. How could he do that to himself when his life and career were more than going well, but were the envy of most? He'd published his last two horror novels with one of the largest publishing houses in the world, Random House. Both books were optioned by major Hollywood production companies. He'd earned starred reviews in Publisher's Weekly and Booklist and the books were glowingly reviewed in the New York Times, NPR, Entertainment Weekly. So many of the important cultural tastemakers had praised his work. His books sold well, though how well was exaggerated by many, as Peter would be too quick to point out, maintaining he was no bestseller and he wasn't quitting his teaching job anytime soon. Regardless, to most outside observers, Peter was living the horror writer's seemingly unattainable dream.

My social media platforms and email inbox were flooded with messages and questions from other writers and readers. Was Peter unhappy? Was he ill? Had something happened to trigger this? Were there things we didn't know about him? Were there any signs? I had no answers for them and I had no answers for myself.

Having been Peter's close friend and co-reader at the

Providence event, I was inundated with interview requests from all manner of press outlets. I rejected almost all of them. On the first night back to my apartment, slurring drunk, I was on the phone I didn't remember answering with a reporter from *CNN*. When he asked if I thought the kind of stuff we wrote might've infected Peter somehow, if this *situation* (the fucking twit actually said "situation") was similar to when heavy metal listeners killed themselves or others, I told him to fuck off, hung up, and committed to breaking all the glasses and dishes in my apartment.

Peter, his life and work, and horror as a genre and as entertainment were discussed on cable networks and online and in print. Less-than half-baked think pieces sprouted like weeds. Everyone had an opinion, and most of the opinions were speculative, lazy armchair psychiatry, and moral pandering pabulum. I blasted social media mis-

sives at the authors of these articles and created accounts at news websites and platforms in order to scorch the comment sections.

The news cycle chewed up Peter and spat him out in a matter of days. The writing community mourned, lamented, introspected, promised tribute stories and anthologies (the proceeds from which would go to Peter's family of course), and limped on with their collective lives after a few weeks. Peter's afterlife would be as the horror community's mystery, martyr, and their cautionary tale, itself a horror story, a twist on the hoary cliché of *be careful what you wish for*.

Then it all blew up again four days ago, after one of the reading's attendees killed himself. Will, the man who'd set up and maintained the event room's sound system, slit his wrists while his girlfriend was at work.

***

After I'd finished poring over the photo, the thank you card and its message, I cannonballed into a bottle of Maker's Mark and spent the rest of the afternoon and evening scrolling through Peter's Facebook page. He had posted and been tagged in hundreds of pictures. There on my screen was Peter at various readings, book events, and conventions, standing at podiums, sitting at long tables in front of a microphone, pen in hand, book splayed out before him like a treasure map, him and a toothy smile, arm around someone's shoulder, glasses filled with amber liquids in hands and raised, and there was Peter with Lauren on a beach, goofy selfies with Maggie sitting on their big green couch, the family on vacation at a rented

lake house, at one of Steph's basketball games, at a sibling's house, niece's birthday parties. I sank deeper and deeper into the bottle and into those bits of color and image from his life. I couldn't help but think that he put too much of himself and his family out there for anyone to gawk at, and I judged him negatively for it as much as I was envious of the attitude that enabled him to share as much as he did. On my phone I only had three photos of Dominick and me together.

I first saw it in a picture of Peter from the night of his latest novel's release event, which was almost exactly two months before he killed himself. The photo was from before the reading/party. He was still at his house and dressed in a black button down shirt and jeans. He stood in front of a red wall in his dining room, eyebrows arched over

his black framed glasses, lopsided smirk, his new novel in one hand and a Narragansett beer can in the other. Peter was a big *Jaws* fan; he'd dressed as Quint the previous Halloween and the can was part of his costume. Below his bent elbow was the shadow of his arm. The shadow began to look odd, a little off, like it didn't quite fit the space that should've been allotted to it. The longer I looked I became more certain a discovery of what I would ultimately see was imminent, but I did not progress beyond a *feeling* of certainty.

I sifted through his hundreds of Facebook pictures a second time. And a third. A pattern initially emerged within the photos from the two months between the release event and the Providence reading, and a subset of those photos in which Peter was alone. Away from the center of focus, which changed from photo to photo, depending on the foreground, the staging, his posture, his expression, the angle of the camera, the lighting, the environment, there was a bit of darkness, or blankness, and maybe at first glance it was simply shadow, or quirks of the photography, but at more glances, more and more glances, it was something else. There was something there in the photos with Peter. There had to be.

I printed out pictures until I ran out of ink toner.

***

I didn't tell Lauren or the Providence police about the thank you card and the photo he mailed. I felt and continue to feel guilty about not telling Lauren, but at the same time, I didn't want her to see that picture of Peter. I know that was not my decision to make, but I made it anyway. He asked that I not show anyone else and I feel bound to do as he requested.

A second attendee of the reading killed herself this afternoon. Rachel was a recent college graduate living in Connecticut with her parents, an aspiring writer, and she swallowed a fistful of her mother's sleeping pills.

***

Saturday night we left Providence early. After a fine afternoon spent in conversation and walking around downtown Providence with Frances and other writers and fans, we skipped out on both the viewing of ten short films and a local brewery's after party that was to feature the unveiling of a Lovecraft beer. I'm not a beer guy. My faith is in whiskey.

Peter and I went to his house, which was an easy forty minute drive. We ate pizza with his family and then we attempted to sneak away into the living room on our own but Steph wanted to show me a new RPG video game that'd been getting a lot of attention. Peter finally kicked Steph out a little after midnight.

We were both working on a third glass of scotch and half-heartedly started in on more talk about books, movies, and industry gossip. I don't know if Peter had planned to finally tell me about the card and photo I hadn't yet received in the mail because I didn't give him a chance. Buzzed and melancholy despite my first enjoyable and anxiety-free afternoon in months, or maybe because of it, I launched into a confessional concerning my current economic situation.

I told him that my teaching two writing courses at a community college and royalties owed by a slew of small presses barely covered the rent, utilities, and now alimony payments. Peter stammered through a sorry and before he could say more, I tried to rescue him by clinking my class against his, saying that I would be okay but I probably wouldn't be coming to very many conventions or readings for a bit. Then I thanked him for letting me crash and complimented his choice of scotch (single malt, and according to the bottle label, fourteen years old, splitting time in whisky oak and cherry oak casks). Peter looked around that giant living room of his that was perched like the victor on top of his two car garage. He scratched at his cheeks and had barely breathed out his *thanks*. I assumed he was embarrassed, even if I hadn't fully intended to make him so.

Now, of course, I can't be sure he was embarrassed. Had I derailed his wanting to talk to me about what he was going through with my own tale of woe?

I don't know what he was thinking on that night or what he was thinking the next morning at breakfast or the next day back in Providence. I'm afraid to know, or more to the point, I'm afraid that I might know now what he'd been thinking or what he might've seen there in the room with him, or with us.

***

Patty called and said I was late and where was I?

Dominick. It was my weekend for Dominick. I told her I was sorry, but I was sick, wasn't feeling well, and didn't want him to catch whatever it was I had. I was lying and I wasn't lying. I asked her to put him on the phone and she hung up instead. I called him and he didn't answer. I left a voicemail message and told him that I loved him and that I'd make it up to him. I wasn't lying and I was lying.

I burned through three more ink cartridges. Upon re-inspection of all the pictures from the two months between the release of his novel and the Providence reading—including photos in which Peter wasn't the only person in the picture—I found darkened areas and I cut them out, leaving only the photo he sent me untouched. I arranged the cutouts like pieces of a jigsaw puzzle. They came close to fitting together into something, a silhouette, a shape, but there was something missing. I tacked the photos with the cut out holes in them to a wall to help keep track of what photos I'd already used. I printed out more pictures. I taped and spliced the darkly colored bits of paper together. In a fit of inspiration, I attempted to recreate the recurring shadows in three dimensions and constructed a bolus, then an obelisk, a crooked tower. Something was missing. I tore it all down. I printed out more photos. Then I made a mask. That seemed to be closer to the truth of things but not fully there.

I took photos of the printed out photos with my phone. I accidentally flipped the screen on one shot and snapped off a picture of my face. My eyes were red and blind. It'd

been so long since trimming my facial hair, my mouth was hidden somewhere beneath the avalanching mustache. From the upward angle, the skin of my neck rolled, forming multiple chins. I looked at the photo and didn't delete it. And I looked again. I focused on the shadow that hung like mist above my left shoulder, or it rested on my shoulder, an abstraction of exhaustion.

There weren't nearly as many pictures of me on my computer. I checked them all. They were okay, and by okay I mean that I wasn't seeing what I saw in Peter's photo and in my accidental selfie.

Did Peter see or feel the shadow, the darkness before he took the picture of himself in his bathroom, or did he only see it after?

I walked into my bathroom, turned the light off, peered into the corners of things, including myself, and I saw nothing and everything. I aimed my camera at the mirror.

***

The Arcade Mall in Providence was purportedly the oldest indoor mall in the United States. Its façade featured a row of Greek columns and marble stairs that led into a naturally lit atrium. Sunlight poured through the metal framed glass ceiling and reflected off the white tile floor, giving the effect of being in an aviary. The second and third floors overlooking the mall featured trendy new apartments or what the proprietors called *micro-lofts*. The shops and restaurants of the first floor mall were an eclectic collection of hipster chic. Across from a combo coffee and spirits bar was the box-sized Lovecraft Museum and Bookstore. The bookstore sold horror and occult books, along with curios related to Lovecraft and weird fiction.

An hour before our reading fifty or so friends, writers, artists, and fans gathered to buy books and meet-and-greet. Peter and I sat at café tables in front of the bookstore. We shook hands, signed books, and took pictures with fans. I was not expecting the level of enthusiasm our reading received, particularly given we were the only authors/readers at what was, ostensibly, a film festival. The brightness within the mall atrium reflected our moods.

Ten minutes before the reading began, Niall (one of the owners of the bookstore and the film festival event planners) asked in what order did we want to read. Without hesitating, Peter said he really wanted to go second. He rambled on for quite a bit saying normally it didn't matter to him and he apologized to me for making it a big deal but, today, he really wanted to go second. He was anxious and afraid, shrinking and receding away from the café table at which I remained seated during our last conversation together. I told Peter it was fine and I would go first even though it wasn't fine.

The room used for the reading was a small common area hidden behind a row of store fronts. There was a black couch and skeletal collection of gray fold up chairs, perhaps enough to seat thirty. The room wasn't well lit despite the two rows of windows. The ceiling was low and white. The walls were stone, stratified, a dark shale. At the back of the room, in the designated reading area, were a red plush chair and a black hooded microphone in a bent metal stand.

After Niall briefly introduced me, I sat in the chair and I read. I read parts of a longer story that I wrote for a bird-themed horror anthology. I've done enough readings to know when a crowd is paying attention. They laughed at the appropriate parts and when I chanced a look into the audience their eyes were on me and not on the floor or out a window or closed. I read for twenty minutes and answered two questions from the audience, one about the film adaptation and one about what I was working on currently. You always had to have an answer for that question even if the real answer was nothing. Then it was Peter's turn.

I walked to the standing-room-only area along a wall behind the audience and near the room's only entrance/exit. When Peter and I passed he said great job and patted my shoulder. I said thanks, and there was a part of me that wanted to say fuck you, I'm not your opening act. I shouldn't have been so petty and angry, but I was. I stood in the back and stewed despite how well the reading and previous hour of book signings went. I was a petulant little asshole and I didn't care.

Peter wore a blue *Jaws* tee shirt and cargo shorts. He didn't sit in the chair but stood in front of the microphone. He towered at the front of the room. He started off thanking people and making jokes but I wasn't really listening. I think he sent a playful jab my way because there was laughter and then he said, no, seriously, it's an honor reading with Jared and he's like a brother to me. Him saying that pissed me off too. Was this the kind of faux-deference, self-important smarm he peddled now that he was publishing with the bigs?

Peter un-shouldered his black bag onto the red chair, bent, and rooted around inside of it. He emerged with a black .22 in his hand. I didn't see him pull out the handgun because I assumed he was retrieving a book from which to read and I was lackadaisically scanning the crowd, picking out who I'd sold and signed books for.

There was a gasp and a few nervous laughs that died so quickly as to have never been. I looked up in time to see him with the barrel in his mouth and his eyes closed. I looked up in time to see him squeeze the trigger and tense up his arms and shoulders and his mouth, bracing himself.

There was a loud pop and I flinched so hard my teeth clicked together. His body dropped and smoke hung in the air in his place, where he used to be, poof, abracadabra, gone. Peter fell back, knocking into the red chair before landing on the floor. One of his feet must've kicked the mic stand because it tipped into the attendees in the first row, and when the mic bounced to the floor feedback shrieked through the speakers. Some of the attendees spilled out of their chairs, trying to scoot back and away from Peter and the gun, others rushed to where his body lay, and I couldn't see him in the immediate aftermath. Everyone was screaming. I pushed through the crowd and stepped over abandoned folding chairs. There was blood on the stone wall at about Peter's height. There was blood on the back of the red chair that he hadn't used. There was blood on the floor under Peter's turned head and his left arm. In my memory that expanding pool of blood resembles a shape that continually shifts.

***

It's been two days since the second envelope arrived. I haven't opened it yet.

During those two days I found photos of the two reading attendees who killed themselves, photos from before and after the reading. I can't look at either set of their photos without crying. There wasn't anything in their before pictures. But there was in their afters.

Two days. I took hundreds more pictures of myself and printed them all out. Every picture had those lingering, lurking, Escher-like shadows, dark forms, or outlines of empty space, that weren't there in any of my pictures previously. They weren't there until they were. They're there in any new photo of me now no matter how or where or when or the angle or how bright or how dark. And they're there with me now even if I can only almost see them.

I carefully cut out the shadow pieces from all the photos. I couldn't pretend they were cancerous cells that could be removed, at least not from me, but maybe I could stop this from spreading to anyone else. Maybe this was what Peter had thought too, back when he'd mailed me his photo. I wanted to call Dominick and explain to him what I was doing, but I couldn't risk it, couldn't risk him.

I was going by feel, by hunch. It was an idea, one that I couldn't shake or stop thinking about, and I had no choice but to see it all the way through. Sometimes ideas were like that.

I stripped down to my underwear and taped and glued the cut out pieces to my body, covering myself, bit by bit, lining up the edges so that they fit together perfectly. Seamlessly. As if there were no seams. I started by covering my right forearm and it turned to shadow, to space, to nothingness. I spent hours and hours applying the pieces to my body. With only my eyes not covered, I shuffled into the bathroom, slow but as inexorable as an advancing glacier. I stood in front of the mirror. I was not there. I could not see me.

I took a picture and I was not in that either. I was gone already.

***

I ignore phone calls and let the battery finally die. There was a knock on my door a few hours ago and I ignored that too. I am sitting at my small kitchen table. They will find me or they won't find me armored in my suit, scaled with bits of shadow.

I finally decide to open the second envelope, the one that arrived after the first one even though Peter had mailed it one day earlier. Time is not an arrow, and if it ever was, it has been broken into pieces, and then the pieces broken into more pieces, and again and again and again.

My shadow-fingers are clumsy, but insistent. Inside the envelope is the same type of thank you card, one of a set. There's no photo. Two sentences written inside the card.

"I had an idea. It won't go away."

The Time Eater

When Roger Borough receives an unexpected call from a mysterious woman, he is summoned into the past by news that an old college friend is dying. When he encounters James Steiner again the floodgates of his unconscious become unlocked, releasing a deluge of memories and fears he has worked hard to forget.

But that's not all.

Their reunion also unearths a secret, a ritual from their shared past that awakened an entity so vast, so outside of space and time, that it shattered their youthful reality.

Now that entity is back.

And it is ravenous and all-devouring . . .

Author: Aaron J. French
Publication Date: January 27, 2017

"RELENTLESS AND UNSETTLING."–GRAHAM MASTERTON

THE TIME EATER

AARON J. FRENCH

INTRODUCTION BY LAIRD BARRON

BEHOLD THE VOID

PHILIP FRACASSI

BEHOLD THE VOID

Nine stories of terror that huddle in the dark space between cosmic horror and the modern weird

Scorned lover acquires bizarre, telekinetic powers

Thief does bloody battle with a Yakuza for the soul of a horse god

A priest must solve the mystery of a century-old serial killer or risk the apocalypse

A newly-married couple discover that relationships-gone-bad can be poisonous, and deadly

A child is forced to make an ultimate choice between letting his parents die or living with the monsters they may become . . .

Author: Philip Fracassi
Publication Date: March 10, 2017

WWW.JOURNALSTONE.COM

MURMURS IN THE DARK

THE REAL AND THE UNREAL

BY DONALD TYSON

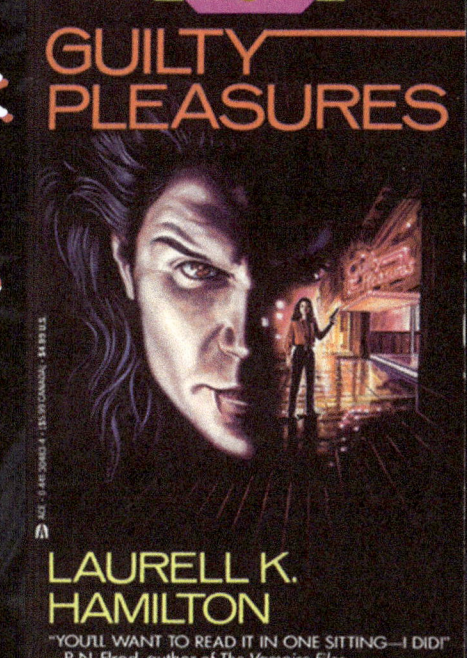

Alternate Realities

I remember how shocked I was when I read Laurell K. Hamilton's novel *Guilty Pleasures* for the first time. Maybe shocked is not quite the right word. Disquieted might be a better way to put it. Nothing in the content of the novel bothered me. It is a well-crafted novel about a woman's interaction with a clan of vampires, the first in Hamilton's popular Anita Blake series.

What disturbed me was that the entire world inside the novel was aware of vampires and other supernatural beings living among them as normal members of society. The novel was set in an alternate reality in which vampires were not only real, but accepted. More than this, it created an entire alternate history in which vampires had for centuries existed alongside human beings.

Looking back, it is hard for me to pin down exactly what I found so disturbing about this concept. I think it was its sheer novelty that discomforted me. It denied all my expectations.

I was well familiar with the idea of vampires, of course. The vampire has been a fixture of Western fiction since John William Polidori wrote his famous story "The Vampyre" on that same fateful night in June of 1816 on which Mary Shelley began writing her ground-breaking horror novel *Frankenstein; or, the Modern Prometheus*. Prior to this the vampire had existed in European literature only in references to ancient myths and folktales.

Vampires were usually assumed to hover about on the fringes of human society. Their material existence was rejected by sceptics within the very stories and novels in which they were featured. They were always presented as uncanny, unnatural, belonging to the other realm, that outland beyond reason and science. Much of the horror of the vampire lies in its nonconformity to everything we take for granted, everything we think we know to be true.

Hamilton's novel broke that barrier between the known and unknown, the natural and the supernatural. In her Anita Blake series the vampires are right here among us, free to prey upon us and manipulate us with their occult powers.

Since the publication of Hamilton's novel in 1993, other fantasy and horror writers have followed her lead. The Southern Vampire Mysteries series by Charlaine Harris is one example, but probably the most famous occult novel series that imitates Hamilton's alternate history concept is the Harry Dresden series by Jim Butcher.

Today it seems very natural to readers to create an alternate world history to accommodate some otherworldly reality. But upon first impression, it is a startling concept that requires some internal adjustment before it can be accommodated. Prior to its introduction, reality was reality, and the supernatural was the supernatural. They interacted at rare intervals, as they do in our actual lives, but they never overlapped.

I should mention that Hamilton did not originate this concept. Others before her experimented with it with varying degrees of success. *The Man In the High Castle* by science fiction writer Philip K. Dick is a prominent example. In this novel, Nazi Germany and Japan won the Second World War and occupy the United States. But Hamilton perfected the perfect normalcy of a world in which the natural and supernatural are seamlessly interlaced.

The Dreamlands of H. P. Lovecraft

There was one other occasion on which my sense of reality was jolted in this same manner by a work of fiction. It occurred when I read my first dreamlands story written by H. P. Lovecraft. Lovecraft wrote two stories and a novel involving his most famous character, Randolph Carter, in which the "experienced dreamer" Carter enters and explores an alternate reality that Lovecraft called the "dreamlands." The stories are "The Silver Key" and "Through the Gates of the Silver Key." The novel is *The Dream Quest of Unknown Kadath*. Lovecraft also wrote other stories devoted to various parts of the dreamlands such as "The Cats of Ulther" and "The White Ship." Collectively these dream stories are known as his Dream Cycle.

I'm not certain, but I believe the first Randolph Carter

I found the idea that dreams could be a landscape both intriguing and difficult to accept. Once I was able to wrap my mind around it, I appreciated its brilliance as a literary concept.

Lovecraft was not entirely original in his dreamlands stories. He was imitating the work of Lord Dunsany, an English writer he greatly admired who wrote dreamlike stories using bejewelled prose. But Lovecraft gave a solid sense of reality to the dreamlands that exists in his stories alone.

H. P. Lovecraft

Bear in mind that I read this Randolph Carter dreamlands story by Lovecraft before I studied the phenomenon of lucid dreaming, and before the creation of the World Wide Web. It is a lot easier for a younger reader to grasp that imaginary worlds may have reality than it was for me. The modern Internet itself is a kind of alternate reality that we enter and leave at will.

I need to emphasize that there was something different in kind between both Hamilton's integration of vampires and other uncanny creatures with our normal reality, and Lovecraft's similar integration of the dream-lands with our waking world, when compared with the

story I read was the "Silver Key." Until reading this story by Lovecraft, I had made the same separation in my mind between reality and dreams that I had made between reality and the supernatural. That is, they were separate realms, one real and one usually dismissed as imaginary, that sometimes touched briefly, resulting in an uncanny incident, but nonetheless remained distinct from each other.

Upon first reading Lovecraft's story, I remember that I could not quite grasp what Lovecraft was getting at. I was like a primitive tribesman in the Amazonian rain forest who sees an airplane fly overhead for the first time, never having heard about such a thing before in his entire life. The eye sees, but the mind cannot quite comprehend what is seen.

There is a story that when the first ships of the Spanish conquistadores arrived in the New World, the natives could not see the ships even when they approached near to the shore. The ships of Spain were so strange to their minds, they had nothing to relate them to, and so for a time at least the ships remained invisible, or at least incomprehensible.

So it was for me upon my first encounter with Lovecraft's experienced dreamer, Randolph Carter. Not that anything within the dreamlands was that strange or difficult to grasp—no, it was the very concept that a man could enter the dreamlands during sleep in the same way he might travel across the sea to a distant foreign land.

conventional fantasy realms so common in pulp fiction written during the first half of the 20th century. In conventional fantasy, the hero travels from the real, everyday world to the fantasy world, which is always somewhere else. It may be distant in space, or in time, or even in dimensions of reality, but it is always removed and apart from our everyday reality.

For example, John Carter, the main character in the Mars novels of Edgar Rice Burroughs, must be actually transported by some magic technology from Earth to Mars. The gulf of space separates the two worlds. The same may be said about his series of fantasy novels about Venus, and the Pellucidar series about a realm that exists within the center of the hollow Earth.

Lovecraft's dreamlands merge with our real world. It is possible to visit a place in the dreamlands that is also a place in reality. Of course the dream place is not exactly the same as the real place, but the two are not separated. They do not merely touch, they interpenetrate each other. It is sometimes possible for dreamers and those who wake to talk to each other in certain special locations where the imposed distinction between reality and the dreamlands becomes vague and ill-defined—for example, in the ancient cottage mentioned in Lovecraft's 1926 story, "The Strange, High House in the Mist."

Astral Planes

At the time I first read of Lovecraft's dreamlands, I knew almost nothing about the practice of astral projection, in which a waking person projects his astral body into a place known as the astral world, or astral plane. Had I been aware of astral projection, I'm sure Lovecraft's story "The Silver Key" would not have startled me so deeply.

The astral plane and Lovecraft's dreamlands are essentially the same place. The astral plane is understood by occultists to be a dimension or realm of reality that overlies our waking reality, touching it at every point. But the astral plane contains things not contained in the real world, and extends beyond the boundaries of our real world.

There is no significant difference between the astral projection of occultists and Lovecraft's dream exploration. His character Randolph Carter was projecting himself into the astral plane, or lucid dreaming, even though Lovecraft never employed these terms.

Theosophy and other occult schools of the West teach that there are many layered astral planes, each related to but unique from all the others. Lovecraft's dreamlands may be regarded as one specific astral plane accessible to the mind of Randolph Carter. Many other beings, both from our earthly reality and from other more alien realities, are able to access this particular astral plane that was explored by Carter. But such astral planes are innumerable.

The fantasy worlds created by Hamilton, Harris, Butcher and other writers may be looked upon as different astral planes—each unique to itself, but at the same time interpenetrating our common physical reality.

The question naturally arises, how much reality do these astral planes possess? Are there really such worlds linked with our world, but displaced dimensionally from our world? Can something done in an astral reality affect anything in the common physical world?

The answer is not quite as obvious as it might seem to cynics. Both physical world and astral world have a common link, and it is the human mind that perceives and interacts with them. As it says in the Emerald Tablet of Hermes Trismegistus:

> What is below is like that which is above,
> And what is above is like that which is below;
> To accomplish the miracle of the One Thing.

Microcosm and macrocosm, the little world and the great world, are connected by the human mind, within which both have their existence. If you believe your physical world does not exist in your mind, you need to re-take Philosophy 101, or maybe just think about the question a little harder. We can know nothing beyond ourselves. Everything we perceive, both near and far, lies within us or we could not perceive it. The physical world—what we usually think of as the "real" word—is a construction and a projection of the mind.

Does anything lie beyond that construction in our mind that we call the physical universe? Maybe. But we can never know anything about it, if it exists, because we can only know what lies within our own mind. If the physical universe has a ground or basis apart from us, we are forever barred from experiencing it.

Astral Projection

Once these concepts are grasped, it becomes easier to consider that there may be an interaction between the "real"

Astral Traveler Sylvan Muldoon

world and the astral world. Certainly, in the literature of the occult, such interactions are common. If you read the 1929 book *The Projection of the Astral Body* by Hereward Carrington and Sylvan Muldoon, you will find many instances in which the astral world became perceptible to those awake and in a normal state of consciousness.

For example, Hereward Carrington wrote in that work of his own experiments with astral projection:

> On a number of occasions I 'willed' to appear to a certain young lady—naturally quite psychic—just as I was falling to sleep. Most of these attempts were apparent failures, but on three occasions she awoke suddenly and saw me standing in the room or sitting on her bed. I remained visible for a few seconds, then 'melted away.'
> —*The Projection of the Astral Body*, Rider and Company, p. 37

It was Lovecraft's genius to recognize that the astral world, or the world of dreams, has no separation from the waking world. It is all around us, all the time. Lovecraft emphasized this concept in his 1920 short story, "From Beyond," which is about a scientist who creates a machine that allows him to perceive the unseen world that surrounds him and the creatures who dwell in it. The observer of the overlapping world that is usually invisible to our sight is only in danger from the creatures that inhabit the other world if he interacts with them, by moving his body in response to them. Of course the astral world revealed by the machine in this story is different from Lovecraft's concept of the dreamlands. Each astral plane is different, and they are innumerable.

In his 1919 story "Beyond the Wall of Sleep" Lovecraft wrote:

> I have frequently wondered if the majority of mankind ever pause to reflect upon the occasionally titanic significance of dreams, and of the obscure world to which they belong. Whilst the greater number of our nocturnal visions are perhaps no more than faint and fantastic reflections of our waking experiences—Freud to the contrary with his puerile symbolism—there are still a certain remainder whose immundane and ethereal character permits of no ordinary interpretation, and whose vaguely exciting and disquieting effect suggests possible minute glimpses into a sphere of mental existence no less important than physical life, yet separated from that life by an all but impassable barrier. From my experience I cannot doubt but that man, when lost to terrestrial consciousness, is indeed sojourning in another and uncorporeal life of far different nature from the life we know; and of which only the slightest and most indistinct memories linger after waking. From those blurred and fragmentary memories we may infer much, yet prove little. We may guess that in dreams life, matter, and vitality, as the earth knows such things, are not necessarily constant; and that time and space do not exist as our waking selves comprehend them. Sometimes I believe that this less material life is our truer life, and that our vain presence on the terraqueous globe is itself the secondary or merely virtual phenomenon.

In Lovecraft's fiction, there is always a threat that the inhabitants of the dreamlands may attack and kill dream explorers. To die in the dreamlands causes a vital shock in the physical body, and may even result in death in this reality. This makes the exploration of the dreamlands more significant than mere fantasy entertainment. It shows that Lovecraft's dreamlands can influence everyday reality in his fictional universe.

Dangers of Astral Projection

Similarly, in astral projection there is said to be potential danger when the traveler interacts with the inhabitants of the astral plane. It is possible that the traveler may be attacked and killed in the astral plane, which might result in death of the body; or prevented from returning to his physical body, which would cause a catatonic state for the empty shell devoid of its animating spirit.

Sylvan Muldoon related in *The Projection of the Astral Body* an encounter with the malicious spirit of a man recently dead. Muldoon wrestled with the spirit, which tried to prevent Muldoon from returning to the region of his physical body. In spite of all its efforts the spirit was unable to stop the reunion of Muldoon's projected astral double with his physical body. Muldoon commented:

> Sceptics may say that this was a nightmare; but I know when I am conscious, and I know what is real when I am conscious. It was no nightmare! It was real! It was as real as any tussle with a flesh-and-blood devil could be.
> —*The Projection of the Astral Body*, p. 293

Today we have a convenient term for what Muldoon experienced, a term that is used to dismiss the importance

and the reality of the event. We call it "sleep paralysis." What a wonderful term, that by its mere utterance can banish all the questions we otherwise might have about this extraordinary experience! Tell a person that they have not really wrestled with a demon on the astral plane, but have merely experienced "sleep paralysis," and all their doubts and fears are sent slinking away like embarrassed school boys.

As it happens, I have had many experiences similar to Muldoon's, and I can support his assertion that his was not an ordinary nightmare. Sleep paralysis, as it is now called, is quite distinct from dreaming. There is an awareness of a malicious presence that approaches ever nearer. Usually this presence cannot be seen, but it can always be distinctly felt in all its loathsome details as it presses against its victim's paralysed body. It presses down upon the legs with a palpable weight, slowly moving itself up the body to the chest, or even covering the face. This causes difficulties in breathing which are not present before the malicious spirit presses on the chest or covers the face.

The victim of this assault—for that is exactly what it is—is unable to move. This is a defense mechanism. In sleep we are usually paralysed so that we do not hurt ourselves by thrashing around while we dream. When we become conscious while still in this paralysed condition, we are naturally helpless against the assault of the type of spirit that in past centuries was known as the Hag, and also as the Mare.

No Separation Between the Astral and the Physical

The lowest astral world resembles the waking world in every respect, apart from small and seemingly insignificant details that allow the astral traveler, or the lucid dreamer, to realize that he has entered the astral world. Oliver Fox mentioned that in one of his dreams he noticed some paving stones arranged in a pattern which he knew they did not possess. This caused him to realize that he was not awake, but dreaming.

> With the realization of this fact, the quality of the dream changed in a manner very difficult to convey to one who has not had this experience. Instantly the vividness of life increased a hundredfold. Never had sea and sky and trees shone with such glamorous beauty; even the commonplace houses seemed alive and mystically beautiful. Never had I felt so absolutely well, so clear-brained, so divinely powerful, so inexpressibly free!
> —Fox, *Astral Projection*, Citadel Press, p. 33

MCGRATH 97

As the astral planes progress, they diverge more and more from the everyday waking world, until at last they lose all common features and become wholly alien. This is one reason they were referred to as "planes." It may be useful to think of them as infinitely thin LP records stacked one on top of the other. At the bottom lies the physical world, and as the stack of disks mounts ever higher, it becomes less and less like the physical world that is its base, until no obvious common links with the physical can be found. The higher planes are esoteric and rarefied in the extreme.

Bear in mind, however, that there is no physical separation between the physical world and even the highest and most rarefied astral plane. All astral planes intersect with the material world, which at its atomic level is not solid but composed only of dancing energy. The solid physical world itself is an illusion, despite how persuasive it can be to we poor human beings with our pathetically limited consciousness.

Accounts differ as to how many astral worlds there are, but it is my own opinion that they are infinite in number, as many as the future dimensions of reality that are said to branch forward from our actions in the present moment in time.

If we accept that the astral planes are infinite, then all fictional worlds that have ever been created in literature are actual realms in the astral cosmos. Somewhere there is a Randolph Carter exploring the dreamlands. Somewhere an Anita Blake hunts rogue vampires. Somewhere a Harry Dresden practices his magic in Chicago.

In an infinite time, an infinite space, an infinite cosmic mind that contains all our minds, the worlds are as many in number as the potential to conceive them.

Seeke not to finde by what device
Men climb from Hell to Paradise,
Nor understand why Satann Fell,
From starrie Paradise to Hell.
For curs't thou art, if thou dost look
To find it in the Divill's Booke

—Jeremiah Staveley, 1595

The ancient city of Morchester with its
fine old cathedral and close where the rooks
caw as they have done for centuries …

A tranquil English scene … but is it? Under the surface dark and terrible things are stirring: a serial killer is on the loose … the Dean's guilty nightmares … a long-dead Bishop of Morchester … a mysterious ring disappears from the cathedral … a famous composer begins his descent into Hell …

A television crew and a celebrated academic conduct a very public search for THE BOKE OF THE DIVILL? One man knows the danger they are in: the mysterious Basil Valentine. But without the help of young Emma Hartley, can he save them?

Thrilling, witty, fantastic, horrifying and strangely profound, this new novel will be available in deluxe lettered and signed & numbered hardcover editions. Coming Fall of 2016!

"Reggie Oliver's writing … is clearly derived not from what he has read but how he has come to see the world … contains some of the best horror prose of the century…. a brooding voice uniquely his own…. by far the most important horror book of the year."

—Dejan Ogjanovic (*Rue Morgue*)

The BOKE of the DIVILL

Reggie Oliver

cover art by
Santiago Caruso

interior illustrations by
Reggie Oliver

DarkRenaissanceBooks.com

Bracken MacLeod

She Dreams of Ghosts and Shadows

> "...men are afraid women will laugh at them... women are afraid men will kill them."
> —Gavin de Becker, The Gift of Fear

She traced the moistened rim of her wineglass with a finger trying to hear the crystal sing. But the shouted conservations over thumping music, and laughing and cheering at the muted game on televisions all kept the high, light tone of the glass from reaching her ears. She gave up, resigned to the idea that the bar's stemware probably wasn't delicate enough to respond to her touch anyway. She lifted the drink and took a sip of cheap wine poured from a too-long open bottle with a cartoon hedgehog or chinchilla or something else nauseatingly cute on the label. The man on the stool next to her shouted over the anonymous song that sounded like it could be country or rock, maybe rap, but definitely exactly like the last song and the next on the random playlist. She tilted her head, moving an ear closer to him. "What?"

He repeated, "What do you *do*?" She didn't know this man and didn't want to judge, but if she had to guess, he was probing because he needed to know how much work it would be to talk to her. He didn't have a look to her like someone who wanted to know what she did because other people's lives genuinely interested him. But then, most people didn't *really* want to know what exactly went into being a dental receptionist or a paralegal. They wanted to put someone else in a context that related to their own. They just wanted a conversation starter. Something to ignite camaraderie like lighting paper under kindling.

"I'm a medium," she said.

"A mediator?"

"A *medium*," she said again, correcting him. His face clouded with confusion, and she took a small amount of pleasure at not being easily put into one of his social boxes. Soon enough, she figured he'd find one into which she fit. But right now, she was outside. She'd come out to relax and not think about work or life or anything other than the glass of pinot grigio in front of her. But then, that was the hazard of going out in public alone. She stalled and finished her last sip of wine, thinking once the glass was empty, she could politely get up and excuse herself without looking like she was trying to snub the guy. The last thing she needed was for him to feel slighted because he was "just trying to be nice" and she didn't feel like having a long conversation about work. The moment frustrated her. She'd had to screw up the will to go out in the first place. It'd been six months since Cory left, and she was tired of sitting home with only their cat—*her* cat now— as a drinking partner. *One glass at Joe's,* she'd thought. It was supposed to be self-care. Just get out of the apartment, get a Buffalo chicken wrap, a glass of pinot, and a healthy reminder that the world continued on, despite the end of her relationship. She told herself, from time to time she needed to be around living people who didn't want something from her, so she wouldn't become a bitter shut-in. So, she'd called Caitlin and asked her to come out and meet her for a drink. Caitlin had said she'd be right there, but it was now over an hour and three glasses of wine past "right there," and it was plain that her friend wasn't coming.

Instead, she sat here at the bar next to this guy in his casual suit and no tie trying to find a demure way to slip away.

He turned to the bartender and held up a finger, dropping it to point at the empty wineglass before she'd even set it down completely. She didn't want him to buy her a drink, but before she could raise her own hand and shake her head, the wine was already pouring. The bartender recorked the bottle and dropped it back in the minifridge under the glowing blue liquor shelves without asking for cash or the guy's card. He had a tab. Her companion—he was her companion now—said something she didn't make out and the bartender reached out and plucked a bottle of something off a shelf that looked like glacial ice, pouring until he made the gesture for "when." The bright azure LEDs along the shelves made it hard to read the labels on anything. Then again, it might not have been the lights. She wondered if he knew the bartender by name. They seemed to have that kind of rapport. She couldn't ever remember seeing him at Joe's before. Not that *she* was a real regular.

He took a drink and leaned closer. His breath smelled like expensive vodka. Normally, she enjoyed that mixture of breath and spirit, especially when it was coming from Cory's close mouth. Tonight, it felt a little too much like having cocktails with a shark. There was a scent of blood under the Grey Goose.

"So, you're like a palm-reader." Not a question.

There it was. The box.

She shook her head. "No. I'm a professional *medium*." He made a face and shrugged as if to say, what's the difference. She sighed and resigned herself to explaining *again*. "I don't tell fortunes. Mostly, I help people talk to relatives and loved ones who've passed on, and help them cope with their grief and loss." *The way I'm trying to do now, by drinking an entire bottle of wine by myself in a college bar.*

He smirked and she braced herself for the patronizing explanation that there's no such thing as ghosts. Instead, he said, "Sounds interesting. How does somebody find themselves in that line of work?" She couldn't tell if he was being condescending or not. He hadn't asked if she had to do post-graduate work, but he didn't seem entirely sincere either. Of course, there weren't ghosts. She read *people* for a living. Got them to open up about their own fears and aspirations, talk about the loved ones they missed, and to tell her first what they wanted her to tell them. Her job was all about getting a sense of people and reflecting what she saw back. But this guy was confounding her. He wasn't giving. He kept asking questions and not offering anything, which put her off balance. She took a sip of the wine he'd ordered.

"It's a..." she almost said "calling." Tilting her head, she said, "Nobody can teach you to be psychic—you either are or you aren't. But if you are, then you can be taught to channel spirits safely."

He leaned back, smiling. "Do you have a card?"

"Why?" she asked.

His smile faded and he paused for a moment before saying, "I'd like to... talk to my mother." His voice became soft and hard to hear in the noise of the bar, but somehow she got every word. "She died last year while I was away on business and I didn't get to say goodbye. But maybe you can help me do that. Right? Reach out and help me say goodbye to her?"

She shook her head trying to clear some of the alcohol buzz clouding her judgment. Cory used to tease her about being a cheap date. She never really got the hang of drinking. She liked a glass of white wine with dinner, or on rare occasions, when she was out with friends, maybe a cocktail—something froofy like a lemon drop or a cosmo, not hard like a martini. Two glasses was her comfort zone. But then, two glasses sometimes were sufficient to lower her inhibitions enough to say yes to a third. And then a fourth would follow. That was not a problem when she was out with her girls, but here she was by herself. Except, she wasn't really by herself. The bar was half full of Tufts students laughing and tying one on before classes tomorrow. She was safe and he wasn't mocking her or mansplaining how the world *really* worked. He wanted a card. He wanted to talk to his mother. Everything was fine.

She turned and reached for her purse hanging off the back of the barstool. Fumbling for a moment with the clasp and then trying to dig the card case out from under her wallet and a half-empty bag of cough lozenges. She faced the bar again, setting the bag in her lap and dug deep. She pulled out a card and held it up, staring at the front for a second before handing it over. He took it with a ready hand, and held it between thumb and forefinger, while his other fingers remained tight in a fist, as though he was holding something else too. He read it aloud. "Carrie Grimwood, Certified Medium and Life Coach. Nice to meet you, Carrie," he said. "I'm Justin." He held out a hand. She took it and gave it a quick shake. His palm was warm and dry and pleasant to touch. He held on a second too long, but let go when she pulled away. He lifted his drink, holding it up and out to her. Though she didn't feel like having more, she didn't want to be rude, so she touched her glass to his and took a drink. The cool semi-sweet liquid rolled over her tongue and she savored it for a moment before swallowing. It was cheap, but like most things alcoholic, any perceived deficiencies in flavor decreased with volume. It had been a while since she'd allowed herself an indulgence like this out in public. Justin seemed nice, if not really her type. Plus, he was a potential customer now. She looked at the face of her cellphone and checked the time. It was early and she wasn't ready to go home to an empty apartment. God damn Cory and Caitlin both. She deserved a nice night out and was going to have it. She decided to finish her drink, have a nice conversation, and then leave. Wasn't this what people went to bars for? To meet other folks and have nice, casual chats. And if Justin got too forward or persistent, she'd just call a cab and have the driver take her the long way home around the block instead of walking. She was a city girl and knew how to take care of herself.

She dropped her phone and the card case in her handbag and slung it back over the back of her chair. "Tell me about your mother," she said. She might have slurred. "Speaking in cursive," is what Cory called it. Justin smiled and began to describe the woman who raised him. At least Carrie thought he did. It was increasingly hard to hear over the din of the bar

did they turn up the music?

and she felt fuzzy, like she'd pressed her head too deep into a pillow. But then she wasn't at home in bed. She was out at the bar. She could hear the music and the cheering. There was shouting and merriment all around. She tried to blink away the disorientation, but her eyes blurred on the second and third blinks, only clearing up on the fourth.

"Are you all right?" he asked.

She nodded and slipped clumsily off the stool onto her feet. "I need to freshen up. Be right back." She took a wobbly step toward the bathroom and stopped, trying to think of what it was she was missing. She reached behind her, slipped her purse off the back of the stool, and continued on. Justin said something like, "I'll be here," or "All the tears," or something like that.

The cramped bathroom was big enough for a single occupant. Carrie slipped in and threw the slide bolt. It was barely one step up from a hook and eye latch, but it made her feel better to think that anyone wanting in would have to make an obvious gesture to get through the door. She leaned over the sink, porcelain brown around the knobs with corrosion and yellow in the basin, and felt ill. But she couldn't puke. Her head started to swim and it felt like the floor pitched under her feet. When she hit her head on the edge of the sink she knew what had moved was her. Straight down. She knelt on the bathroom floor, hands planted in spilled sink water and trodden piss from the toilet stall a few feet away. The edges of her vision dimmed again as she tried to make sense of the familiar things scattered around her knees. A lipstick, lozenges, glasses case, and wallet. She fumbled and picked up the silver business card case with the cloisonné enamel flower on the front.

I spilled… I spilled my purse.

Carrie shoved her things back into her bag and tried to stand. Her legs were weak and unsteady, but with the help of the sink, she got to her feet without falling again. She turned and splashed water in her face before looking in the cloudy mirror. She felt embarrassed to be this drunk out in public. But she'd been drunk plenty of times. This wasn't the same. This felt different.

He drugged me.

It was time to go.

She slung the bag over her shoulder and reached for the slide bolt. The clacking sound of it in its bracket made her wince. It seemed so much louder than everything. Like a signal screaming, I'M COMING OUT! I'M BACK HERE! She hesitated a moment before opening the door and peeking out. A group of college kids were huddled around the digital jukebox giggling about the music they were trying to select, blocking her view of Justin toward the front of the bar. That suited her. Still, she had to walk past him if she was going to leave. The idea made her stomach threaten to rebel again. She could happily abandon the light hoodie she'd left draped over the back of her chair if there was another way out. But she couldn't see one.

"Through here."

The voice was thin and soft, but it carried over the noise like it had been whispered directly in her ear. She whipped her head around, ready to slam the door shut and scream for help. But no one was standing next to the door. She heard it again. "Through here." Carrie looked in the direction of the sound and saw a woman standing in the kitchen dressed like she was out for an early morning run, not a night on the town. She lifted a hand and beckoned Carrie with a finger. "This way," the woman whispered. And then one of the cooks in the kitchen walked through her. She shuddered like disturbed mist and then settled again. Dark bruises on one side of her face and body seemed to grow darker and then fade again. She beckoned with more urgency. Carrie staggered out of the bathroom and into the restaurant kitchen. Her shoes slipped on the grease coated floor mats and she lurched toward the back door, propped open with a milk crate. "¡Oye! No puedes salir por ahí!" She ignored the cook and kept going, following the woman in the running shorts and bruises.

The air outside was brisk, but not cutting. She lurched to the left and started running up the block away from the front of the restaurant and Mass Ave. with its bright lights and wide sidewalks. She wanted to get lost in the shadows, disappear like a spirit. She looked back over her shoulder and saw a dark figure standing on the distant corner under Joe's awning light. It was Justin, looking around. Looking for her. She ducked into a yard and crouched behind a rhododendron, trying to make herself small. The misty woman appeared in front of her, her indistinct face still seemingly full of worry, and whispered, "You can't stop. Not here." She was right. Whatever Justin had put in her drink was working its magic. Carrie felt certain that running and making her heart pump hard would only spread whatever it was through her bloodstream faster. But her choices were try to get home, or hide and pass out anyway in these bushes. She preferred to be behind a deadbolt instead of a bush, if she could make it.

She straightened up and slipped into the backyard and clumsily climbed over a fence into the neighbor's garden. She was moving farther away from her house, but she wasn't on the streets, and she could backtrack easily enough as long as Justin didn't know where she was. Ahead, she saw a couple of people standing on the sidewalk out in front of the house she crept around. They were also blurry and seemed to have a faint shimmer in the dark. They each held a finger to their lips and pointed away toward the playground where Caitlin took the kids from her daycare. It was deserted and dark, and she ran toward it, stumbling on the uneven sidewalk broken by decades of growing tree roots breaking through the concrete. If she fell, she wouldn't get back up. She knew this as well as she knew anything else. If she fell, she was done.

The woman in the running shorts was gone, as was the couple on the sidewalk. Replaced by a child in the dark playground sitting motionless on a swing, staring at her. Like the others, outside in the dark, she seemed surrounded by a pale light, pulling her out of the scene just enough to suggest she didn't belong. This was not her place.

"Who are you?" Carrie asked.

"I'm no one," the girl said. Not, no one you know. *No one.* She peered around past Carrie's hip and added, "He's coming this way. He can hear us." She hopped off the swing. Despite her leaving it, the seat and chain remained still as if she'd never touched them. The child held out a hand. Carrie reached for it, expecting hers to pass through like the cook walking through the runner. Instead, she felt a solid, small hand slip into her palm. For a second, she felt like she couldn't breathe and was trapped in something holding her still and tight, crushing her. Then the sensation faded and the girl smiled. Her gray skin tinted a light brown for a moment before she lost color in the shadows again, like some image from a black and white movie

escaped into the world. She pulled and Carrie followed.

She was able to move faster and with a surer foot while holding on to the child. They slipped out of the playground, deeper into the neighborhood, taking side streets Carrie had never traveled before. Her surroundings grew less familiar with each step, but she felt lighter and safer as the child led her away.

They turned a corner and the streets opened up unexpectedly onto what looked like a small town square. Wide open lanes instead of narrow city streets encircled a park with a bandstand gazebo in the center and slat benches all around. She looked back, trying to orient herself to this part of the city which she didn't know existed. But what was behind was lost in the blur of her deranging senses.

"Where are we?" she said.

"It's a short cut," the girl replied, pulling her along.

The earth lurched under her like it had in the restaurant bathroom and she staggered a step, trying to keep her feet. She lost hold of the child and stood alone in the middle of the small common, exposed and cold. Much colder than she had been. She turned, looking for the way to go, looking for the girl or another spirit to help guide her, but they had all gone. In the distance up a dark avenue, she saw a shadow. She knew better than to call out to it. It wasn't one of her ghosts. It was him. She could feel it, even if she couldn't see him clearly. She ran away, toward a street lined with tall trees and Victorian houses set far apart

from one another. This was not Cambridge any more. It reminded her of her Nama's neighborhood in Vermont, but that wasn't a shortcut—it was the long way around. Wherever she was, it wasn't home, and the fear of being found by the approaching shade was only slightly greater than the terror of not knowing where this was. So, she ran. Out of the common onto a side street that felt like it led in the direction of her apartment, though she couldn't tell anymore.

Everything was wrong.

She skidded to a stop halfway down the lane. At the end of the block stood an old woman in a nightgown. Not her Nama. A ghost, shimmering pale in the gloom.

Unlike the others, Carrie didn't get the sense she was there to help. This woman felt the opposite. Waves of bad intention crashed off of her like thunder. The old woman stared at her with an expression of open hatred. Her knife slit mouth opened and she emitted a long wail that hurt Carrie's ears and made her disorientation worse. The drug in her blood brought fog and blurred her eyes. It made her legs wobbly and arms weak. But it was the howl that made her feel like dying.

Clapping her hands to her ears, she cast a frantic glance over her shoulder. The distant shape drew nearer, still in formless shadow, but looming larger with every step. The yards on either side of the street were impenetrably dark. The road suggested only two ways to go: toward the approaching shape, or the old woman. Knowing deep in her guts that the void following her guaranteed oblivion, she took a step forward, and then another. The old woman's face screwed up with rage and she opened her mouth wider, her wail never breaking for a breath. The maw gaped wide, revealing an expanse that contained neither tongue nor throat, but a deep nothingness like timeless space, and Carrie was suddenly terrified of being swallowed by the crone and trapped in a dark, eternal nullity. She ducked right and tripped over a low fence, tumbling into the cold, wet lawn of a silent home. Her purse spilled again, her things scattering out silently into the grass. She scrambled, trying not to stay down, but finding it difficult to push up. Gravity was stronger here. She was heavier, and being prone was easier than standing and running or fighting. The desire to stay down and rest was almost as powerful as the impulse to escape. The equality of surrender and revolt warred in her. And surrender began to prevail.

"I found you. This way!" The runner's voice returned. She looked around for the first ghost and saw nothing. The runner called out again, and this time Carrie saw her. She was peeking out from behind the house next door, as if she too wanted to hide from the woman with the abyss in her mouth. Carrie got up on her hands and knees and pushed again, crawling toward the runner until she had the energy to stand. She stood and shuffled until she found it in her to run. She ran until she found the other woman and reached out for her.

The runner grabbed her wrist and Carrie felt a looming force like a city bus bearing down on both of them. She screamed and tried to dodge, but the woman held on, and the force passed through them as if they were never there, or it wasn't. The runner looked at her, and the darkness Carrie had seen hide her face returned before fading again. Though she still couldn't make out her features. "This way. Don't be afraid." Carrie wished that was possible.

Together, they ran until the neighborhood houses grew thick and the streets were narrow and familiar again. The woman pointed to the end of the block and said, "That way."

"You're not coming?"

The runner shook her head. "I can't go *that* way."

"Why not? What's there?"

The woman drifted away on the breeze. A faint hint of a word that might have been "home" disappearing with her.

"Wait! I need you!" There was no answer. No runner, no child. No help. Carrie looked in the direction the runner's ghost had pointed and saw nothing. No houses or streets, no playground or gazebo, just the deep darkness of the old woman's mouth, of the shadow pursuing her, of eternal nothingness, and she was afraid of the dark. "I can't go in there," she said. Tears blurred her heavy-lidded eyes and she repeated herself, though there was no one to answer her or even hear. "I can't go in there. Don't make me do it."

In the distance, a familiar howl rose up.

She hurled herself into the void.

The cold grew warm as everything around her closed in with a lightless intimacy. She felt it against her like the softness of a mattress and heavy covers. She moved, though it was a struggle for her arms and legs. She couldn't feel the ground or see ahead of her. It felt like she was walking, but she might have been sinking underwater or floating away in space. She held up her hand to look, center herself in reality, but it was a dark blur. The shadow world was thick and surrounded her, dimming her shine.

What had at first been a not-unpleasant warmth grew uncomfortable and then painful. The heat pressed against her, felt like scalding water in her lungs when she tried to take a breath. Getting a deep breath seemed impossible, so she took short, small gasps of air. It tasted bad. It smelled. Like… alcohol.

She tried to move again, but the sensation of heaviness increased and pressed against her, leaving her still, trapped in the dark where there was no up or down, and she had no idea where she was going, if she was moving at all. The sensation of lying down returned, and she wondered if she'd fallen again. Tripped over an invisible obstacle in the void and was struggling once more against gravity and her heavy blood. She pushed forward with her palms and the darkness pushed back, bending her arms against her will. That was it. She'd fallen and was face down. If she wasn't walking, she needed to pull herself along through the… shortcut. Home was on the other side. Home and safety. The girl. The couple. The runner. They'd brought her here, and they were helpers, trying to rescue her from the shade, from Justin and his drugs, and they wouldn't throw her in the crone's mouth. They wouldn't sacrifice her to the darkness. She had to believe that. She held on to the thought of them glowing ever so slightly, leading her away from danger. Because they were the very last thing in the world she could imagine. Everything else was gone in the dark.

And so was she.

She gave up and lay down deep in the void and allowed it to take her and leave her with nothing of herself but this last feeling of rest.

And there was nothing.

***

She awoke in her bed. Her head ached and her stomach was sour with hangover. She felt a little like throwing up and was sweaty and weak. But she felt a wave of relief wash over her as she saw the morning light outside making her white window sheers glow. The hydraulic hiss of a kneeling bus pierced the air as it lowered to accept passengers at the stop in front of her apartment. Behind it, the steady drone of traffic passing by and the sounds of the corner gas station next door. Marcos's voice carried into her room as he asked someone at the pumps if it was going to be cash or credit.

She'd made it home. Her spirits had guided her through the night and she made it home into bed, and was safe. The dark had been her room and her bed, and falling into sleep under her heavy duvet covering her head. And everything in the world was all right because here she was. By herself. Just like she started.

Another push of nausea swirled in her belly, and she pulled her knees up to ride out the cramp. She kicked off the covers and let the brisk chill of her drafty apartment dry the sweat from her body. The cool sensation on her bare skin helped. It made the queasiness easier to bear.

Bare skin.

No pajamas.

Too drunk to change into them.

The feeling of needing to vomit came back stronger. She rolled onto her other side and lowered a leg over the edge of her bed. She sat up and hugged herself, working up the will and energy to stand. In the corner she saw her clothes lying in a pile. Cory had called it the "floordrobe." Carrie hated that and always folded her things and put them away or in the hamper. But then, she didn't always drink an entire bottle of wine

and get roofied

and pass out in bed after

running through a spectral world

staggering home.

She looked at the nightstand to see exactly how late she was for work, though she'd already made the decision in that instant to email her clients and reschedule, then spend the rest of the day in bed nursing her hangover and thinking of nasty texts she could send Caitlin for standing her up. In front of the glowing red clock face sat her card, perfectly aligned with both the number display and the edge of the table. With a trembling hand she reached out for it, afraid what feeling it might inspire, recalling the sensation of being crushed when she took the child's hand and the force that passed through her when the runner had grabbed her. But here, in this moment, under the tips of her fingers she felt nothing but cardstock. It slipped off the table with a dry rasp and she crushed it in her hand.

There was no child or couple or runner.

There was no such thing as ghosts.

Photo courtesy of Peter Levenda

LURKING IN SHADOW:
A CONVERSATION WITH
PETER LEVENDA

BY AARON J. FRENCH

Peter Levenda writes occult history, what is sometimes referred to as para-politics, or even conspiracy theory (this latter term developed by the CIA for tactical usage). His foundational trilogy, *Sinister Forces: A Grimoire of American Political Witchcraft*, tracks events and connects dots between the supernatural and natural worlds, peering into corners most researchers leave uninspected. He is, perhaps, best known for his book *Unholy Alliance*, which describes the relation of esotericism to Nazi occultism. However, he has also been associated with H.P. Lovecraft and the "Simon Necronomicon," a grimoire that derives its title from Lovecraft's fabled *Necronomicon*. It has been suggested that Peter is himself "Simon," the author of the book, but Peter has flatly denied this on several occasions, stating he is merely an acquaintance of the enigmatic "Simon." Whatever the case, he has certainly lived an extraordinary life, and I recently had the pleasure of interviewing Mr. Levenda for the *Dark Discoveries* theme of Supernaturalism.

***

Aaron J. French: Thanks, Peter, for taking the time to sit down with *Dark Discoveries*. We are big fans of your work. As you discuss in your article in this issue, you got your start writing in this genre with the *Sinister Forces* trilogy. Tell us a little about your journey with those books, what the experience was like, and how you felt when you finally completed them?

Peter Levenda: It all started with Watergate, actually. Even the phrase—Sinister Forces—comes from Watergate, as I mention in the article. But the idea for the book (and I had written it as a single volume) came about when I read a series of two short articles by Craig Karpel in the *Village Voice* entitled "Patriotic Witchcraft." This was in the 1970s. It tied together Manson, Nixon, Disneyland, and so much else in only a few thousand words but it detonated something in my consciousness. In a sense, I saw "the Matrix" when I finished reading Karpel. I realized then that you couldn't describe all of reality by using the traditional linear narrative approach. There were simply too many moving parts, and elements of what people call "conspiracy theory" are actually the spores of a meta-reality that is impinging on our own, leaving traces here and there and not only as odd coincidences or synchronicities but which have just as much of an effect on our world as actual conspiracies.

When the two—actual conspiracies, legally defined;

and the "sinister forces" of my study— combine, you are introduced to another level of understanding completely. We like to think we are in total control of our environment, and for the most part that is a workable hypothesis. But our naturalistic, materialistic paradigm cannot account for the fact that Maurice Maeterlinck accurately foresaw the details of the Kennedy assassination before Kennedy was even born; or that Lee Harvey Oswald was surrounded by people with connections to The Nine. Or even that I once belonged to the same pseudo-church as David Ferrie, Jack Martin, Carl Stanley and Tommy Baumler. Or that I once worked in the same small office in Queens with Arthur Hochberg, former CIA agent and colleague of E. Howard Hunt. None of this is proof of a conspiracy from any normal, academic, legal perspective. And yet…

So I began to research traditional conspiracy theories as well as deep politics, forgotten history, covert ops, and extended that field to include quantum theory, consciousness studies, and even UFO lore. I even traveled to Canada to get a copy of Phil Agee's book, *Inside the Company: A CIA Diary*, when it was unobtainable in the US. All with a view to using only fully-documented sources in order to build a picture that was at once solid from an evidentiary point of view and completely new. If we are only blind men describing an elephant based on whatever part of its anatomy we are touching, I wanted to compare the experiences of all of them to see if I could draw a picture of the Beast. It was an exhilarating and frustrating 25 years of my life, and when all the research was completed (or as much as it could be at that point) I sat down in my apartment in Kuala Lumpur and wrote it all in a feverish state over the period of almost a year. And then… 9/11 occurred and it all began to feel just a tad surreal.

AJF: Your interests all intersect at this cross-section of politics, the occult, and conspiracy theory. Some of your work also focuses on WWII with *Unholy Alliance: A History of Nazi Involvement with the Occult* (2002) and *The Hitler Legacy* (2014). What was it about

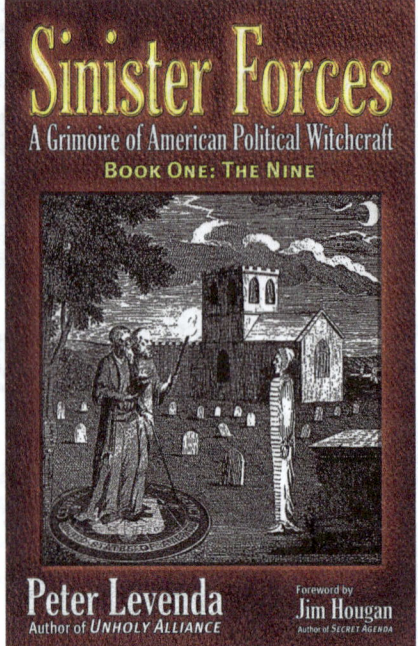

the WWII subject that caught your attention, and what did you manage to dig up in your research?

PL: The whole Nazi angle came about because the Nazis seemed like they had married science and esotericism (at least, the SS had) and understood the value of secular ritual, such as the Nuremberg rallies. Basically we are talking about Emile Durkheim and Max Weber taken to their logical conclusions. Then there were all those books speculating about Nazi occultism, some of which were poorly researched and unsupported by any kind of documentation. Was there anything there at all? Pauwels and Bergier had us all hopping back in the 1960s with their *Morning of the Magicians*, but how much of it was "real?" Was weird fiction becoming weird non-fiction? What was going on?

Around that time I became fascinated by the work of Ladislas Farago, the WW II historian who was unfairly castigated for the book he wrote about his search for Martin Bormann: *Aftermath*. He wrote about a place called Colonia Dignidad, in Chile, and the way he described it made me determined to go down there and see the place for myself. This I did, in 1979. Also around that time I made many trips to the National Archives and the Library of Congress, going through the microfilm records of the Captured German Documents section and it is there that I saw the actual documentation of the SS Ahnenerbe and all their esoteric studies, reports, experiments, and expeditions. It was real, and no one had been there before me to actually look at the original material.

I was stunned by this. We had all this published speculation about Nazi occultism, and here was the actual proof. When combined with my own interviews of Nazis in the US, and Klansmen, and assorted fellow travelers, as well as my research trip to Chile, I began to form a picture of the extent of the Nazi presence in the world and the effect they were having on the political systems of Latin American and Middle Eastern countries. I began to understand that the true believers among the Nazis would not suddenly become "converted" to American democracy and capitalism just because they had lost the war. They would simply move their theater of operations to Egypt, Syria, Argentina, Chile, Paraguay, etc. and continue on from there. When I realized they were being assisted to some degree by our own government, the implications were profound. I had to keep looking, and that meant I had to keep publishing.

AJF: You have written two other books, which I am tempted to call practical books, on the subjects of alchemy, spiritual transformation, and esotericism. These are *Stairway to Heaven: Chinese Alchemists, Jewish Kabbalists, and the Art of Spiritual Transformation* (2008) and *The Tantric Alchemist: Thomas Vaughan and the Indian Tantric Tradition* (2015). Tell us about those book and how they differed in approach from some of your other work. Are you a practitioner yourself? An alchemist maybe?

PL: Alchemy is one of those subjects that have both "real" and "unreal" components, like my understanding of the "sinister forces." If one begins to take a serious interest in alchemy, one gradually begins to understand the political process too and all that "spooky action at a distance." Alchemy is about understanding reality on multiple levels, and the requirement to use a meta-language to do so. If you have an understanding of what I wrote in the two books you mentioned, you can apply that understanding to *Sinister Forces* and see what I am suggesting in a whole new light. I am a great fan of Ioan Coulianu and find that his interest in Giordano Bruno and the idea of the "magical bond" as being Eros is an idea that can be applied to both politics and alchemy equally. *Tantric Alchemist* was a labor of love for almost as long as I was working on *Sinister Forces*.

Aleister Crowley

H. P. Lovecraft

Longer, actually, since I first became fascinated by the subject in 1968 and studied Chinese in the early 1970s in order to read alchemical texts that had not yet been translated. You can thank Kenneth Rexroth for that. *Stairway to Heaven* began as my Master's thesis in religious studies and was considerably expanded for publication. As for whether or not I am an alchemist myself, that would be telling! (Actually, there is no good way to answer that question.)

AJF: The readers of *Dark Discoveries* are probably most familiar with your work on H.P. Lovecraft. *The Dark Lord: H.P. Lovecraft, Kenneth Grant, and the Typhonian Tradition in Magic* (2013) is a unique book and a fascinating expedition into the worlds of Lovecraft, the occult, and Kenneth Grant. And you draw some interesting analogues between the lives and events of Lovecraft and Aleister Crowley, then link it in with the history of the *Ordo Templi Orientis* and modern occultism. How did this project come about? Perhaps you could touch on a few of the relevant points you describe your book.

PL: In the late 1970s and early 1980s I was in contact with a lot of people in the "Occult Renaissance" taking place in New York City at that time. Numerous among them were members of several OTO factions as well as people interested in hardcore magical philosophy and practice. Robert Anton Wilson had made Crowley and Thelema sexy, linking it with Timothy Leary and even with conspiracy theory (in his famous *Illuminatus!* trilogy). One of the most influential writers on deep magic (perhaps the unseparated Siamese twin of deep politics) was Kenneth Grant, author of what would become the three Typhonian trilogies. Grant wrote with command of the subject and was able to expand the ideas in Crowley's work with detailed discussions of Afro-Caribbean and South Asian occult practices. We all devoured Grant's work, because it seemed to provide a window onto Crowleyan occultism from the perspective of a life-long practitioner. The problem with Grant, though, was that he was often indecipherable. He assumed a knowledge of Sanskrit and Tantric literature that his audience was simply not able to provide. One of his more important references—one that consumed a great deal of speculation on the part of Crowleyan occultists—was the concept of the kalas.

Grant wrote that these were mystical essences that emanated from women generally and in particular from those women who were initiates of the system. There were sixteen of them, and the accomplished magician was able to gather these essences on specially-constructed metal plates. It was all very obscure, if somewhat titillating. The problem was: no one knew what the hell he was talking about.

That is only one example. There are many others. I gradually came to realize that what Grant's work required was a concordance of some sort. The fact that there were nine books in total on this system meant that the task would be enormous, so I decided to focus on several of the more important references in his work just as a kind of service to those who were reading Grant and scratching their heads. So I chose the Tantric elements (of which I knew a certain amount, as evidenced by my *Tantric Temples: Eros and Magic in Java*) and some of the Afro-Caribbean elements, with a lot of explanation of the Golden Dawn themes that appear in Crowley's work—notably in *The Book of the Law*—which are never explained.

But there was another aspect to Grant's work as well, and that was the Lovecraftian element. Grant saw in Lovecraft a kind of unconscious medium or channel for occult ideas and forces, and when I took a closer look I was quite surprised to discover that there were definite connections—in terms of language, concepts, and even dates—between Crowley's work (notably his *Holy Books*) and Lovecraft's oeuvre. Lovecraft had written—in "The Call of Cthulhu"—that artists and other sensitives were the first to hear the "Call," and I wondered if Lovecraft himself was one of those.

All of these various themes came together in *The Dark Lord*. I believe it is the only work on the subject that (a) identifies the 16 kalas by name and by quality; (b) demonstrates the links that exist between Lovecraft's tales, particularly "The Call of Cthulhu," and Crowley's *Holy Books*; and (c) goes to some length to show how Golden Dawn themes and rituals are an inextricable element of Crowley's own writings and rituals.

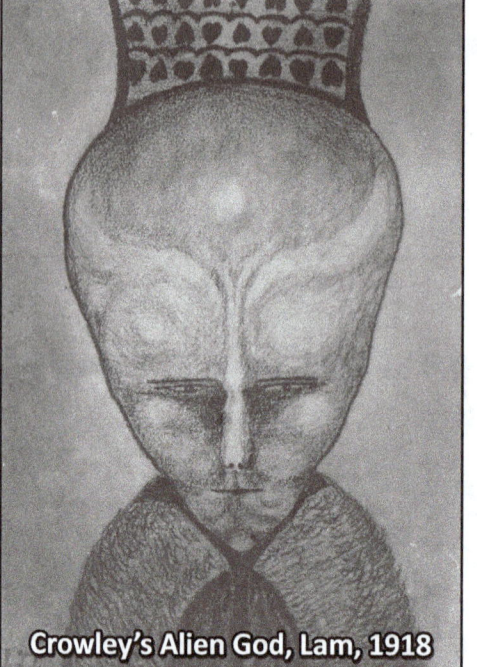
Crowley's Alien God, Lam, 1918

AJF: You have a new project featuring Lovecraftian themes that came out in December 2016 called *The Lovecraft Code*. But this is a work of fiction. Is this your first novel, your first piece of weird fiction, or have you tried your hand at this before? What was the genesis of this project?

PL: It's not exactly my first novel. I have been writing novels since the early 1970s. But it is my first published novel. I had written several versions of it over the years, and been forced to amend and expand it considerably due to the world situation (which is very much part of the plot). It's weird fiction, but the type that you don't realize is weird until you're pretty far into it.

I was very impressed with HPL's "Call of Cthulhu" for a lot of reasons. First is the fact that Lovecraft—almost alone of his peers—is quite specific as to dates and places in his work. That places his stories in a definite timeline with reference points to actual events that were taking place around the stories. Secondly, he wrote that tale from a variety of different perspectives: Providence, Louisiana, and points north and east. It is a tale that stretches around the globe, and that made me wonder: what if that story was taking place today? How would it be the same? How would it be different? And what if Professor Emeritus George Angell had a descendant living today, scion of the famous Angell family of Providence? And then I discovered that there was such a descendant: David Angell, the well-known TV writer and producer involved with such hits as *Cheers*, *Wings*, and *Frasier*. David Angell and his wife died on 9/11/2001 when their plane crashed into the North Tower of the WTC. And thereby *The Lovecraft Code* was born.

AJF: That's fascinating. You also seem to cycle back to familiar themes and territory in your work every few years or so to revisit them, update your material. Is this something you do deliberately, or does the emergence of new research compel you back?

PL: It's new research, for the most part. My books are parts of a "grand project" to tell a different sort of history/interpretation of America and the world. That includes the fiction and non-fiction, and even my book on China trade, *The Mao of Business*. I don't see the world in categories or boxes—though many do, of course—and by writing on a wide variety of subjects and then cycling around to tell more of these subjects in greater detail and from different perspectives I hope to convince the reader to appreciate that literary genres are a bureaucratic convention by people suffering from the sort of affliction that requires them to separate the peas from the carrots on their plate.

Reality is not like that. It's more like succotash (which is an unfortunate analogy, but there you go).

AJF: *Sekret Machines: Gods: An official investigation of the UFO phenomenon* is another new project coming out in 2017, co-authored with Tom DeLonge of Blink 182 and a foreword by Jacques Vallee. This looks amazing. Tell us about it, and also tell us how you and Tom happened to start working together.

PL: Tom contacted me at the end of 2015, largely on the strength of *Sinister Forces* as well as my Amsterdam presentation on the "Secret Space Program" (which turned out to be much more popular than I had anticipated). He wanted a collaborator for the non-fiction aspect of the Sekret Machines project; he had already identified the author of the fictional series, Professor A. J. Hartley. The Project is quite ambitious—involving not only the books but also a documentary film and much else besides—and Tom was able to recruit a cabal of individuals from various walks of life and different levels of government, military and industry to act as sounding boards and to provide their own unique perspective. We want to go a step further than many Ufologists have taken, and that is to begin on the premise that the UFO Phenomenon is real and go from there. That means no more tedious lists of UFO sightings going back a hundred or more years (although we do reference a few of them from time to time in order to tell a somewhat different story). We want to jump-start a new interpretation process and inject new energy into the subject, hoping to attract those who had never really taken all this seriously before. We hope that our sincerity, hard work, and

enthusiasm will rub off on a lot of people who either have become tired of all the books already written (which often seem to recycle a lot of the same information) or who have never considered the implications of the Phenomenon in their own work or their own professional life (such as genetics, physics, biology, philosophy, anthropology, etc.).

Sekret Machines: Gods is the first volume of my trilogy. The second and third are *Man* and *War*, respectively. *Gods* takes the point of view that we do not need to "prove" ancient alien interference or influence in such things as the building of the Great Pyramid or the Nazca lines, etc. because that (we believe) is a kind of misdirection. Ancient alien theorists will always be arguing with scientists and archaeologists over these things, and often the former will be shown to be in error in their assumptions. That devalues

the field and turns off the more scientific and skeptical. Instead, we say: "Look at what the ancient people *said*, in their scriptures and other important writings. The key is there." There are themes that run through the sacred texts of ancient peoples that are easily identifiable and which don't require some specialized translation of the odd cuneiform combination or a debatable Hebrew phoneme. The overall themes are surprisingly consistent, within certain limits of course, and that is what excites us.

AJF: Well, we are definitely looking forward to that one. I have to now ask you about this: The material of you work has always, to one degree or another, involved the hidden or occult aspects of history as it flows through the course of time. These are aspects that most people don't believe in or simply ignore. But it is clear in this post 9-11 world that reality is becoming much stranger. Why do you think this is so? I've heard you say you don't really like to discuss 9/11, but I would be interested if you had any thoughts you might share on that.

PL: When it comes to 9/11 I have always asked: *cui bono*? Who benefited from the attack? For the United States, and particularly for George W. Bush, it was a Reichstag Fire. It doesn't matter in the end who caused the Reichstag Fire *or* 9/11: the results are what really matter. The Reichstag Fire enabled Hitler to assume complete control of the German government. 9/11 resulted in the Patriot Act, airport cavity searches (not really, but soon maybe) and the invasions of Afghanistan and Iraq and the ensuing catastrophe.

On the cultural level, the impact was enormous. It

reset a lot of our buttons, and that always has an effect on consciousness and on our understanding of reality. I was living in Kuala Lumpur at the time, and I heard Americans being interviewed on TV asking "Why do they hate us?" As someone who has traveled extensively around the world my whole life, I was surprised by the question. I was more surprised by the way we managed to fold the 9/11 attacks into our worldview after that. The loss of a sense of security is probably the first step towards enlightenment. After all, we initiate Freemasons by having them blindfolded and at the point of a sword. And Freemasons were influential in the American Revolution that started this country.

America has been involved in a lot of good works overseas, but she has also been involved in "regime change" going back as long as I have been alive. We've done that from a position of strength and from assuring our own people that they were safe and secure (as long as they stayed home! I didn't get the memo, obviously). Now that has changed, and it is causing some of our people to ask uncomfortable questions about America's profile in the world and about American responsibility and accountability for its foreign policies. Do we own these policies now, or do we abandon any pretense of caring about them and demand instead more guns and a further relaxation of privacy laws, etc.? After all, understanding foreign policy is hard. You need languages, knowledge of history, religion, etc. But it doesn't have to be that hard. We can demand our government display a certain degree of enlightened approach to the problem of foreign policy and that does not mean we have to be wimps about it. We have to be smart and realize that not every problem is a nail that can be solved with a hammer.

An interesting aspect of the UFO Phenomenon is that its very existence is a critique of our notions of authority and security. It's a theme we examine in some detail in the series. It also raises questions about colonialism and racism. Science fiction authors and moviemakers have been raising these questions a lot in the past 50 years or so and especially so in recent years; it is time to use these critiques as templates for asking questions about human conduct and attitudes.

And, anyway, Ufology provides us with a whole new way of looking at the concept of "foreign policy!"

AJF: Another sort of hyperreal and surreal event is the election of Donald Trump as the 45th U.S. president. Would you care to share your thoughts on this? I am most interested in hearing how you might tie this event in with your past work on occult forces, hidden aspects of history, and the more supernatural features of reality. What does this election mean, and where is humanity headed?

PL There is way too much to unpack here. Let me just raise one important point, and that is the role of Steve Bannon and Breitbart in the campaign.

I know some otherwise very intelligent people who claim that Breitbart is their news source of choice. To me, that is a lot like saying Alex Jones is their social studies teacher. When I was a wee lad, conspiracy theory was a leftist kind of milieu, especially with regard to the JFK

assassination. Gradually it became the province of the alt-right. You can't rely on "news" that is politically-determined, and you can't rely on "news" from institutions that regard it as a way to sell gold futures and crackpot herbal remedies. Edward R. Murrow is spinning frantically in his grave right now. Walter Cronkite is next to him, mumbling "I thought we were winning this thing." That Breitbart should be considered a viable news source is simply obscene. Their journalistic standards are confined to creating an emotional response in their readership rather than informing them and allowing them to make up their own minds. It's taken the entertainment model to its logical conclusion. And their information is so highly contaminated that if they had any journalistic integrity at all they would be issuing retractions every few minutes.

Trump was the conspiracy theory candidate, and not in a good way.

That is not to say that the mainstream media is above reproach. Far from it. But we can't be forced to make a choice between a rock and a hard place. We have to demand—or at least seek out—reliable sources of information on which to base our conclusions. The problem is: that takes work. We have grown up in a culture that has abandoned the study of rhetoric, logic, and the other classical virtues. We have forgotten how to think, and how to challenge assumptions. We believe that having access to data on our smartphones means we are better informed than our ancestors; but data is not knowledge any more than a pile of ingredients on a kitchen counter is a meal. I find myself embroiled in arguments with people for whom anything they read on the Internet is truth. Search engines are an ideal breeding ground for conspiracy theories since the results are not challenged or prioritized in terms of reliability. What we need is what the Evangelicals call "discernment" in order to tell the demons from the angels, the bad data from the good. People whose exposure to the world at large is limited to their own small towns develop very bizarre ideas about the world outside, and these ideas are created, fueled and managed by conspiracy theories. That's often true anywhere in the world, but especially in a country like ours that is huge and geographically rather isolated. Doubt about the reliability of the mainstream media has led to an uncritical adoption of sites like Breitbart and Drudge. Their readers want someone else to do the work for them. They don't realize that the Internet has changed forever the system of responsibility and placed it back on our own shoulders. We are responsible now, for better or for worse, for our own information. And we are not prepared to handle that responsibility. We don't have the intellectual tools. We are the sorcerer's apprentices, and the brooms are dancing around our heads, totally out of control.

AJF: Thank you for sharing your thoughts. Now finally, what else are you working on, if anything? And please tell our readers where they can find out more about you and pick up your books.

 I'm always working, man. Work, work, work. I'm Mel Brooks as the governor in *Blazing Saddles*.

Seriously, though: I am still deeply embedded in the Tom DeLonge project. I am also writing the sequel to *The Lovecraft Code* (if I get that far!). And I have a lot of other projects on the back burner, as well. It is possible that I will manage to get some of my other fictional work published in the next few years, too.

My books are all found on Amazon, of course, and on the Barnes and Noble site. My website—which I update periodically (if by "period" we mean geological period!)—is peterlevenda.com and I was also forced this year to go on Facebook, Twitter and Instagram. When I say "forced" I mean that quite literally. Social media is one of the tools that the Sekret Machines project employs to get the word out, and while authors have been using social media for a while now I have been one of the last holdouts. It is time-consuming and for someone who researches and writes as much as I do, anything that consumes time is anathema for it robs you of concentration as well as of time. But, hey, you know. Anything for the cause! And I have been gratified to read some of my readers' comments on my work and what it has meant to them, and that's a good thing (as Martha would say). On the other hand, I have also been identified as an evil disinfo agent out to manipulate the hearts and minds of the innocent, or something. It's amazing how many people have a negative opinion about me who have never read my books. And that is the curse of social media.

Where is The Exorcist, now that we need him?

◇◇◇◇◇◇◆◇◇◇◇◇◇

Get Out Your Violins

By Peter Levenda

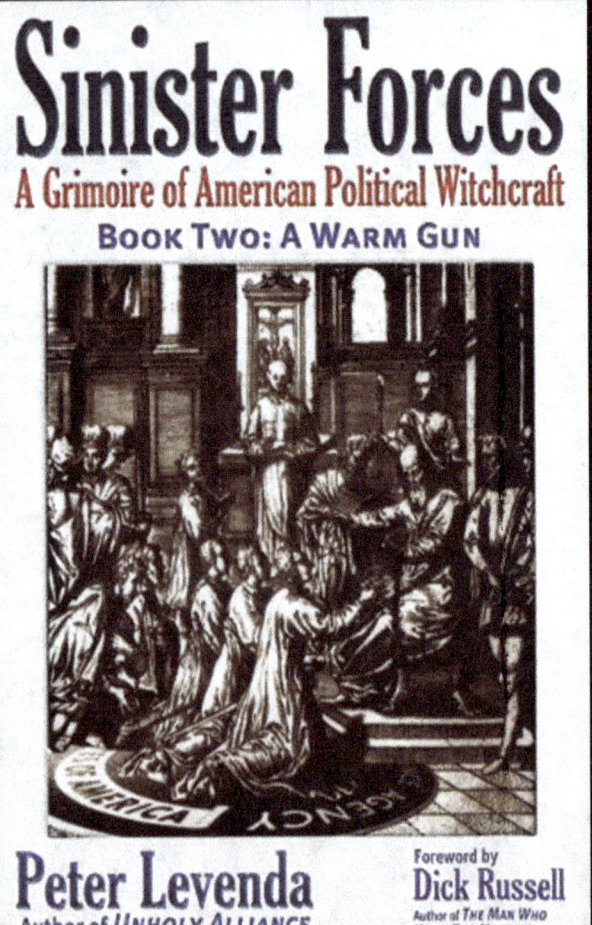

Sinister Forces
A Grimoire of American Political Witchcraft
BOOK TWO: A WARM GUN

Peter Levenda
Author of *UNHOLY ALLIANCE*

Foreword by
Dick Russell
Author of *THE MAN WHO KNEW TOO MUCH*

Over the past ten years or so people have asked me to clarify what I mean by "sinister forces," the title of a non-fiction trilogy I published back in 2005. Unfortunately, I don't think that these forces are easily defined. Like the astronomers who discovered the existence of Pluto by realizing that something unseen was affecting the orbit of Neptune, one has to notice how persons, places and events are connected in inexplicable ways in order to become aware of the existence of this otherwise invisible presence.

We use the term synchronicity to characterize what Jung called an "acausal connecting principle," and that's good but it's a little like telling a cancer patient they have a tumor that is causing their distress without ever linking the tumor to its underlying disease. Is synchronicity *sui generis*? Or does it represent the existence of some other force in the universe?

Objects in the natural world can be connected in ways that are not reflective of cause-and-effect. Color is one such connecting feature. A sunflower is yellow, and we perceive the sun to be yellow. Both are also round. There is no cause-and-effect relationship there, but occultists have often claimed that the sunflower and the sun share some characteristics in common. This is known as the doctrine of correspondences. For that reason Mars, as the red planet, is related to iron (in its rusted state, apparently), blood, passion, and war. The connecting principle is acausal, like synchronicity. Is it possible that the ancient doctrine of correspondences is one way of looking at synchronicity and, by extension, illuminate what is meant by "sinister forces?"

***

Astrology is one method that relies heavily on the doctrine of correspondences, in which elements of the microcosm are connected—correspond to—elements of the macrocosm. Parts of the human body are related to specific planets and signs; parts of the world we experience—the natural world as well as the political world—are similarly connected. The experience of synchronicity may be simply that of becoming suddenly and momentarily aware of this connection. It is, in Kabbalistic terms (and the Kabbalah is the source *par excellence* of correspondences), the experience of *tikkun olam*: the repairing of the world, the bringing together of the sparks.

My use of the term "sinister forces" was inspired by none other than Alexander Haig, who blamed the missing 18-1/2 minutes of an Oval Office tape on "sinister forces." This was during the Watergate era, and the tapes were part of then-President Richard Nixon's own taping system. Those missing minutes from a conversation that took place on June 20, 1973 were crucial, for they would have revealed what the White House knew about the Watergate break-in: a caper that tied together E. Howard Hunt, Gordon Liddy, the CIA, the FBI, Operation Mongoose, and what Nixon called "the whole Bay of Pigs thing." Sinister forces, indeed.

But what piqued my curiosity is just what Haig meant by "sinister forces." Was it an allusion to political enemies? Something fairly mundane in that case? It was then that I discovered the term was used by a wide variety of

individuals—mostly military and intelligence types—to denote invisible influences powerful enough to change the course of history. For instance, in a speech General Douglas MacArthur had referred to the "sinister forces" of some other galaxy that might invade the Earth in the foreseeable future. Even the fictional Inspector Clouseau of the *Pink Panther* movies referenced "sinister forces."

In Haig's case, the statement was widely reported in the Washington *Post* and other news outlets of the time and his reference to "sinister forces" was identified by reporters as his "devil theory." Thus, the media picked up on the subtext of the statement and recognized that it was intended as an allusion to supernatural forces and specifically to demonic ones.

Remember that the man making this statement was the former commander of all NATO forces and the national security advisor to the President of the United States.

And that all of this was happening at the height of the Cold War.

***

Ronald Reagan would eventually describe the Soviet Union in equally apocalyptic terms, calling it the "evil empire." Nancy Reagan, his astrology-obsessed spouse, was thus on intimate terms with the doctrine of correspondences and perhaps no more so than in the days following the assassination attempt on her husband by the Jodie Foster-obsessed fan, John Hinckley. Jodie Foster, of course, had come to wide acclaim for her role in *Taxi*

Driver: a film based on the diary of Arthur Bremer, the man who attempted the assassination of presidential contender George Wallace in 1972 (after missing a chance to assassinate Richard Nixon, his original target, instead).

(It was reported in the underground press at the time that Watergate Plumbers G. Gordon Liddy and E. Howard Hunt were the first two officials to arrive at Bremer's apartment in the hours after the assassination attempt, even before the police.)

Both Arthur Bremer and John Hinckley are currently out of prison and psychiatric ward, respectively. Bremer got parole in 2007, and Hinckley was released into house arrest this past year.

But getting back to Nixon and "sinister forces."

Richard Nixon met his future spouse, Thelma "Pat" Ryan, during some amateur theatricals in Whittier, California in 1938. The play was called *The Dark Tower*, and the plot concerns a man who uses hypnosis to commit crimes involving the manipulation of women. A career criminal, he is expert at this type of suggestion and one of his wives committed suicide after she signed over her estate to him. In the play, he is about to commit an act of embezzlement on a wife who believed he had been dead for years when he is himself murdered.

The play is replete with classical and Biblical references, none of which would have been lost on an audience in 1933 but which would probably escape the same today. The use of hypnosis to have others kill on your behalf is pretty much the plot of the Robert F. Kennedy assassination by a hypnotized Sirhan B. Sirhan. The villain of the

play—"Stanley Vance"—had served time in San Quentin: the same prison that would see Sirhan Sirhan on death row for the Bobby Kennedy assassination (as well as host Charles Manson, Richard "Night Stalker" Ramirez, and many other notables). The assassination of Bobby Kennedy in 1968 set the stage for the Nixon presidential victory that year. Both Nixon and Pat Ryan had roles in the 1938 Whittier Community Center production and were thus familiar with the play's theme of hypnosis as a weapon, as well as the usefulness of an actor's training in carrying out a successful assassination. (Vance is murdered by one of the other characters who is a professional stage actor and who adopts a new persona complete with costume, make-up and foreign accent in order to lure the villain to his death.)

As is well-known, horror author Stephen King began publishing his *Dark Tower* novels in 1982 and they have no connection to the 1933 play by Algonquin Round Table regulars: the famous playwrights George S. Kaufman and Alexander Woollcott. For King, the Dark Tower represents a kind of singularity in time and space. Perhaps, in terms of American politics, the Kaufman and Woollcott play represents something similar. Many elements of the Nixonian underworld are present in the play, even to the extent of involving the major player, Nixon, himself.

The play does contain references to the Devil, to breaking the Devil's spell, casting out the Devil, and selling one's soul to the Devil. In one case, it was the rumored murder of Vance by gunshot that was described as "The spell had been broken," and "The devil had been cast out"

because that is when his wife suddenly came to her senses and began to succeed at her career as actress, abandoning her meek personality for the vivacity of a true thespian. And that was just in the first few pages of Act One.

The villain quotes a Biblical verse, taken from Matthew 25:13 but amended slightly. He says, "We know neither the day nor the hour when the bridegroom cometh." It is an obvious reference to himself, as the husband of the actress, who had been missing for years and presumed dead by gunshot. However, the actual reading is "Ye know neither the day nor the hour when the Son of Man comes," although the "Son of Man" indeed is identified as the "bridegroom" in another part of the same verse. This conflation of Son of Man with bridegroom would have passed by without notice except that "Son of Man" resonates with Man Son, or Manson: the man who used suggestion, drugs, and hypnotic control to manipulate women into committing murder. It should be remembered that it was no one less than President Richard Nixon who declared Manson guilty of the Tate/La Bianca killings while the trial was still in process, thus nearly causing a mistrial when Charlie waved the newspaper headlines in front of the jury.

And Stanley Vance is satanic in other ways. Beyond identifying himself with the Son of Man, he also refers to himself as Enoch Arden. That is a name that would be lost on most people today, as it is a reference to a poem by Tennyson that was later set to music by Richard Strauss. Enoch Arden was a man who left his wife and family so that he could obtain employment overseas in order to provide for them. He is shipwrecked and spends years alone

on a desert island before finally returning home, only to discover that his wife has remarried. He does not want to ruin her happiness, so does not reveal himself to her and instead dies of a broken heart.

The similarities to the ancient Greek tale of Ulysses are great, of course, but the name itself is a reference to the Biblical figure of Enoch: the prophet who lived for 365 years and then disappeared off the face of the Earth. Enoch would become the model for the Kabbalistic figure of Metatron: the humanoid figure who sits on the throne at the penultimate stage of the celestial ascent: the final terrifying obstacle before the mystic can attain direct contact with God. If the mystic mistakes Metatron for God, the consequences are dire. Stanley Vance does worse: he mistakes himself for Enoch.

It is also Enoch who would give us the infamous Books of Enoch: occult texts that detail the inner workings of reality, the cataloguing of spiritual forces, and the methods for manipulating the world around the magician. This is perhaps a great deal closer to what Stanley Vance thinks of himself, for he is a kind of black magician who enters the play like a pail of cold water splashed on everyone he meets and immediately takes over the entire proceedings, including especially re-exerting his mysterious influence over his wife who again becomes meek and submissive at once.

Stanley Vance is taking Biblical verses and turning them upside down by using them to refer to himself: a man neither Jesus nor Enoch. Thus, when he is finally murdered by his wife's brother—in disguise as an exotic European gentleman, but whose real name is the rather suggestive Damon Wells—no one seems too upset and, indeed, it ends on a happy note. Literally, with a flourish at the piano.

Stanley only had power over women. Men seemed to be immune. But the twentieth century had just come out of World War One when *The Dark Tower* was published. By the 1950s we would experience a more industrialized form of Vance's methods in the phenomenon of "brainwashing." And that would give rise to another iteration of the same meme: the Manchurian Candidate. The book by Richard Condon would become the film by John Frankenheimer, a film that would be pulled out of circulation in November of 1963 when a real assassination took place in the streets of Dallas that seemed too similar in some ways to the plot of the film.

Five years later, and Frankenheimer would hold a celebratory dinner party at his Malibu home for Robert F. Kennedy who was winning the California primary. It was June 4, 1968. Bobby would leave dinner to go to the Ambassador Hotel in Los Angeles where he would be shot later that same evening, after midnight on June 5, 1968.

Frankenheimer's other dinner guests that night included Sharon Tate and Roman Polanski. Tate would be murdered in August the following year by Manson's followers. Her husband Polanski, of course, had directed *Rosemary's Baby*, the film about a satanic cult in New York City based on the novel of the same name, which was released on June 12, 1968: precisely a week after the assassination.

Lovecraft tells us—in "The Call of Cthulhu"—that artists are the first ones to sense the call of that dreaded High Priest of the Ancient Ones. This probably should be extended to include novelists and filmmakers, too.

***

The tight little knot of Nixon, JFK, RFK, Manson, Sirhan, Hinckley, Bremer, Reagan… would get tighter and tighter in so many ways, as I describe in *Sinister Forces*. But what of us normal people? People who are not political operatives, government agents, or mass murderers? Do the sinister forces affect us, too?

While writing *Sinister Forces*—much of it done in Kuala Lumpur, Malaysia—I often had need of source material that I was not able to obtain. I had brought cartons of documents and references (and books) with me to Malaysia but there was never enough. This was the late 1990s, and Internet sources were not as comprehensive as they are today (and Internet connections not as fast or as reliable in Southeast Asia at that time).

But there was an odd phenomenon that took me by the hand in that tropical wonderland of Hindu temples, ornate mosques, and Buddhist monasteries. I would find myself down a side street in some never-before-seen neighborhood and encounter a worn and sun-stained book rack made of rusted wire and full of cheap romance novels in Malay or Chinese or Tamil covered in dust… and a small collection of scholarly works on Charles Manson. In

English.

On another occasion, I would come across—in a completely different part of the city—Ingo Swann's book *Penetration*. One might agree this is a rare thing to find anywhere, even more so in Kuala friggin' Lumpur.

And then there was the time I found a stash of works on the Salem witchcraft trials… just when I needed them and didn't even know those specific titles existed.

Other writers have described this same phenomenon. We don't want to belabor it too much, in case we break it or lose it. We're superstitious, which is another way of talking about synchronicity and sinister forces. Suffice it to say that the doctrine of correspondences—that old medieval rabbit trick—is one perfectly serviceable way of looking at how synchronicity works, both on the world stage and in one's local environment. Perhaps it describes the way our brains work, by categorizing information according to shape, color, sound, etc. in a clever play on references that uses our nervous system as a bow across the violin strings of reality. It is not just information; information by itself is static. There is an energy there, a movement from one point to another, a connection drawn between impossible objects and events, and once you are playing that violin you never want it to stop.

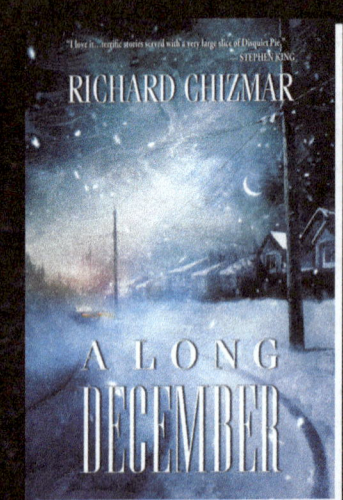
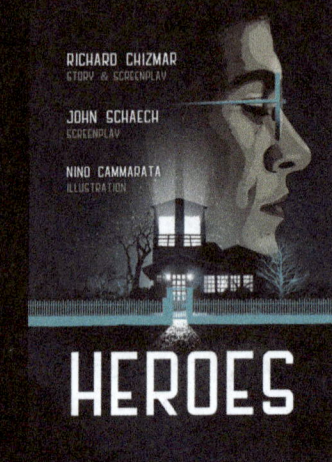
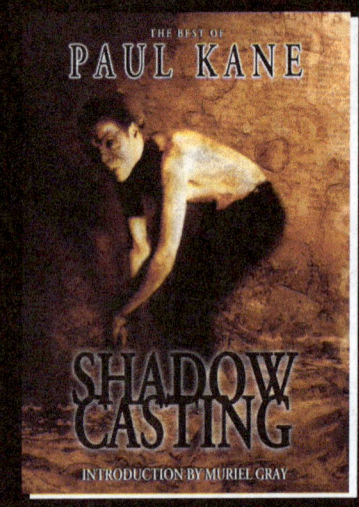
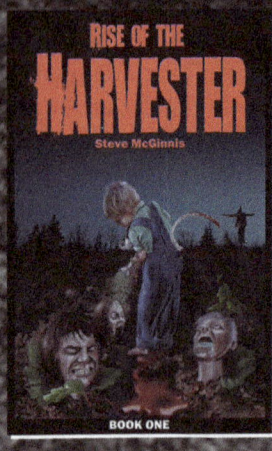

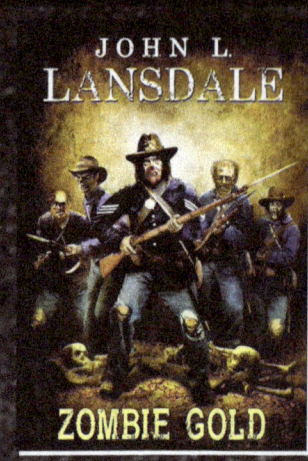
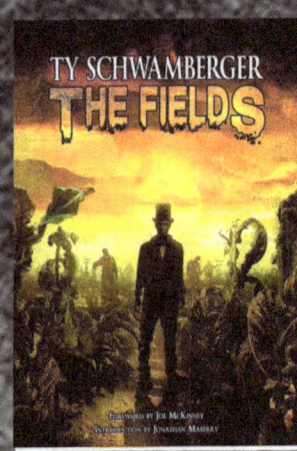

THE BLACK BARONY

ANOTHER WORD FOR SUPERNATURAL IS WILDERNESS

BY LAIRD BARRON

1. SOMETHING SCARY

Another word for supernatural is wilderness. I didn't come to that right away; it was a process that occurred over many reckless years. The process is ongoing. There are depths to the conclusion that feel like looking down into a vertical shaft and occasionally a cold draft prickles my flesh.

Why do you write horror, Laird? It's an obvious question (accusation), and one that tends to exhaust authors of any genre. I've warmed to it of late, here on the mid-career threshold. Circumspection becomes a preoccupation the farther into the wilderness you go. Make no mistake, at least in my experience, this writing career is a journey that carries me inexorably toward the edge of known territory. I spend as much time alone with my thoughts as I ever did tramping around backwoods Alaska.

Provenance is important, albeit not in the regard a casual observer might presume. Writing is one of those professions that can be undertaken and perfected despite (or due to) a veritable shit-storm of a youth. No experience, good or bad, and no time spent on earth, is truly wasted

"You're travelling through another dimension. A dimension, not only of sight and sound, but of mind. A journey into a wondrous land whose boundaries are that of imagination. Next stop, the Twilight Zone!"

Rod Serling

if one considers that everything is ultimately grist for the creative mill. Provenance is important because, deep down, everybody loves a good origin story.

And so I've become keenly interested in what makes those of us whom are for the dark tick. Looking back, I realize that my parents, if not superstitious with a capital S, were credulous with a capital C when it came to the occulted universe, which incidentally covers 99.9 percent of reality. Their credulousness and its manifestations had a potent subconscious effect on my development, especially as an artist. My origin story is steeped in folklore, Christian fundamentalism, shadow people, genius loci, and doppelgangers. Last time we met, I talked about my mother's faith and how her beliefs continue to ripple through my life. In one sense, this essay is a companion piece, or the next chapter. This go around, I'll focus on folklore and sinister doubles as accomplices in the strange case of Laird Barron.

The Twilight Zone was a cornerstone of my early childhood development prior to my family's relocation to the hinterlands of Alaska. It remained popular on the homestead as one of the few programs suited to our lunchbox-sized black and white television. *Twilight Zone: The Movie* (and the 1980s revival of the series) was a highly-anticipated event, but I didn't screen it until the end of the decade. In those days, my parents frequently made the trip into civilization to attend business, leaving my little brother Jason and I to tend the home fires and care for the kennel of huskies. Consequently, I didn't take in many first run movies as a teen.

The Twilight Zone ties into a reference I made in a previous column about my dad's fondness for testing his children with spooky theoretical scenarios. In this case, Dad battened onto the "wanna see something really scary?" bit from the opening scene wherein hitchhiker Dan Aykroyd plays a dangerous game with the poor Samaritan behind the wheel.

Dad used variations of that phrase when tormenting us kids about the evils of the world, which ranged from trespassers and wild animals, to things that go bump in the night. The term that stuck was Something Scary—as in, *hey, kids, here's Something Scary. We don't have any food!* Or, *hey kids, here's Something Scary to ponder: What if those new neighbors in the cabin down the river are child-murdering maniacs? I saw them creeping around the wood lot this morning. By the way, your mom and I are heading into town for a few days. Good luck!*

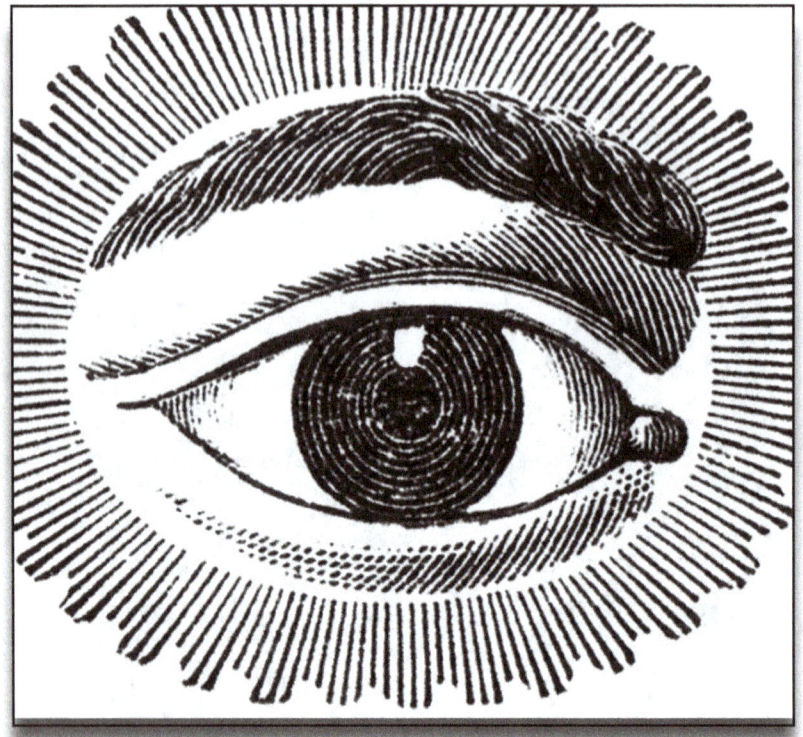

Alaska (and I'm sure plenty of other places blessed with extreme geography) has an effect on people; the atmosphere can be oppressive as the creeping insanity of Stephen King's *The Shining*, although written in prosaic lowercase. We call it Seasonal Affective Disorder, manic depression, and in rarer instances, homicidal-mania. Those worthies notwithstanding, paranoia is king in the Land of the Midnight Sun.

I spent the 1970s through the early '90s instate. What seemed normal looks a bit stranger in hindsight. But damn, we took weirdness for granted; some of us relished it. By no means the majority of the population, nonetheless, a significant measure of people in my circle, which included tycoons and bottom feeders alike, accepted to one degree or another the plausibility of alien abduction, missing time, inimical woodland spirits, black helicopters, black ops sites in the mountains, the Iliamna Lake Sea Monster, and shadow people. The Satanic Panic hit the Matanuska Valley as hard as it did anywhere else except possibly California. Last I heard, Alex Jones-style talk radio is the

go-to A.M. choice by a segment of the population who purchase their tinfoil in bulk.

Just about every person I ever met up north had at least one "hand on the Bible, this really happened" story to tell, provided they were drunk enough, stoned enough, or bored enough, to lay it on me. It's easy to write people (starting with Mom and Dad) off as confused. Science has shown the brain is a flawed, flawed miracle, witness accounts are often wrong, and people lie. In the end, the truth matters far less than the perception of our natural world impinged upon by forces beyond our understanding.

2. Double-Double

Mom swore to the existence of shadow people. Dad claimed to have lost nearly twenty-four hours during the 1979 Iditarod. An earnest middleclass couple told me they were abducted by aliens while vacationing in the Kenai area. A popular riverboat freighter once related a tale of missing time similar to my father's, except the freighter was visited in his remote cabin by a man in a black suit prior to the blank space in his memory.

My personal interactions with the ineffable have generally been naturalistic. Night terrors plagued my youth; considering our close to the bone subsistence lifestyle, it's little wonder. The shadows thinned as I reached my majority. Like claws, they still reach out to me every now and again. Usually in the form of the most exquisitely vivid nightmares imaginable. As the man says, *wait, there's more.* You see, what comes out of the wilderness is a reflection of what we bring into its embrace.

I have a doppelgänger. That much has become clear over the past twenty-odd years. Obviously, there are cases of mistaken identity, innocent and expected confusion. I've written off most incidents as such. However, several of these sightings when taken in the context of a larger pattern continue to mystify me.

Among many other places, I worked on and off at a fish processing plant in Anchorage, AK during my youth. The plant was bordered by a railroad track. Walking on the track or fooling around with cargo flats, etc. was instant termination from the company. On two occasions people accused me of clambering around the parked locomotive. The accusers were relative strangers (300 people worked at the factory) and had no motive to harm me. In fact, when confronted by HR and myself, they swore to their testimony. One fellow even apologized for getting me in trouble—he just felt it was his duty. I'm a pretty distinctive looking person, extremely easy to ID in broad daylight, I'm sure. Of course, I never went anywhere near those tracks.

I wrote off the incident.

A couple of years later I was walking back from lunch and this huge man accosted me. Now the fish factory was located in an industrial area adjacent to the airport. This man was delivering a semi load of whatever to a warehouse. The trucker was in his late 50s and simply massive. He wore a leather biker vest with no shirt. Lots of muscles, lots of tattoos. Extremely grizzled and forbidding—the man could've played a heavy in an action flick. He was chatting with a receiving clerk when he saw me walking by. The trucker frantically called to get my attention. I'd never seen him before, but he was so insistent I met him halfway. This man, who I'd heard speaking perfect English, started babbling at me in a com-

bination of English and I don't know what as he crushed my hand in both of his. There were tears in his eyes and he repeated, "Oh my God, it's you!" and "How did you get here?" and when he realized I didn't understand, "1955! 1955!" and "You were there!" As if he were trying to convince me that I was who he thought I was. Eventually, he stared at me, wiped his eyes and said solemnly, "Remember, you were there. It was you." Then he patted me on the arm, his expression melancholy. He resumed a perfectly gruff truck driver type conversation with the poor clerk who'd been standing there with his mouth open.

Again, I wrote off the incident, although it bothered me for years.

I used to take a martial arts class in Seattle. I walked or rode the bus everywhere. I also carried a metal grip strengthener everywhere I went. This thing looked kind of like a foot long harp with four massive springs. Some joker at my former fish plant job painted it neon pink. So one evening I'm at the dojo and one of my classmates, a mechanical engineer, asked what the hell I'd been doing wandering the streets at 5am that morning. I'd been dead asleep and told him so. Other guys wear patches in the big city—he must've caught a glimpse and mistook someone else for me. My friend was adamant. "Nobody else I know wears a patch and lugs a giant pink hand gripper." He'd pulled over and called to the figure. I guess my double

grinned, waved and then disappeared down an alley. And frankly, my friend never did quite believe I was on the level about the whole deal. A year or so later, one of the police officers who attended class swore he saw me across town at night. Same thing, except I carried a blackthorn cane, having ditched the gripper. This one I had an alibi for—I'd been at dinner with friends that evening.

Now I'd finally decided something rather peculiar was occurring.

The last one I'll mention (and there are several more) occurred a year or so later. I'd been working for a tree service. My job was to run the ground lines, cut rounds, feed the chipper, all kinds of backbreaking fun. I never climbed, however. I went into my favorite coffee shop on a day off, late afternoon. The barista, who I'd been buying coffee from for ages, expressed surprise at my arrival. She'd just seen me several miles away (on her way to work) about halfway up a humungous tree cutting branches and lowering them on a line. I told her it was my day off. Erin, my future wife, explained we'd been at her apartment all day. The barista shook her head. "No, it was you," she said. She'd been stopped in traffic, or at a stop sign, I don't recall, but I'd leaned way out and made a point to smile and wave at her. There was no question in her mind.

The other thing is, in retrospect, the three Seattle folks later admitted that whoever they'd seen had seemed unmistakable, but had acted in an odd, sly manner.

I don't know what it means. Maybe whatever's in the Yentna River seeped into me and has released like a slow-drip poison over the decades. Maybe something sinister and real is in play. The only ritual I know to deal with the weird, is to write about it, to name it.

3. Outro

Back to the beginning, and back into *The Twilight Zone;* an iteration darker, more rural and more desperate than anything Rod Serling could've bargained for.

You wanna see something really scary? asks Dan Aykroyd, mild-mannered hitcher during the opening scene of *Twilight Zone: The Movie.* Any sane person would answer, *I'm trapped driving with a stranger in a car on a lonesome*

stretch of highway in the dead of night.
Naw, motherfucker, I assuredly do not
want to see something really scary. Let me
slow down to forty-five and let you out.
Instead, the driver (Albert Brooks)
plays along; he pulls over, and as the
camera cuts away from Aykroyd's
ghoulish transformation, the driver
begins to scream. The high desert that
surrounds them keeps its counsel in
the shriek of a bird of prey and the
low, soft sweep of night unraveling
into a void. Forget it's a cheesy horror flick—the filmmakers nailed the
sentiment in one swing. We apes are
free to imagine what we will, apply
significance as we will, to live, die,
root in the mud, and go mad. The wilderness (be it tundra, a cold-burning
constellation, or the black hallway that
travels through your cozy little home)
doesn't care about human (or inhuman) drama.

It never has.

The Endless Corridor

William Sotheran

Reggie Oliver

Before my book about him was published you could be excused for never having heard of William Sotheran. God, that sounds arrogant! I apologise— No, I don't! It's a fact.

If you *had* known about him before then, it would almost certainly have been through an eight line quotation of his verse in a celebrated essay by Thomas de Quincey entitled "Of Art and Madness" in *The Edinburgh Review* of December 1823:

> I roamed the endless corridor of Fame,
> To seek a niche, a statue, or a name;
> But none could find that might belong to me:
> I wondered if I was, or e'er could be.
> We have our hour and leave a fleeting trace:
> A stone-carved name, a tear upon a face;
> Even before our mortal frame's decay
> The stone has cracked, the tear is wiped away.

These lines and a few more besides can sometimes be found in old anthologies or books of quotations. They come from a poem of about 1500 lines entitled *The Castle of Oblivion* which was published in 1817, the year of its author's death.

That date, 1817, I am almost ashamed to say, was what really started it. If you are, like me, a young academic, at the start of her career, you will be all too aware of the need to publish. You simply cannot climb the greasy pole in the world of scholarship without having at least one "seminal study" to your name. In addition, it has become increasingly necessary for you to have what is called "impact"; in other words you must make a discovery or come up with an idea that is noticed in the world beyond higher education. An article in one of the broadsheet Sunday papers, or better still a radio or television program, preferably with you as presenter, will do the trick. Then you will become an asset to your university or college; you will be valued; you will be promoted. Fail to make an impact and you become expendable. That is why I embarked on a study of the poet William Sotheran, with the bicentenary of both his death and the publication of his major work looming.

I lecture in English Literature at Wessex University and I specialise in the Romantics. As you can imagine the subject has been fairly well covered. You can't move for studies of Byron, Keats, Shelley, Coleridge, Wordsworth and the like. The trick is to break new ground, to find some minor but significant figure who has not been "done" before. So I thought my luck was in when a couple of years ago I stumbled on Sotheran.

Briefly, William Sotheran (1793-1817) was the younger son of a baronet, Sir Selwyn Sotheran. He was well connected, his mother being a Wellesley and a sister of the Duke of Wellington. It was perhaps from her side of the family that he inherited the urge to excel from an early age, which he did. At eighteen he composed a tragedy in verse, *Belisarius*, which showed such promise that it was accepted for performance at Covent Garden with John Philip Kemble in the title role. (It lasted three nights.) At Oxford he continued to write verse, and, after Oxford, took holy orders, the traditional career choice of the aristocratic younger son. But he seems to have been of a restless temperament, and in 1816 he embarked on a tour of the continent, then recovering from the Napoleonic wars. Shortly after his return in January 1817, he began to show signs of mental instability. Then in August of that year while travelling by mail coach from London to Bath to take up a position of curate in the parish of Fonthill, he made an unprovoked attack on a woman with whom he happened to be travelling. Family influence saved him from criminal prosecution, and he was confined to a private asylum where he died a few months later from causes unknown. Syphilitic dementia has been put forward as a possible cause.

Shortly before his death, his best known work *The Castle of Oblivion* was published. I won't go into detail; you will have to read it yourself because I genuinely think it is worth reading. I am not promoting it simply to further my academic career. But if you are going to understand or believe what happened to me I have to say something about it. De Quincey, in his famous essay, while admiring it, obviously believed it to be the product of an unbalanced mind, but I am not so sure. True, the poem was published while Sotheran was in an asylum but we have no idea exactly when he wrote it, though a rather oblique reference in the poem to Waterloo and Napoleon's final exile fixes the date of composition as no earlier than 1815.

It is in the form of an allegorical epic. The hero, sometimes referred to as "the poet", but in other parts of the poem speaking in the first person, is in the process of climbing a mountain which in one passage is called Parnassus. It is clear that the actual mountain in Greece of that name is not intended, and that *Parnassus* is used for its mythical association with Apollo and the Muses. The poet meets with various adventures on his way up and when he thinks he is very near the summit, he suddenly finds that the whole of the top of the mountain is crowned by a great and ancient fortress, the eponymous *Castle of Oblivion*. The poet enters the castle and there things get very weird indeed. The poem begins to resemble a contemporary Gothic novel of the most lurid kind and the hero has a succession of horrific and bizarre escapades involving flying skeletons, giant toads dressed as monks, strange shifts in perspective, and, worse still… No! You'll just have to read it for yourself! Eventually the poet makes his escape but the experience has shattered him and he retires to, as Sotheran puts it, "a hermitage obscure", there to live out the rest of this life, the final couplets reading:

> Down lonely paths in some sequestered glade
> Where yew trees cast their melancholy shade
> He wanders now, a neighbour of the dead
> His deeds dishonoured and his verse unread.

It is on the basis of the episodes in the castle that De Quincey decided that *The Castle of Oblivion* must be the work of someone who was already insane. Nowadays our view of what is sane and what is not is more nuanced and besides, I think I can grasp a kind of meaning behind all that strangeness. Or I thought I could. Maybe. Where was I?

Well, it is almost two years ago now since I began seriously researching Sotheran, and, almost immediately, I had the most extraordinary piece of luck. Luck? Was it luck? Oh, hell, judge for yourselves!

I had gone to London to visit the British Library which holds the only extant printed copy of Sotheran's tragedy *Belisarius*. It's pretty hard going, as most verse dramas from the early 19th century are, though it is an astonishingly accomplished piece of work for an eighteen-year-old. The only sign of real dramatic life comes in the final act when the great Byzantine general Belisarius is seen blind, forgotten and disgraced, begging at the Pincian Gate in Rome. (This was a popular legend beloved of painters and opera composers: history tells a different story, but never mind.) His last speech ends as follows:

For Time, the only conqueror at last,
Extinguishes the lamp of glorious fame
And with a shrug of his great sable robe
Enfolds the world in universal night. (He expires.)

Even in this early work Sotheran seems to have had an almost pathological obsession with fame and the transience of reputation. We imagine it is only our age that is celebrity obsessed, but we are wrong. I was beginning to think that I had the key to his character and art. I made notes; I jotted down quotations. I experienced the thrill that all academics feel when they believe they have a thesis, an original focus for their studies—a book!

I emerged from the British Library at around five. It was an inky October evening. The sky hung low and threatened rain; in spite of which I was feeling rather exultant. Then, as I was crossing the Concourse with the great bronze statue of Newton in it, a male voice just behind me said:

"Hey, madam! You dropped this!" And a grubby copy of the *Daily Mail* was thrust into my hand.

Madam! I am thirty-two; I am unmarried and I have never been called "madam" in my life before. And I never read the *Daily Mail*! Nobody at Wessex University would allow themselves to be seen dead with the *Daily Mail:* it's *The Guardian* or nothing.

I caught only a brief glimpse of the man who had given me the paper. He looked like some sort of tramp. I had an impression of lank, straggling hair over a long rusty black greatcoat and dark, lugubrious eyes. By the time I had recovered myself sufficiently to repudiate the doubtful gift, he had shuffled off somewhere. I might have thrown the wretched newspaper into a nearby bin, only I had a long train journey back to Wessex ahead of me and I felt in need of some light reading after the adolescent glooms of *Belisarius*.

As it turned out, what with the crowds on the underground, a delay in a tunnel, and a consequent rush to catch the 5.30 from Paddington, it was only when I was safely on the train to Morchester that I had the leisure to look at my *Daily Mail*. I began to leaf through it irritably, now thoroughly angry that I had meekly accepted it from a total stranger. To add to my annoyance, I noticed that it wasn't even today's newspaper: it was two days old. I was just about to throw it away when my eye caught a headline.

NONE OF YOUR "FRACKING" BUSINESS SAYS PEER

As it happens, my partner Julia is head of Environmental Studies at Wessex and so naturally I take an interest in such matters.

Apparently a certain Lord Glimham was allowing a company to prospect for shale gas on his estate and the locals, assisted by various environmental groups, were objecting strongly. Glimham had responded to their protests dismissively by saying that it was "nobody else's ******* business" and this had inflamed the situation still further. A photograph of his Lordship showed an overweight, red-faced, truculent-looking person of about fifty in a tweed Norfolk jacket; an easy man to hate, I thought. Then, further down the page a paragraph made my heart jump.

In the nearby village of Glimham Parva there have been various demonstrations. Lord Glimham's effigy has been burnt on the Green and the inn sign of the local pub, The Sotheran Arms, *has been defaced, Sotheran being Lord Glimham's family name.*

Could it be…? I got out my tablet and began to google frantically. Yes, it was the same family. William's elder brother George had been a cabinet minister in Sir Robert Peel's 1841 administration and was consequently raised to the peerage. He took his title from the family estates at Glimham. The present Lord Glimham was the fifth Baron and still lived at the ancient family seat of Glimham Hall where William Sotheran had been raised. Could there still be papers relating to William Sotheran in the ancestral home?

As soon as I got back to my flat in Morchester I began to compose a letter to Lord Glimham. It was my partner Julia who suggested that I should gently hint that it might improve his Lordship's tarnished image if it were known that he was helping me in my researches. I sent the letter on University of Wessex headed notepaper but I included my own mobile number and email address.

To my amazement, only two days after I had sent the letter, I had a phone call on my mobile.

"Glimham here. What's all this about William Sotheran?"

The voice was loud, braying, assertive—why do posh people have such loud voices?—but I detected a certain hesitancy, a vulnerability even, under the bluster. Arrogance is nearly always a carapace. Within a few minutes I found I was being invited down to Glimham the following Friday. When I told Julia about it, all excitement, she looked at me quizzically.

"You're not going to leave me, are you, for this William Sotheran?"

It was a joke, of course, and we both laughed, but I thought that Julia spoke not entirely in jest.

At the gates of the Glimham estate I encountered a huddle of protesters watched over by a single glum policeman. There was a smattering of young people, but most of them were very middle class retired types with grey hair. They had Thermos flasks and camp stools with them for rest and refreshment. They shouted "No more fracking!" at me as I passed through the gates and onto the long drive up to the house. I felt vaguely guilty that I had not responded to them in some way.

I drove through a mixture of park and farmland until, in a dip, I found Glimham Hall. It was not an architectural gem: a plain Queen Anne box of red brick, like a doll's house, with a few ill-advised Victorian additions and excrescences. As soon as I was parked on the gravel drive in front of the Victorian limestone portico Lord Glimham in his green tweed Norfolk jacket emerged to greet me. I had taken the trouble to arrive precisely at the time agreed.

I had not expected to like Glimham, and I didn't, but at least you knew where you were: some way beneath him admittedly. He treated me rather as if I were a high class plumber come to look at his drains. He ushered me into the drawing room where his wife, a skeletal blonde who might once have been beautiful, offered me a small cup of coffee and then never spoke again.

"To tell the truth," said Glimham who was not one for polite preliminaries. "We don't talk much about William in the family." It was as if William Sotheran were still around, a disgraced uncle perhaps. "But I think we have some papers relating to him. Do you suppose they could be valuable?"

"Very much so," I said. I knew that he was talking of commercial value and I meant value of another kind, but I did not enlighten him.

"Nobody seems to realise how much it costs to keep a place like this going. I'm hanging on by the skin of my teeth. That's what those unspeakably ghastly people at the gate can't understand. I don't want a lot of frackers all over my land, any more than they do, but I'm at the end of my tether. If the fracking chaps don't come up with the goods I'll have to sell up. Glimham has been in the family for over three hundred years, you know."

I nodded sympathetically: it was a point of view.

I had barely finished my coffee when he was taking me through to "the library", a long room lined floor to ceiling with bookcases above oak muniment cupboards. Apart from a shelf of Dick Francis thrillers and sporting manuals none of the books looked as if they had been read or even handled for a hundred years or so.

Glimham pointed to a desk on which reposed a number of deed boxes.

"Funny thing," he said. "I had to scout around before you came, to see what there was about old William. Thought I'd have a devil of a job finding anything, but my black Lab Stephen began snuffling and pawing at one of those cupboards." He pointed to a row of muniment cupboards. "So I unlocked it and these boxes practically fell out. Inside, family papers and stuff about William. Got it in one, thanks to a Labrador! Old Steve's a bloody good gun dog; but I never imagined he was keen on literature. Eh? Eh?" He seemed immensely pleased by his joke and I was happy to join in the laughter. I was very excited by this time. "Well, I'll leave you to it. Yell if you want anything. Serena, the wife, will be around somewhere." And he quitted the library.

The papers were in complete disorder. Wills, bills, deeds, letters, even old newspaper clippings had been crammed into boxes and forgotten. I was as frustrated by the confusion as I was thrilled by the occasional serendipitous discovery.

Details of William Sotheran's life emerged haphazardly. A long account of Sotheran's assault on the woman in the carriage written by a lawyer for the Sotheran family revealed that his frenzied attack seemed to have been triggered by the lady taking out a small hand mirror from her reticule and scrutinising herself in it. A letter from the keeper of the asylum to which he was confined as a result of this incident writes to the family to say that: "his conduct is generally sober and gentlemanly, unless he finds himself in proximity with a looking glass upon which he becomes extremely agitated and sometimes violent. On being asked why this harmless domestic item should occasion such alarm, he replied mysteriously that it was not so much what he saw in a mirror that troubled him as what he did *not* see. I have pressed him to explain further, but he will not."

I found also fragments of his writing, early drafts of some of his poems, all in the same hand which I took to be his. But undoubtedly the most interesting and valuable manuscript of his that I found was in prose. It appeared to be an account of his travels abroad in 1816. Some of it consists of jottings of dates and places, along with a few descriptive notes, but there are longer passages in the form of a journal as well. I had the feeling that he had intended to work it up into a publishable work, but circumstances prevented him. At the head of the manuscript, he tries out various titles: *The Wandering Poet, The Bard Abroad* and *Childe William's Pilgrimage*, this last heavily crossed out. Perhaps he felt that the nod towards Lord Byron's recent work (which, notoriously, made him famous overnight) to be too slavish.

Towards the end of this manuscript there is a passage of sustained narrative, parts of which I must quote:

"My uncle Sir Henry Wellesley [British Ambassador to Spain at the time] received me kindly. He told me that thanks to his brother and my Uncle, the Duke of Wellington to whom Spain owed a great debt for its liberation from the Corsican Tyrant, I was to be in high favour with the Spanish people, its court and its nobility. I expressed my wish to see the wonders of this great country and, in particular, its monasteries and religious institutions which, as an ordained priest of the church, albeit of England and not Rome, must interest me greatly. That my concern was more Romantic than Religious, that I had a yearning to behold:

The Horrid crags by toppling convent crown'd
The cork-trees hoar that clothe the shaggy steep… [Byron. *Childe Harold's Pilgrimage* I.19] — I concealed from my noble kinsman.

"Within a few days he had assigned me to the most noble Marquis de Santa Cruz and his brother the Grand Prior of San Isidore as my conductors and companions. Far from being reluctant to the task they seemed most eager to oblige. That their court and ecclesiastical duties were so light, or so wearisome, that they had the leisure and the eagerness to conduct a young English gentleman around the monasteries of Spain was a source of great astonishment to me, but my uncle informed me that it had been the wish of His Majesty himself King Ferdinand VII, that I should be so honoured. The Marquis was a small meagre man, somewhat in awe of his much larger wife from whom he was doubtless happy to escape. His younger brother the Grand Prior was built on an altogether grander scale as befitted his rank. As neither gentleman was anxious to forego an atom of the comforts and conveniences habitual to their stations in life we set off accompanied by a great array of carriages, mule-drivers, grooms and acolytes, together with my servant Marston and my Arabian steed, Salamanca, a present from my esteemed Uncle, the Duke. We formed altogether a caravan which, camels and dromedaries excepted, would have cut no unworthy figure on the route to Mecca."

There is much more in the same ironic style but I want to cut to an incident a little further on in the journal.

"Our reception by the monks of Alcala had exceeded even the Grand Prior's expectations and we set out late that morning for Guadalajara with heavy hearts and even fuller stomachs. It was a hot day and I found the interior of the carriage oppressive, and its close air, perfumed by the bodily exhalations of my noble companions' offensive. While they were disposed to sleep or, as my Lord Prior expressed it, to 'silent prayer and meditation,' I was for air and exercise. I therefore asked permission of my conductors to take my Arabian and ride ahead of the caravan. They, with some humorous remarks about the impetuosity of young Englishmen in midday sun, readily gave permission. Marston saddled Salamanca and I set off.

"My courser, pampered by the rich provender with which he had been so abundantly supplied by the good monks of Alcala, set no bounds to his exertions, even though the morning sun, unclouded, was approaching its zenith. We followed the road to Guadalajara as it crossed a wide and empty plain, at full stretch. Like Phaethon I felt myself:

With flying speed outstrip the Eastern wind
And leave the breezes of the morn behind

[Ovid, Metamorphoses II ll 158-9 trans Samuel Garth]

"Like Phaethon, perhaps, I scorched myself in my reckless career, but never had I felt an atmosphere so elastic, so full of life and light. I was on fire with the poetry of motion and longed to translate my sensations into deathless verse. At last Salamanca began to tire and I was able to curb his velocity. We found ourselves entering a valley with mountains on either side. One of these mountains I saw was crowned with a fine set of buildings which I took to be a monastery or convent. Some of it was in a state of decay but the main part of the structure looked sound, with a handsome bell tower and a platform on which to walk. I stopped altogether and tied Salamanca to a nearby olive tree in order to gaze in astonishment at this edifice, for it seemed too lonely and remote to sustain a thriving community. No other human dwelling could be seen for miles and the plain across which I had just ridden so precipitously was almost barren of vegetation. I was just wondering if it could possibly be inhabited when I heard the Angelus sound from the bell tower and presently I saw a hooded figure appear on the platform. He wore the black cowl of the Benedictine order.

"He stood alone and, though he was above a quarter of a mile away and the cowl obscured much of his face, I had the overwhelming impression that he was staring at me. I stared back at him and for near half an hour we remained thus occupied in mutual contemplation. What my thoughts were during this mysterious exercise I have no recollection. Then the cowled figure turned and began to glide towards what I took to be the monastery church and was lost from sight. I felt a strong urge to make my way up to the monastery and seek entry, but prudence restrained me. Besides, the heat of the day and my exertions had overwhelmed me with profound exhaustion. I sought the meagre shade of the olive tree to which Salamanca was tethered, sat myself down under it and, despite the discomfort of the stony ground, fell into a doze.

"I was awakened suddenly by the cries of the muleteers who formed the advance guard of our little caravan. I roused myself and, with a sore and throbbing head, sought out my guardians' carriage which, for all its foetid atmosphere, would provide me with more comfort and shade than my previous resting place.

"The Marquis and the Grand Prior greeted me with expressions of considerable relief. They had been worried in case I had ridden too far and become lost in this wilderness. I thanked them for their concern and then pointed out to them the monastery on the hill to their right. I saw the Marquis throw a quick glance at his brother the Grand Prior who crossed himself. I asked him to tell me something of the place. The Grand Prior told me that it was the Benedictine Priory of St Simeon but that it had been long since abandoned as being too remote and inconvenient even for the most ascetic of that order. Not so I replied, for I had seen a black monk of the Benedictine order standing upon that very platform yonder, and I pointed. Again the brothers exchanged agitated glances and the Grand Prior shook his head and said I must have been mistaken and perhaps the heat had affected my senses. Might we not at least see if the place was indeed deserted, I asked? No, indeed, the Grand Prior replied for we were expected at Guadalajara before nightfall and must be on our way.

"I did not dispute with him further because I was still suffering from the effects of my exhaustion and the heat. In fact I was beginning to feel somewhat unwell. I climbed into the carriage, sat down and almost at once fell into a heavy swoon or sleep and knew no more until we were at the very gates of the Monastery of San Pedro at Guadalajara.

"There I remained for several days, though I cannot remember much about it. The heat had so affected me that I fell sick of a fever which disordered my brain. A young novice Fray Antonio who had been appointed to look after me told me after my recovery that during this period when I was not asleep I was delirious. During my sickness, according to Fray Antonio, I had risen from my bed many times with the avowed intention of climbing a mountain and it was all he could do to restrain me. I had insisted to him that the mountain was called Parnassus which, he informed me in his simplicity, he had never heard of and was certainly not in Spain. On hearing this I could not forbear to laugh which seemed to wound him, but I embraced my novice and told him he was an exceedingly good fellow and we were friends again.

"My noble and reverend conductors during this time had deserted me in order to inspect a parcel of land which the Marquis wished to buy, so that I was left to my own devices. This suited me well for it took me some time to recover my spirits and the monastery at Guadalajara, in fact a Franciscan friary, was quiet and airy, a solemn, plain building but not destitute of wholesome comforts.

"I was nonetheless curious about my experiences and I asked one of the older friars, Fray Juan, about the Priory of St Simeon. He seemed reluctant to speak but when I pressed him he told me that the place had acquired an evil reputation and had been abandoned before the French came. Guerillas had for a time used it as a refuge during the war with Napoleon but even they had deserted it. I asked what was the nature of the evil that had inhabited it, but Fray Juan said only that the isolation of the Priory had turned the heads of its inhabitants who had previously had the reputation of extreme asceticism and holiness. I asked him if he was quite sure that the Priory was now unoccupied. He hesitated a moment and then said in a most determined manner that it was.

"I wonder if it was that hesitation which decided me; I cannot say, but I became resolved to visit St Simeon. My guardians, I was informed, were not to return for some days, so I was at liberty to please myself. I summoned my servant Marston who, during my illness, had gainfully employed himself in a liaison with a local innkeeper's daughter, and commanded him to prepare Salamanca for an early start the following day. He looked at me doubtfully, but when I told him he need not accompany me, he was all smiles.

"I set off the following morning before dawn so as to avoid if at all possible the midday heat. The day was fresh and first light was empurpling the Jarmara Hills as I rode out. I crossed the Henares River and gave my Arabian its head. I felt the bliss of youth and the prospect of glory, yet why I had embarked upon such a doubtful venture I cannot say.

"The sun was approaching the full blaze of noon when I came to the valley and the mount of St Simeon. Whether it was my own light-headedness or the recuperative powers of the Franciscan Friary, I was feeling no ill effects from the heat. I crossed a small stream, allowing Salamanca to drink his fill from the crystal waters then, leading my horse by the reins, I began to climb a wide, stony track towards the monastery of St Simeon.

"Close to, the edifice seemed more vast in extent and more ruinous than I had previously supposed. I stopped before a gateway, half tumbled, and showing the pockmarks of shot on its two great pillars, doubtless a memento of its recent incarnation as a guerilla fortress. I would have led my steed through this gate into the inner courtyard had not Salamanca utterly refused to proceed a step further into the monastery precincts. Accordingly I tied my Arabian to a gnarled bush that sprang from a confusion of fallen masonry and proceeded inside alone and on foot.

"The structures that I encountered within the monastery wall had once been magnificent, but were now in a state of melancholy ruination. Weeds erupted from every crack and crevice of the marble flagged pavement which I crossed to reach the main entrance. This was in the form of an elaborately carved ogival arch framing double doors of oak bound with elaborate iron arabesques. The wood was

scorched and rotted, and one half of the door had fallen away from its hinges. Beyond these portals I could see little light and no trace of human occupation. I could hear nothing but the wind and the beating of my own heart.

"I stood for some time at the entrance while I seriously considered my position. It was beginning to seem increasingly probable to me that the vision of the black monk on the monastery battlements a few days before was nothing but a delusion, 'proceeding from the heat-oppressed brain'. St Simeon was a deserted ruin and I should leave this scene of horrid desolation forthwith. Yet there is something that craves the strange sensations that such prospects engender in the poetic soul.

…This is not solitude: 'tis but to hold
Converse with savage Nature, and view her force unrolled
[*Childe Harold* II.25—adapted, or misremembered by Sotheran?]

"I thrust aside the decaying oak doors and entered a great vaulted hall lit by arched windows now cracked and open to the air beyond, but once richly decked with coloured glass of which only a few fragments remained

to bejewel the ruined pavement. My footsteps echoed but nothing else was there to stain the silence.

"I had come to the foot of a great staircase and was just about to mount it when I heard a noise behind me. It was no more than an exhalation of breath but it was as sharp as a sting in that immemorial stillness. I turned and saw standing some ten feet away from me a cowled figure, the same, I was sure, that I had seen on the monastery battlements a few days before. His hood was up and shadowed most of his face, though I could see that it was lean, clean-shaven and bone-white in colour. The eyes dwelt unseen in cavernous sockets under heavy brows.

"In my best halting Spanish I greeted him and begged his pardon for my intrusion. The monk spoke not a word. I bowed and he bowed in return, a low but dignified obeisance, then gestured to me to follow him. I did not venture to engage him in further conversation, suspecting that perhaps his order had bound him to silence.

"He led me through a succession of halls and passageways, each one vaster, gloomier and more ruined than the last, until finally he ushered me into a great corridor lit by a succession of beams of light coming from circular apertures in the groined vaulting of its roof. The corridor appeared to have no end, and I observed that there were figures coming towards me from a distance. Then I realised that the figures approaching were myself and my ghostly conductor. We had entered from a side door and there were mirrors at either end of the corridor to create the illusion of an infinite recession into a dim obscurity of space.

"I turned to ask the monk the significance of this astonishing effect, but he merely put his finger to his lips and, with the gentlest push in the small of my back, propelled me towards one of the mirrors which were of the finest Venetian make, curious possessions for a house of prayer and penitence. When I was within five feet of the glass he indicated that I should stop and observe what was before me.

"I saw myself framed by the mirror; behind me another image of myself, behind that another and so on in an infinite regression, each one dimmer and gloomier than the last until I faded into a grey green obscurity. It was, of course, as I saw it first, a purely natural phenomenon, while at the same time being wholly illusory. I was staring not into infinity but at a piece of glass backed by a mercury and tin amalgam. The contemplation of this spectacle so absorbed me for some moments that I forgot entirely about the monk until I noticed that his image could not be seen in the glass. I turned round and saw that he was standing directly behind me so that I had obscured any reflection of him.

"I was about to make some remark when he put a finger to his lips again and pointed at the mirror. I turned back and once more, this time with strong inner misgivings, gazed at myself multiplied in the mirror.

"The sight I beheld was different from my last encounter with it, though at first I could not discern where the difference lay. By slightly shifting my position in relation to the mirror, I could see more clearly the second image of myself behind the first, and it was then that I received a shock. The second image was the difference. Not only was it dimmer, but it seemed older. At first I tried to dismiss it as a passing illusion, but there were lines on the face which were not present in my most immediate reflection. The hair, moreover was more disordered and had the taint of grey in it. I looked at the third image which seemed older still. Deep grooves of disappointed hopes curved around my lips and darkened my eyes. My hair was not only greyer but had begun to thin. I blinked, passed my hand over my face but the illusion—if it was an illusion—remained. Down the endless corridor I stared as each succeeding reflection of myself diminished and decayed until, far in the unreal distance, I could see, faint and small, but still discernible, a grinning skull and skeleton to which a few rags of decayed flesh still adhered. I cried out in horror and the echo shrieked back at me a thousand times. When I turned from the mirror I saw that the monk was gone. I was alone.

"I ran and found that I was running towards my infinite self in the opposite direction. This filled me with such terror that it confounded my senses for a while, and some time elapsed before I recovered my wits sufficiently to find the exit from the endless corridor. The monastery had become a labyrinth to my wounded mind and for a long while I blundered through decaying passages and chambers, and through vast ruined halls until at last I found my way out into the open air where, to my astonishment, the sun was already beginning to decline into a cloudy and ensanguined west.

"I untethered and mounted Salamanca who seemed to welcome my arrival and we set off at once on the long ride to Guadalajara. I truly believe that it was my faithful horse rather than I who found the way back to our Franciscan sanctuary. We arrived before its gates in starlight and under a moon without whose guiding illumination Salamanca and I would have been utterly lost."

There is more in this journal, but it is mostly fragmentary. Some of it shows evidence of a deeply troubled mind, but I don't need to quote further. I had taken scans of these and other pages. It was evening and I had not eaten all day. Needless to say my hosts offered no refreshment. When I took my leave of Lord Glimham and the skeletal blonde whom I took to be Serena, Lady Glimham, they looked at me searchingly, almost in a concerned way. Glimham asked if the Sotheran papers were "worth selling" and I replied, again ambiguously, that they were of great value.

As I drove my car down towards the entrance gates the evening sun was low and shone almost directly in my face, masked only by a belt of spidery trees. The protesters were still at the gates, sitting on camp stools and regaling themselves with sandwiches and Thermos tea. I felt a pang of hunger and, in a momentary loss of concentration, swerved towards them almost hitting an elderly lady who fell off her stool. The rest shook their fists and yelled at me. To them it had been a deliberate attack on their righteous cause. I felt dazed and confused. It was as if someone or something had taken momentary possession of the steering wheel.

Nothing, except a faint but persistent sense of unease, could restrain the sense of exhilaration I felt over the next few weeks. I wrote some chapters and a synopsis, then approached a publisher who showed enthusiasm for the project. All was going well, or seemed to be. It was Julia who alerted me to the fact that I was working too hard, lecturing and giving tutorials during the day, writing in the evenings, sparing no thought for myself or others. My work on Sotheran had almost finished before I paid her any attention.

One evening, on returning from a seminar on Byron, I took a bath. I had begun to pay conscious attention to my exhaustion but still denied it to the world. A bath, I thought, would dissolve anxieties. I am still young enough to believe in simple remedies.

The area of the bath is surrounded on three sides by mirrors, an idea of Julia's. I have never cared much for the sight of myself naked and I have always had an aversion to the endless reflection that Sotheran writes about in his memoir. Indeed the image had preyed upon me, and this may explain what appeared to happen next.

The bath had done me good. Cares from the day had dissolved. I rose out of the water and, without giving it much thought, cleared the steam from the mirrors that surrounded me. Before taking my towel I studied myself in the glass. I had lost weight recently and was preparing to be pleasantly surprised by what had become of my figure.

The heat of the water had made my skin pinker than usual, and I looked with interest at the infinite recessions of my body in the glass. I found it hard to focus my eyes on the grey-green distance. It was my partner Julia who had put the mirrors up. She liked the paradox of the mirror world which was at once entirely real and completely false. It was, she said, the simplest and most profound of art installations.

I seemed to be looking at a stranger. It was me, of course, the features were recognisable, but I could claim no ownership over my reflection. The eyes were cold and lustreless: their weariness was ancient. And each succeeding image in the infinitely long line was increasingly strange until, at the apex of the endless vista, I saw something shadowy and utterly alien with two points of darkness for eyes. Then that thing began to advance and all sense of perspective collapsed. It was not me at all but a dark man in a rusty black suit with a white stock around his throat. He was running down the endless corridor towards me, lank hair waving in a mythical breeze, while my own image shuddered in the vaporous heat. His lugubrious eyes were hungry to possess me while I was beginning to lose all that I was. I could barely see myself; in a moment I might not exist at all.

A hand on my shoulder; arms around me as I collapsed: it was Julia. She was by me as I recovered, slowly, as far as I am able. I still am but do not know if I will be. I cannot be what I was: that is certain.

Now I have achieved my "impact". My book *The Endless Corridor: William Sotheran, Doomed Romantic* has been published by Bloomsbury, and John Carey has reviewed it favourably in the *Sunday Times*. I have presented a *Radio 3* documentary about Sotheran and my lectureship at Wessex University has been renewed. But Julia walked out on me two days ago, giving no reason, though maybe I can guess. I am chained to a madman. I owe Sotheran, and he is not about to forget my obligation to him. He beckons to me from the Endless Corridor where Fame and Oblivion are one.

REVISING HORROR:
AN INTERVIEW WITH
ELLEN DATLOW

BY CHRIS KELSO

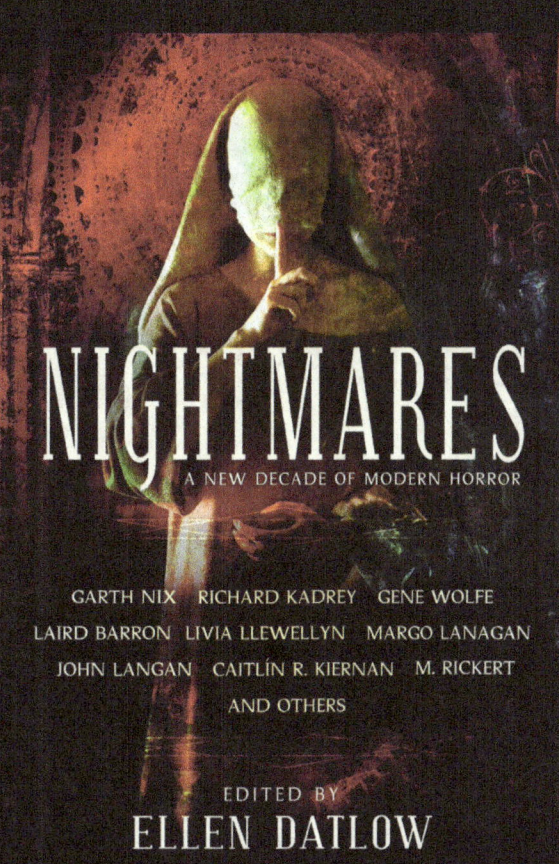

Photo courtesy of Ellen Datlow

After over thirty-five years in the editing game, there aren't many people out there more respected or critically lauded than Ellen Datlow. In a long, prestigious career *(that's seen her win seven Hugo Awards, ten World Fantasy Awards, two British Fantasy Awards, five Bram Stokers, three Shirley Jacksons, and twelve Locus Awards)* Datlow has cemented herself as something of an institution in the field of science fiction, fantasy, and horror, our very own arbiter for great writing and truly terrifying tales.

With over ninety anthologies to her name, the New York native is considered by many to be the leading authority on which authors we should all be reading within those genres—and it's difficult to dispute this claim.

***

Chris Kelso: Ellen, you always hear people asking authors which other writers inspired them, but do you have any particular editorial influences? Anyone's approach or style that you really admired or motivated you to head down a similar path so enthusiastically?

Ellen Datlow: Judith Merril, Maxwell Perkins, and Harlan Ellison. Merril for her Bests of the Year, which included fiction from all types of magazines

and reprinted stories by Bernard Malamud, Isaac Bashevis Singer, Romain Gary, Muriel Spark, Bertrand Russell, Jules Feiffer, and John D. McDonald, and many other writers not known for their SF, paving the way for the blurring of genre boundaries. Maxwell Perkins for his dedication and encouragement to some of the United States' greatest novelists. Harlan Ellison for pushing writers into then-taboo territory with *Dangerous Visions* and *Again, Dangerous Visions*.

CK: Your eighth *Best Horror of the Year* volume was recently published, and I was wondering—what's the screening process like for a project of that magnitude? I mean, you must receive thousands of entries from eager candidates? Do people send you stories or do you actively seek them out?

ED: I don't solicit "entries." I solicit *publishers* to send me their magazines/files of stories from websites, entire anthologies and collections. The only reason I should be sent an individual submission is if I can't get the material through the publisher. Contributors should be pushing their publishers to send me and every other year's best editor their books/stories. I rarely read self-published work, unless it's by someone already established by having first published traditionally.

NIGHTMARES
A NEW DECADE OF MODERN HORROR

GARTH NIX   RICHARD KADREY   GENE WOLFE

LAIRD BARRON   LIVIA LLEWELLYN   MARGO LANAGAN

JOHN LANGAN   CAITLÍN R. KIERNAN   M. RICKERT

AND OTHERS

EDITED BY

ELLEN DATLOW

CK: *Nightmares: A New Decade of Modern Horror,* **a companion anthology to** *Darkness: Two Decades of Modern Horror,* **recently hit the shelves—I'm curious about your experience compiling that book. Do you encounter a lot of hurdles in the editing process? Has there ever been a backlash from a writer you turned down or refused to work with?'**

ED: I was eager to edit an anthology of newer stories as soon as *Darkness* was published in 2010. But Tachyon, my publishers, convinced me to wait until I could cover the next ten years: 2005-2015. No obstacles—it's just difficult to pick the best of the best, which essentially is what the two volumes represent in my mind.

Sometimes, when editing a best of the year, I can't acquire the rights to a story I'd like to use, for one reason or another. That always bothers me because it means that this one, terrific story that I love won't be shared with my readers. (Of course they might have read the story wherever it was originally published).

When editing an original anthology, sometimes writers on whom I've been counting don't come through with their story. Or the story doesn't work for the anthology, and I've got to turn it down. This is the reason that I and many other editors of original anthologies ask about one third more writers than we actually need for any given anthology. We know that about one third will drop out.

Back in my *OMNI* magazine days I received a few nasty rants by rejected writers, all of whom swore they'd never send me another story. They did, all of them within about three years. And not one ever acknowledged his assholery nor apologized.

FEATURING STORIES BY

NATHAN BALLINGRUD
LAIRD BARRON
BRIAN EVENSON
GEMMA FILES
STEPHEN GRAHAM JONES
CAITLÍN R. KIERNAN
ALISON LITTLEWOOD
GARTH NIX
ROBERT SHEARMAN
GENEVIEVE VALENTINE

AND MANY OTHERS

THE BEST
HORROR
OF THE YEAR

VOLUME EIGHT

EDITED BY
ELLEN DATLOW

CK: The anthology *Children of Lovecraft* came out this year too. How has the book performed commercially and has the reception been what you expected—I know it was released by Dark Horse who are seen as primarily a publisher of graphic novels?

ED: This is my third Lovecraftian anthology (the reprint anthology *Lovecraft's Monsters* was published in 2014 by Tachyon) and my second for Dark Horse—the first was *Lovecraft Unbound* back in 2009. They've published single-author collections and several novels in the past and so far have been supportive of the anthologies of mine that they've published.

I don't know how the book is doing commercially—I won't know for quite a while, but generally, Lovecraftian anthologies and novels continue to sell and sell, which is why my editor asked me to edit this second one for them.

CK: I'm sure you're asked this a lot, but what are your thoughts on H.P. Lovecraft himself? He's come under some heavy criticism from certain corners of the horror community for his personal ideologies; do you think it's easy to separate the art from the artist?

ED: Lovecraft was a racist and anti-Semite. There's no arguing against that. And his work's influence on weird/dark fiction and weird/dark fiction writers is also unassailable. I've recently responded to a question from another interviewer essentially explaining that I read Lovecraft when I was very young and was not cognizant (nor interested in) metaphor or symbolism in fiction. And I knew nothing about Lovecraft the person—was unaware of the scholarship on him or his correspondence or his poetry. Basically all I knew were the stories and novels set in his mythos. I appreciated the cosmic horror he depicted. In a way it's poetic justice that so many writers—of all sexes, races, and ethnicities—are using his works as a playground to create new stories and new themes, rather than slavishly imitate them as so many of his "circle" did, way back when.

CK: People see you as something of a gatekeeper in the field of horror and science fiction, do you ever feel the pressure of that responsibility? Does this provide a driving force when compiling an anthology, knowing you have a certain weight of audience expectation on your shoulders?

ED: Every editor is a gatekeeper. That's a large portion of any acquisition editor's job: to make choices. To decide what goes into a magazine, a webzine, an anthology—and what doesn't. There are plenty of other short story editors and markets out in the world so if one editor turns down a story, the writer just needs to send it to another one.

I'm a reader first and foremost. I'm a reader who loves short stories and loves working with writers on their work to help them make it better. I'm lucky that most of my anthologies sell well enough that I can continue to edit new ones. I please my readers by pleasing myself, which is why I'll only work on a theme that I believe will generate really interesting stories.

CK: It's difficult for young writers in a market that's become so over-saturated—do you have any tips for people who want desperately to stand out from the crowd?

ED: Write your heart out and submit to markets that have a high profile. Don't give your work away because very few "for love" markets have any distribution. Keep writing, keep submitting work. If you seek feedback, first make sure you trust whoever is giving it to you. Don't send out first drafts. Once you finish a story, let it sit for a little while (not too long). Reread it. Revise if you feel it needs it. Then send it out. Do not wait for a response. Write your next story. Rinse and repeat.

CK: What advice would you give a writer who maybe wants to feature in one of your anthology projects? Is there a style that appeals to you or that you find repellent?

ED: First of all, I don't read unsolicited manuscripts. If a writer is published in a venue I check out while reading for the *Best Horror of the Year* (and that's most magazines/anthologies that publish sf/f/h and even crime/mysteries) I'll likely start noticing their work and one day I might solicit a story from them for something else.

What I buy depends on what anthology theme I'm working on. When I solicit stories I send out guidelines to the writers in whom I'm interested. In those guidelines I usually give an idea of what I do and don't want. And as I start to acquire stories for that anthology and it fills up, I'll contact the writers who have promised me stories to let them know that I don't want to see any more… such and such type of story.

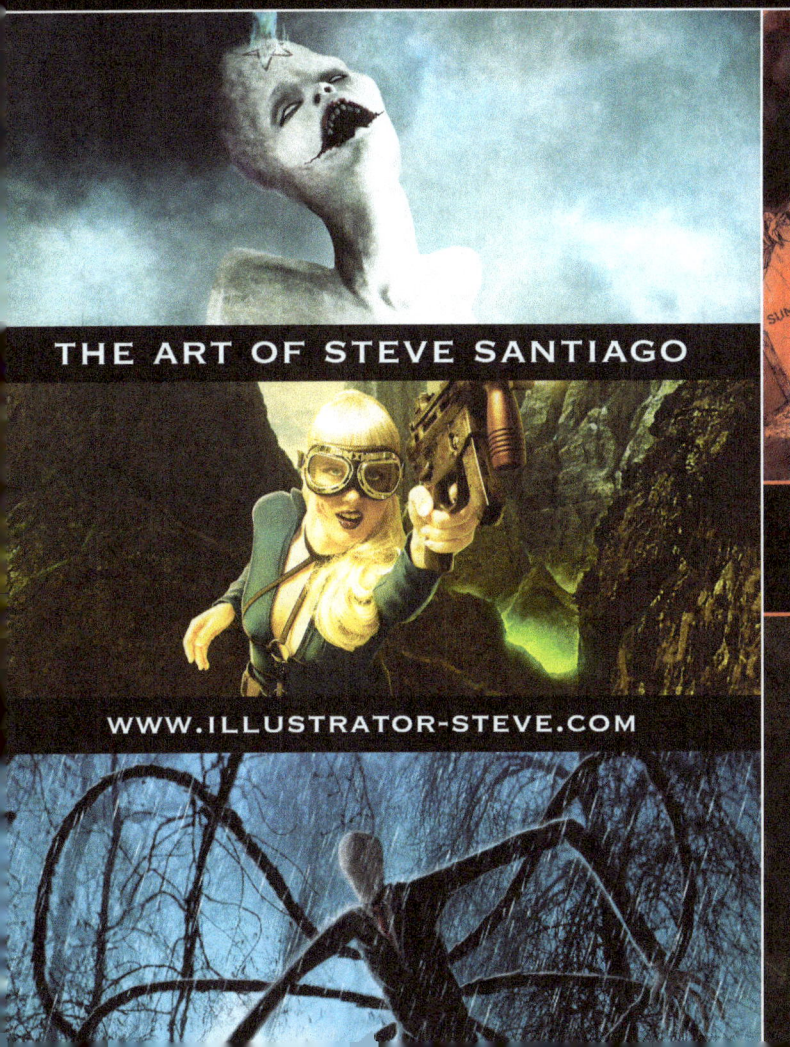

TheHieroglyphs of Blood and Bone
Visionary new voice in weird fiction Michael Griffin

When Guy's marriage of two decades unravels, he's driven from his previously stable domestic life and ends up renting a room in the houseboat of his much younger co-worker Karl. Pushed outside his comfort zone, Guy tries to follow Karl's example, until he ends up exploring entirely new frontiers, both natural and uncanny.

He finally encounters the enigmatic Lily, who offers to share with Guy her own arcane language, a mix of incomprehensible symbols, rough bits of nature and dark pleasures of the flesh. Guy finds himself obsessed, as if powerless under Lily's spell.

Will he recognize in time the many secrets she keeps hidden in plain sight, or will allow himself to be pulled downstream toward an inescapable vortex?

Publication Date: February 24, 2017

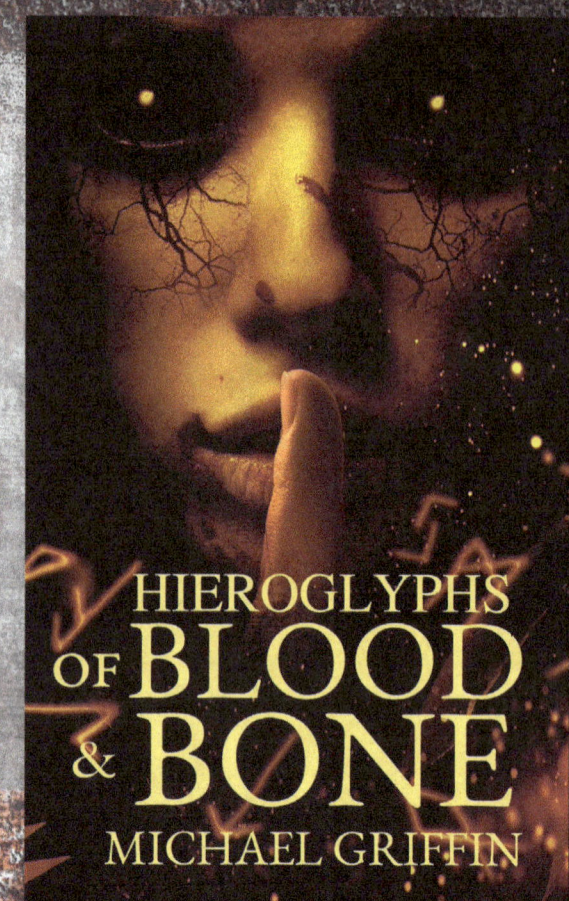

HIEROGLYPHS
OF BLOOD
& BONE
MICHAEL GRIFFIN

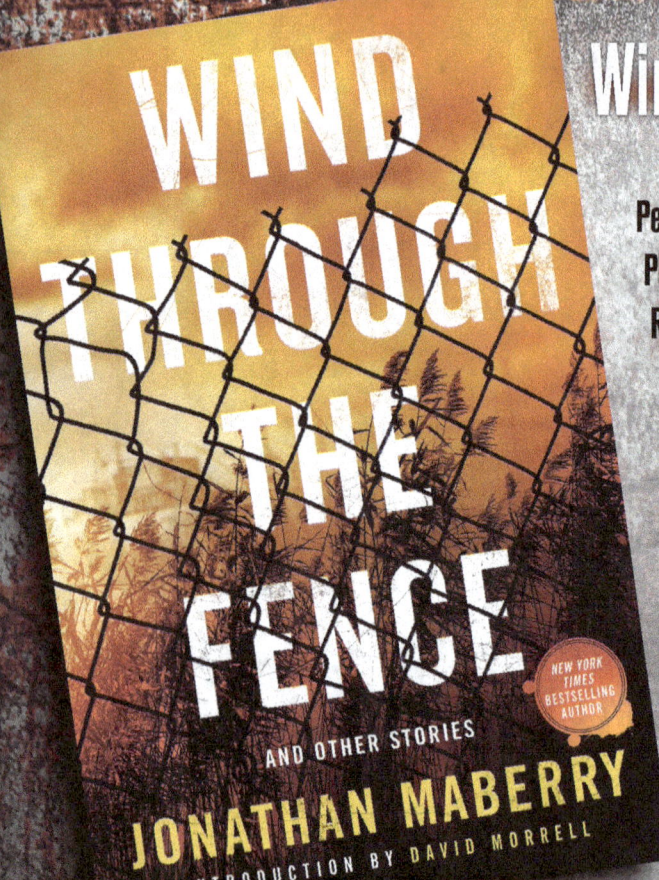

WIND THROUGH THE FENCE
AND OTHER STORIES
JONATHAN MABERRY
INTRODUCTION BY DAVID MORRELL

Wind Through the Fence
And Other Stories

Pegleg and Paddy Save the World

Plan 7 from L.A.

Red Dreams

Saint John

She's Got a Ticket to Ride

Spellcaster 2.0

T. Rhymer – Written with Gregory Frost

The Cobbler of Oz

The Things That Live in Cages

The Vanishing Assassin

The Wind through the Fence

Faces

Publication Date: February 10, 2017

FANTASIA FILM FESTIVAL REVIEWS

BY NANCY KILPATRICK

FEAR YOUR DREAMS

BEFORE I WAKE

IN THEATERS THIS FALL

For three weeks every year I vanish. You will not find me. I am imprisoned in a dark room, locked to a seat, unable to move, every few minutes silently cringing in terror; escape is impossible. And I love every second of it.

If you've been fortunate enough to attend a horror film festival, you know what I'm talking about. And if you haven't, this is an experience you need. Nowhere else will you find so many dark films from around the world, including your own backyard, that will alter your perception of the genre through the work of visionary directors and scriptwriters you will not have heard of, and actors you will have not previously seen. At such festivals you will encounter alternative films that challenge the somewhat stale boundaries set by Hollywood. This is the future of horror cinema.

The festival I hit every July has just celebrated its twentieth year, making it one of the oldest genre festivals in the world. Year one was devoted to Asian films. Years two through twenty have been split between Asian and Horror/DarkFantasy/Fantasy/ SciFi films, with many overlaps. These were and are the predilections of the guys who started *Fantasia*, Pierre Corbeil and Mitch Davis being two of the kingpins, opening Montrealers to international genre films the citizens of this city would otherwise never get to see. Tony Timpone has shown up annually for more than a decade to introduce the best of the best to the large and highly enthusiastic crowds.

About 120 films are screened, half in our beloved dark genre. It's a challenge to see as many films as possible, which would be around 60 to 70, and likely no mortal can cope with so many flicks over such a short time span and live to tell about it. Wimp that I am, I generally manage to view about 30 to 40 films.

Over the two decades of *Fantasia* I've seen the premiers of some amazing cinema, films that have gone on to catch worldwide attention. Here are a few you will recognize:

LET THE RIGHT ONE IN (2008 Sweden - Swedish with English subtitles) Based on the book *Let Me In* by John Ajvide Lindqvist. Matt Reeves remade it in English in 2010 as *Let Me In*. Awards: won 55 and even more nominations.

[REC] (2007 Spain - Spanish with English subtitles) John Erick Dowdle remade it in English in 2008 as *Quarantine*. Awards: won 15, and as many nominations.

RINGU (1998 Japan - Japanese with English subtitles) Screenplay by Hiroshi Takahashi. Remade in 2002 by Gord Verbinski as *The Ring*. Awards: 6, plus a slew of nominations.

JUAN OF THE DEAD (2011 Cuba - Spanish with English subtitles) Awards won: 7, plus nominations.

TROLLHUNTER (2010 Norway - Norwegian with English subtitles) Awards won: 3 plus 7 nominations.

CITADEL (2012 Ireland/Scotland - English) Awards won: 9 plus an equal number of nominations.

ABSENTIA (2011 USA - English). Awards won: over 20.

***

Here are my selections of the best films from *Fantasia*, year 20.

MUST SEE:

Before I Wake (US) A couple grieving the death of their eight year old son reach the stage where they are able to take in a foster child. The boy is sweet, loving, respectful... and deeply disturbed. Eight-year-old Cody (Jacob Trembly)

is terrified to fall asleep because his dreams become reality, some lovely, some horrific nightmares, with a ruthless monster out to get him that Cory calls Canker Man. This is a good psychological horror story packed with thrills and chills and creepiness—think M. Night Shyamalan's best movies. The casting is excellent, with Kate Bosworth starring. Mike Flanagan, the director/writer, is known for his previous films include *Occulus*; *Hush*; and *Absentia*. He's clearly on the rise. Expect this one to appear in a theater near you. *****

Beware the Slenderman (USA) This is a chilling documentary and you will likely recall the news stories of young people obsessed with the online character Slenderman. In 2014, two twelve-year-old girls from a small Wisconsin town brutally stabbed their friend because the tall, slim, faceless Slenderman told them to. It's a long, detailed documentary but so well done your time won't be wasted. Crammed with direct material—interviews with the girls' parents, police interrogations, courtroom video, videos of the girls talking about Slenderman and their crime—the film culminates with the diagnosis of one girl as schizophrenic. The story stops when the judge decides whether or not to try the girls as juveniles or adults. It's a heart-wrenching story, one that shows the vulnerability of an age where reality and fantasy blur, especially for those with a propensity to lose touch with the former. Irene Taylor Brodsky directs this disturbing documentary. *****

Embers (US/Poland - English) This film was one of my favs. A post apocalyptic world where the virally-infected

lose their memory. We follow several characters who seem to know some things by instinct but not details of their lives, not who they know, not their own names. There is a strong sense of menace in this trust-no-one world gone awry. In the midst of hell on earth, two people unaffected by the plague have been hiding in a posh bunker for 9 years. This movie begs the question: is it better to be free in an infected world or safe but existing like the living dead in a prison-like environment? Claire Carré wrote the screenplay and directed. Sundance loved it, and so did I. *****

I, Olga Hepnarova (Czech Republic/Poland/Slovakia - English subtitles) Petr Kazda and Tomas Weinreb co-wrote the screenplay and directed this film which reminds me of *Christine F*, a fictionalized story of a true-life tragedy. Shot in b&w, the cinematography captures the Cold War era and the occupation of what was then Czechoslovakia. Olga is a grimly compelling and twisted young woman who was brutalized at home, in institutions and by society in general. A passive chain-smoking victim, nothing brings her joy, including several lesbian flings. One day this perfect victim snaps and we see on screen what recently occurred on the *Promenade des Anglais* in Nice, France. Olga's letters and diaries detailing her horrific experiences survived to become the basis of this story. Her story and the outcome proved so traumatic for the citizens of both the Czech Republic and Slovakia that it wasn't talked about, much less made into a film until very recently. Olga made history as the last woman to be executed in Czechoslovakia. Hers is a haunting tale of a terrifyingly alienated character

portrayed by rising star Michalina Olszanska. *****

Superpowerless (US - in English) What happens to a superhero who hits middle age and finds that his powers have waned? Bob (Josiah Polhemus) *was* an icon, but no longer. He cannot fight crime anymore, and he's been all but forgotten; he doesn't know what to do with himself. He tries intervening in a mugging and comes away with a black eye. His wife suggests he write a book about his exploits, but his sidekick has already done that, landing a bestseller. This is a fun film featuring a schlunky ex-super-hero who, like just about every human on the planet, has to contend with the fact that he's no longer trim, fit, coura-geous and twenty. It's a well-executed coming-of-middle-age story that leaves the special effects behind. Is it horror? If you're over 30, yes. *****

We Go On (US - English) Mike Grissom (Clark Freeman) is afraid of everything, but mainly death, and he offers $30,000 through a newspaper ad to anyone who can prove to him that there is life after death. Three people hit the shortlist, all scam artists or crazies, and then a 4th surfaces through an untraceable phone call. Mike meets the man who takes him to see a ghost. But this ghost is demanding and until Mike commits the horrible act that the ghost insists upon, he will be haunted day and night. Co-directors Andry Mitton and Jesse Holland have made a smart and unique film with a solid spooky plot full of twists and turns—refreshing in a ghost story. *****

SHOULD SEE:

Demon (Poland/Israel - English subtitles) Peter (Itay Tiran) leaves London to marry his best friend's sister Zaneta (Agnieszka Zulewska), who he has been dating via Skype. Odd things begin to happen from the get-go in this isolated village and when he unearths bones that no one else can find, he becomes possessed. The late Polish direc-tor Marcin Wrona wrote and directed a tale which utilizes the Jewish legend of the *dybbuk*, or unquiet spirit. Nicely shot in a rather creepy old house where all hell breaks loose at the wedding-from-hell-reception. ****

Let Me Make You a Martyr (US - English) With charac-ters named Pope, Charon, Father Francis, viewers should grasp the allegorical significance of this gritty base-line-human story. There are no real likeable characters, no real winners and everyone seems to be a loser, but these malefactors are interestingly portrayed in a world of hard drugs and violence, where familial revenge is the norm. Think a *Sons of Anarchy* tone (and hey!, Nico Nicotera who plays lead Drew Glass in this movie is a veteran of S of A, as is Mark Boone Junior, who plays Larry Glass). If you liked the gritty feel of *True Detective*, that sultry, sweaty, so-much is rotting climate, this one is for you. Marilyn Mansion has a small but pivotal role and you won't recog-nize him, which is probably a good thing. Corey Asraf and John Swab directed their first film over five years (Swab wrote the screenplay). Many have hated this dystopian movie, I didn't. It's hard and cruel, yes, a portal into the decaying and violent world of low-lifes, so be forewarned: once you view it, you'll need a shower for your body and some bleach for your brain. ****

Little Sister (US - English) Not an obvious horror film but so many of the elements are there that it will appeal to those who like dark and offbeat. It's been described as both improbably pure-hearted and magnificently demented. The story falls into the humorous horror sub-genre of quirky films about dysfunctional families, but this one offers a twist. Colleen Lunsford (Addison Timlin), former goth, now a novice nun, returns home to visit her pot-smoking parents and especially her post-traumatic-stressed-out-ex-military brother. It's a wacky black comedy that is also strangely heart-warming in a dark and cryptic way. See it if you enjoy eccentrics cavorting around Halloween. ****1/2

Realive (Spain - in English) Mateo Gil wrote and directed this film. He has a long list of movies he's directed, and written for, staring among others, Tom Cruise (*Vanilla Sky*) and Penelope Cruise (*Open Your Eyes*). In this mod-

creepy and so much the type I've been hoping for in a film: dark eerie music combined with dark unforgiving nature, the undertone isolation and extreme witchiness. Elena, a young, single mother from a Slavic country, takes a job in Scandinavia at a house located in a remote region. The couple she works for live without electricity or other modern conveniences. Her three year contract is hard: drawing water from a well, growing and cooking vegetarian dishes, washing, cleaning, every manual labor chore imaginable—but she needs the money for her son. The husband seems a decent guy, but the wife is severely depressed—their child has died recently. They offer Elena a surrogacy deal—once she delivers the baby, she will leave with enough money to buy an apartment for herself and her son. The couple will have a child, and the wife will no longer be in mourning. A win-win. What could possibly go wrong? This is a Bergmanesque vision of *Rosemary's Baby* in a rural setting, blurred reality blended with hallucinations, and for Elena,

ern *Frankenstein* offering, Marc (Tom Hughes) discovers he has a fast-moving and terminal cancer. He possesses wealth and charm, he loves life and he loves his girlfriend and good friends and in an effort to hold onto what he has, all his money goes into being preserved cryonically post-expiration, to be revived when a cure is found. But the future isn't what he imagined. They've rebuilt his body but memories of his past life seep through his consciousness to haunt him, including his long-time love and what happened to her. As *Frankenstein* was made great under the control of Mary Shelley's pen, this film, in the hands of such a thoughtful director and writer, explores an existential philosophy tinged with the horror of a future world that feels strangely unemotional and inhuman. A terrific updating of a classic. ****1/2

Shelly (Denmark/Sweden - in English) There is a lovely lead-in to the story through the opening shots, wonderfully

no way out. Horrific through building creepiness. ****

Tank 432 (UK - English) Military paranoia to the max. No one knows where they are or why they are there except the log-book recording leader of this grisly band of soldiers trapped in enemy territory with two prisoners in tow and a dangerous enemy they can't see. Is the enemy real, or unreal? It is definitely *not* what it appears to be, when it appears at all. Massive confusion and hallucinations create a lattice of the mental and physical disintegration of tough but frightened soldiers trapped in a tank. Such a situation can only lead to violence, and this movie layers it on. Written and directed by Nick Gillespie. ****

The Alchemist Cookbook (US - English) Sean (Ty Hickson, who has been in four previous movies including *Gimme the Loot*) took his cat Casper and moved to a trailer deep in the woods. It's everyone's fantasy: live in nature, off the grid, do as you like when you like, please your-self. A friend brings him supplies on occasion, including his medication—except for this time, when he forgot the pills. Isolation leads to alienation and Sean, a guy with a chemical bent, makes bombs and studies alchemy for fun. He tries to summon a demon so he can give himself over in exchange for wealth that will truly make him independent. Admirably, Hickson covers the gamut of emotions in this character study of a tormented man who is losing it as he plays with the demonic—a demon that plays back! Screenplay and direction in this his fourth film is by Joel Potrykus, whose work has been compared to early Jim Jarmusch. ****

The Lure (Poland - English subtitles) Michalina Olszanska (from *I, Olga Hepnarova*) co-stars in a Polish Bollywood-style movie/musical of two mermaid sisters wanting to check out living on land for a change. But there

you gets: Black face; hoochie-koochie girls; men shot out of cannons; men and women catapulted through the air inside boxes; high diving into tiny tanks; escape artists freeing themselves from straightjackets and other bonds to escape flames; belly dancers, hula dancers, strip tease dancers, giants and midgets, knife and axe throwers and bow and arrow shooters, their weapons targeted to sur-round a woman's body; a woman throwing knives at her toddler; lions, tigers, monkeys, horses, donkeys, zebras, bulls, bears, elephants—sane people will root for the ani-mals; wrestling; four-way blind-folded boxing; lady box-ers; child boxing a kangaroo; boys from the age of five or six boxing each other to tears; monkey bands; dancing bears, bike riding bears, horse-riding monkeys and lions; elephant bands; cake-eating pandas; soccer-playing dogs; unicycle riding monkeys; clowns of all types; clown box-ing; midget clown boxing; acrobats of every persuasion; tossing toddlers from hand to hand at the edge of a build-

is much more to their dark side than just having a fish tail. They work in a nightclub with a host of weirdos, so there's plenty of song, nudity and sex. And smoking, lots and lots of smoking in this 50s style film. This is the Everything-I've-Always-Wanted-to-Know-About-Mermaids   film you've been waiting for. It's a totally fresh story, weird and wacky and ultimately horrific. This is director Agnieszka Smoczynska's debut film. ****

The Show of Shows (Iceland/UK - silent with subtitles here and there) A melange of painstakingly researched archival footage of circuses and sideshow acts that are compellingly seedy. It's the kind of stuff you can't stop watching. By today's standards, some of this is politi-cally incorrect. But the footage is from the 1930s to 1950s, decades where carnivals and oddities were big entertain-ment around the world, and if you can't cut the times some slack, this isn't for you. You pays your money and

ing over a highway... and so much more. This is a world of the past, what entertained your grand and great grand-parents, which is probably why they seemed so stoic. ****

Women Who Kill (US - English) A funny well-made black comedy featuring Morgan (Ingrid Jungermann) and her ex-girlfriend Jean (Ann Carr) who host a podcast called *Women Who Kill*—their focus: female serial killers. Jungermann, with a couple of TV series under her belt, has been touted as one of the best new directors. Here, she directs and co-stars in this hilarious and well-written movie. Out of a communal world of eccentric lesbian char-acters, paranoia and horror build—Morgan's new lover just might be another serial killer. It is a darkly fun film, completely quirky, the dialogue crisp, the plot unique, and I'm betting that you haven't seen anything like this before. ****1/2

COULD SEE:

Bed of the Dead (Canada - English) Jeff Maher and Cody Calahan wrote the screenplay, and the former directed. Two young couples celebrating a birthday go to a fetish club and rent room 18. Of course the real room number is 13. Good film for the college kegger crowd who won't be too worried about why these characters didn't leave the haunted bed of retribution when they had the chance. ***

Goran (Croatia - English subtitles) An extremely passive going-nowhere-guy drives a taxi for a living. He has a blind but beautiful adoring girlfriend who has a rich dad, and that should be enough for any guy, but it isn't for Goran. He can't seem to grasp the good life and hold on. He manages to make a mess in many directions, destroying more than his own life in the most violent way. Directed by Nevio Marasovic, screenplay by Gjermund. ***

Lace Crater (US - English) A group of millennials weekend in a posh house in the Hamptons. Naturally they drink and take drugs, forcing mildly depressed Ruth (Lindsay Burge), who is recovering from a nasty breakup, to go sleep in the guest house alone. Reputedly haunted, it *is* haunted but by a relaxed and casual ghost wearing a burlap bag over his head. One thing leads to another and flesh and spirit meld as intimacy develops. After this tryst, every aspect of Ruth's life changes, and not for the better. Harrison Atkins wrote and directed an unusual and bleak ghost story. I'm still not sure, though, why he titled it *Lace Crater*. ***

She's Allergic to Cats (US - English) Michael Pinkney (Michael Pinkney—hey, it's an indie!) lives a messy life. He grooms dogs and cats but is really a frustrated filmmaker. This guy can't get anything right. His dream is to make a film based on King's *Carrie*, but using cats instead of people, which shows you how off-kilter he is. His filthy, rat-infested apartment in LA adds to his despair. But then he meets Cora (Sonja Kinski—daughter of Nastassja, granddaughter of Klaus), the woman of his dreams. She is strange and dark and off-beat like him. She might even understand him—until the messiness of his life catches up with him, and it's not pretty. ***

FROM THE TWISTED MINDS
WHO BROUGHT YOU *BITE*

BED OF THE DEAD

The Unseen (Canada - English) A strange story of Bob (Aden Young, star of TV's *Rectify*), a man with a family secret. Set in a Canadian far-north logging area, Bob must return to a small city where his daughter has gone missing. Meanwhile, he is slowly vanishing. It's a strangely long film that doesn't need all this time to accomplish what it intends, but maybe it will be further edited by the time you see it on *Netflix*. ***1/2

The Dark Tapes (US - English) This is *not* a *Fantasia* film but I saw the screener. It's horror with some nifty plot twists, a bit of other genres tossed in. The film has been described as a cross between *V/H/S* and *The Twilight Zone* and I think that's pretty accurate. Michael McQuown and Emmy nominee Vincent J. Guastini directed. Three known actresses star: Cortney Palm (*Sushi Girl, Zombeavers,* and *Death House*); Emilia Ares Zoryan (*V/H/S: Viral*); and TV actress Brittany Underwood. This is a cam movie, in four parts, a found-footage film, the overview a search for demons, scientific rational and other logic going only so far when there's a demon at your door. Look for it in 2017.

Karla was ten years old when she lost her left eye. Her brother had been playing with a BB gun in the backyard and she unfortunately got in the way when he was defending his imaginary log cabin from pretend Indians. An excruciating pain zinged through her eye, and she fell to the ground, shrieking at such a wild and high pitch that her brother began to laugh at the craziness of it all. Too many *Road Runner* cartoons had convinced him that she would just happily bounce back up on her feet in no time, but Karla continued to writhe in agony.

Her mother shot out like a banshee from the kitchen, snatched the BB gun from her brother's hands and ran to Karla. Scooping her up, she carried Karla inside to the living room couch.

Chaos reigned after that. An ambulance arrived. Medics fussed over her and then, with sirens wailing, rushed her to the hospital ER department. Nurses and doctors closed in and surrounded her. Finally, the bliss of painkillers and tranquilizers took hold and she drifted off to an uneasy sleep.

When she finally awoke to the mumble of adult voices, her mother's tear-stained face was the first thing she saw. There was a bulky bandage over her left eye. Her mother told her that the doctors couldn't save it—that her eye had been blasted into strawberry jelly by the BB. In doctors' terms, it had been eviscerated. They would have to wait until the wound healed completely, then they could fit her with an ocular prosthesis, otherwise known as a glass eye.

That was it. She was a one-eyed girl and life would never be the same again.

Karla was fitted with an artificial eye a year later, having to endure the inevitable taunts at school in the meantime because of her eye patch. Nicknames like Jolly Rodger and Pirate Girl got old very quickly.

Dr Deakins, the venerable ocularist who fitted her glass eye, did an exceptional job. The sapphire colour of the fake matched her right blue eye perfectly. However, as entertainers as diverse as Sammy Davis Jr. and Peter Falk had discovered, the effect wasn't exactly lifelike. Karla always appeared as if she wasn't quite looking right at you, but at something in the distance. But she didn't care. At least she didn't have to wear the damn eye patch anymore.

Fast-forward 15 years. Karla had gone through a few eyes in the intervening decade and a half because she wasn't eligible for a permanent porous ocular prosthesis, due to the risk of inflection. Finally she had to change ocularists when Dr Deakins retired. After a difficult search, as good ocularists were few and far between, she found a new guy in the city called Dr. Markham who seemed to fit the bill. He was almost too young and handsome to be a real doctor, but he possessed an intelligent gravitas that belied his years. However, she found Dr Markham's fascination for her empty eye socket slightly creepy, as if he found her more attractive eyeless than not. Notwithstanding her monocularism, Karla was a beautiful woman: lovely face, slim figure, radiant blonde hair. However, her self-consciousness about her eye made her dress down so people wouldn't notice her.

Dr Markham told Karla about the new inroads in ocularism. There were now revolutionary kinds of prostheses that were more lifelike and more comfortable. He had a guy in Chinatown that was such a wayward genius that he made Hannibal Chew—the geneticist who made the Replicant's realistic synthetic eyes in *Blade Runner*—look like an amateur. (Although of course, Hannibal Chew was just a fictional character and Dr Markham's boffin was the real thing.) The new procedure would only take a couple hours in his office, instead of a long operation under full anaesthetic. Karla enthusiastically ordered her new orb and hoped for the best.

A week later, she arrived at Dr Markham's office for her procedure. It was a late appointment, the last in the day. She entered the waiting room, puzzled to see that the receptionist had already gone home. Dr Markham emerged from his office and smiled her through the door.

With a flourish, he presented Karla with her new eye, which nestled like a jewel in an intricately detailed black velvet box decorated with Chinese hieroglyphs. It was astonishingly beautiful, almost like that dreamed-for diamond engagement ring that she knew in her heart she would never be offered. Who would ever want to marry a one-eyed girl?

Dr Markham escorted Karla to the luxurious DRE Milano H50 Procedure Chair where he performed all his out-patient operations. Her head rested in a surgical articulated pillow that contained a friction lock lever to keep her head in place.

He pushed a button and the lounge chair glided into a position almost parallel to the ground. As Karla made herself comfortable, Dr Markham sat on a stool next to the procedure chair. He asked her a few questions about what medication she was currently on, whether she suffered from allergies, anything else that might be relevant. Then he used a guarded eye speculum to keep her eye open, examining her socket closely with a flashlight. He attached an oxygen feed to her nostrils and then, via a winged infusion set, he injected a cocktail of Buscopan, Fentanyl and Midazolam into the vein in the crook of her right elbow.

As the sedatives flowed through her veins, Karla instantly relaxed. She was beyond caring as Dr Markham secured her into position with sturdy leather straps so it was impossible for her to move her body as well as her head. He explained that he didn't want her to make any sudden movements that might jeopardize the procedure.

Karla closed her good eye and waited for the insertion of her new ocular prosthesis to begin. Instead, something warm and wet was thrust into her empty eye socket. It started to wiggle around and she tried to scream, but Dr Markham stifled her cries with his hand.

Her one good eye popped open and she was horrified to see that not only did Dr Markham have his tongue down her eye socket, his other hand was sliding inside her blouse, twisting and pinching her nipple. He moved his hand down and pushed her panties aside, thrusting his gloved fingers inside her.

Karla moaned in horror, but her noises of helplessness just spurred Dr Markham on. His movements became more urgent. He removed his tongue from her eye socket and kissed her, all the while vigorously masturbating her until she came helplessly.

He stopped as soon as she came. It was as if nothing had happened. Dr Markham changed his gloves, swabbed out Karla's eye socket with Povidone-Iodine, an ocular antiseptic, and inserted her new prosthesis. He adjusted her clothes and then injected her with another cocktail of drugs, which sent her off into a state of half-consciousness and unreality.

An hour later, Karla came to. She was still on the chair, but the leather straps had disappeared. She glanced over to see Dr Markham at his desk, writing notes on the procedure.

"What… what happened?" Karla whispered hoarsely. She tried to get out of the chair. Dr Markham jumped up and came to her side, solicitously helping her.

"You just conked out," he said, smiling. "You've been having a little snooze for the last 40 minutes or so. So, how does that new eye feel?"

Karla looked at him suspiciously. He looked so innocent and above-board, like butter wouldn't melt between his thighs. Did she simply dream the assault?

Dr Markham took her by the arm and helped her to a nearby chair. "Have you ever had that kind of procedural medicine before?" he asked. "Perhaps it didn't sit well with you. Do you feel dizzy? Headache?"

"No, I'm fine," Karla said. She knew what had really happened to her, but she realized that the situation was hopeless. Everything that occurred could be explained as a reaction to the drugs. There was no proof of sexual assault, unless the CSI guys could pop her eye out and try to find a hint of Dr Markham's DNA still residing in her eye socket. Although the antiseptic probably took care of any residual epithelials from this pervert's tongue.

Karla could also smell the faint whiff of disinfectant coming up from her cleavage. This guy was thorough, if nothing else.

"I've got to go home right now," she said.

"Of course, do you want me to call you a cab?"

"I'll just grab one on the street," she replied.

She got up too quickly and her knees buckled. Dr Markham grabbed her by the arm and steered her to a mirror on the wall.

"You can't go before you see your new prosthesis," he said with a proud grin.

Karla looked in the mirror. There it was: perfect, magical, iridescent. Her new eye had an inexplicable charisma and glamour that her real eye lacked. For a few moments, she just stared at it, the horrors of her procedure and Dr Markham's violation fading for a bit while she was mesmerized by her new orb.

Finally, she left and staggered out into the dying light of the day. It was 8 PM on a beautiful summer's evening, but she didn't care. The memories of Dr Markham assaulting her came back in little electric shocks of horror. All she could think of is how she could get revenge on someone she should have been able to trust. What. A. Bastard.

Karla got drunk that night, glugging down a whole bottle of Chardonnay on her own, something she rarely did and probably not the wisest course of action after having all those drugs in her system, but she didn't care.

She felt angry at herself. How could she have been so stupid? She should have known that something was up as soon as she walked in and saw that the receptionist was gone. She should have confronted Dr Markham, but he would have denied everything and called her a fantasist, or said that she was dreaming, or that she was hallucinating because of a reaction to the drugs. She was also afraid that someone that fearless about attacking his patients might turn violent if challenged.

In the end, Karla kept reminding herself that this whole situation hadn't been her fault. He was the pervert. She was the victim.

That night, after being plagued by imaginary conversations with Dr Markham, culminating in a court case and her dramatically taking the stand, Karla finally fell into a troubled, nightmare-filled sleep, populated by a devilishly handsome mirror-eyed doctor sporting an eyeball at the tip of his tongue.

Karla woke up the next day with the mother of all hangovers. It felt like lightning was slicing through her brain and the vision in her good eye was blurred. Her problem with floaters—the reflections of dead cells floating in the vitreous humour of the eyeball—was acute. Occasionally one floater would catch the light of the sun and take on a darkly crystalline form, as if the monolith from the film *2001* was making a guest appearance in her eyeball. It always scared her a bit when the floaters became more persistent than usual. The last thing she needed was problems in her good eye.

Karla took a shower and grabbed a cup of coffee, supremely glad that it was a Saturday and she wouldn't have to show up at work: a dead-end job as an accountant's assistant.

She was gazing out the window, playing the floater game, seeing if she could spot the biggest one darting around her eyeball like a mosquito on speed, when she noticed something else. Something unusual. A wavering light source from the left had appeared. She was so used to her monocularism that anything coming in from the far left hand side was shocking. She whipped her head around and immediately regretted it. Her brain screamed in pain.

Karla resumed looking out the window. Again, something seemed to be on the edge of her vision on the left. But that was impossible. She shouldn't be able to see from that angle, because she only had one good eye.

Then it moved. A figure of light, golden light. It shimmered gold, then ruby, then emerald, then sapphire. Jewel colours, fascinating, scintillating, beautiful. A supernatural kaleidoscope swirling and twirling, sucking her in, until it was all she could see.

Karla panicked. She shut her eyes and shook her head violently, ignoring the throbbing pain in her skull. What the hell was going on? Her left eye was gone, dead, nothing to see, no way to see, the optical nerve lifeless.

She cautiously opened her right eye. All was well… nothing sinister there. Now the left eye… slowly. Nothing. Karla realized that she had been holding her breath. She sighed with relief.

Then suddenly the scary, shocking entity, shimmering malevolently now, was back. Karla started to hyperventilate with fear. The thing raised its arm (tentacle, feeler, who knew?) and waved at her.

Karla bit her tongue to suppress her natural reaction to scream. She shut her left eye again and the thing vanished. She smacked her hand over her left eye and scanned the room with her right: nothing.

She decided to do the opposite, placing her hand over her right eye and cautiously opening her left. It was back. The thing had retreated a little, as if it sensed that Karla was distraught. Perhaps the little panicky moaning noises that she was making without realizing it warned the creature off.

Karla put both hands in front of her eyes, shutting off visual contact with the world, and began to weep with her one good eye. What had that mad scientist done to her? This new kind of ocular prosthesis… was it causing hallucinations? Did Dr Markham not just want to assault her sexually, but drive her crazy as well?

She kept her left eye shut as she got up and shuffled miserably to the table where she'd left her purse. She fished around until she found her eye patch. She was just about to put it on when she mistakenly opened her left eye.

It was still there. It was trying to communicate with her. She felt a sudden intimate connection with the little golden being. It wanted to help her. It wanted to help her seek revenge. Karla smiled in gratitude.

***

Dr Markham specialized in seeing patients who possessed the more odd and outré ophthalmological problems on the spectrum. Occasionally, he'd pick out a special case that excited him. He could sniff out the weak and vulnerable ones easily. Like a wolf snuffling at the edge of a flock of sheep, he could almost sense the susceptible patients who wouldn't kick up a fuss if he chose to explore his fantasies with them. He could count on them to keep quiet, because they weren't confident enough to complain, to even consider that he had actually attacked them during their procedure.

Dr Markham especially enjoyed his time with Karla Alexander, or "Patient K" as he liked to call her. She was so responsive, even under the meds. He wondered if he would see her again. If she had enjoyed their encounter as much as he had. He dreamed of his tongue delving into her empty eye socket and lasciviously exploring her ocular cavity. It turned him on more than so-called normal sex.

It was the end of the day the following Friday. All his patients had been seen, his receptionist had gone home and he was tidying up his office. Dr Markham heard the outside door open and wondered who it could be. He went to his private office door, opened it and was startled and (secretly thrilled) to see "Patient K" standing in the reception room. For a minute, he thought that it was because she couldn't stay away, that at last he'd found his dream patient who took as much pleasure in his fantasies as he did. His cock hardened at the thought of another sexual escapade with this gorgeously ruined woman.

However, Karla had different ideas. She smiled at Dr Markham, putting him at ease, and walked into his office. He turned to shut and lock the door. Before he could

turn around, Karla hit him in the back of the head with a medium-sized meat tenderizer that she had taken from her handbag.

Dr Markham slumped to the floor, out for the count. Karla put the crowbar back in her bag, slipped on a pair of rubber gloves and then put on one of Dr Markham's surgical gowns.

She dragged him over to his procedure chair and after a few tries managed to manhandle him into the chair. She

searched through his desk and cabinets and finally found the leather straps that he'd used to bind her and did the same to him.

By the time that Dr Markham had groggily come to, he was securely tied down on the chair, which had been moved into a position parallel to the floor. Karla had duct-taped his mouth shut to keep him quiet, not that anyone could have helped him, since the building was long empty.

All the time that Karla was getting Dr Markham ready, her little shimmering friend in her left eye was cheerfully directing her actions in a kind of weird sign language that only she could understand. She could see perfectly out of both eyes now, with the exception of her friend dancing away in the far left hand corner. Sometimes, if it was

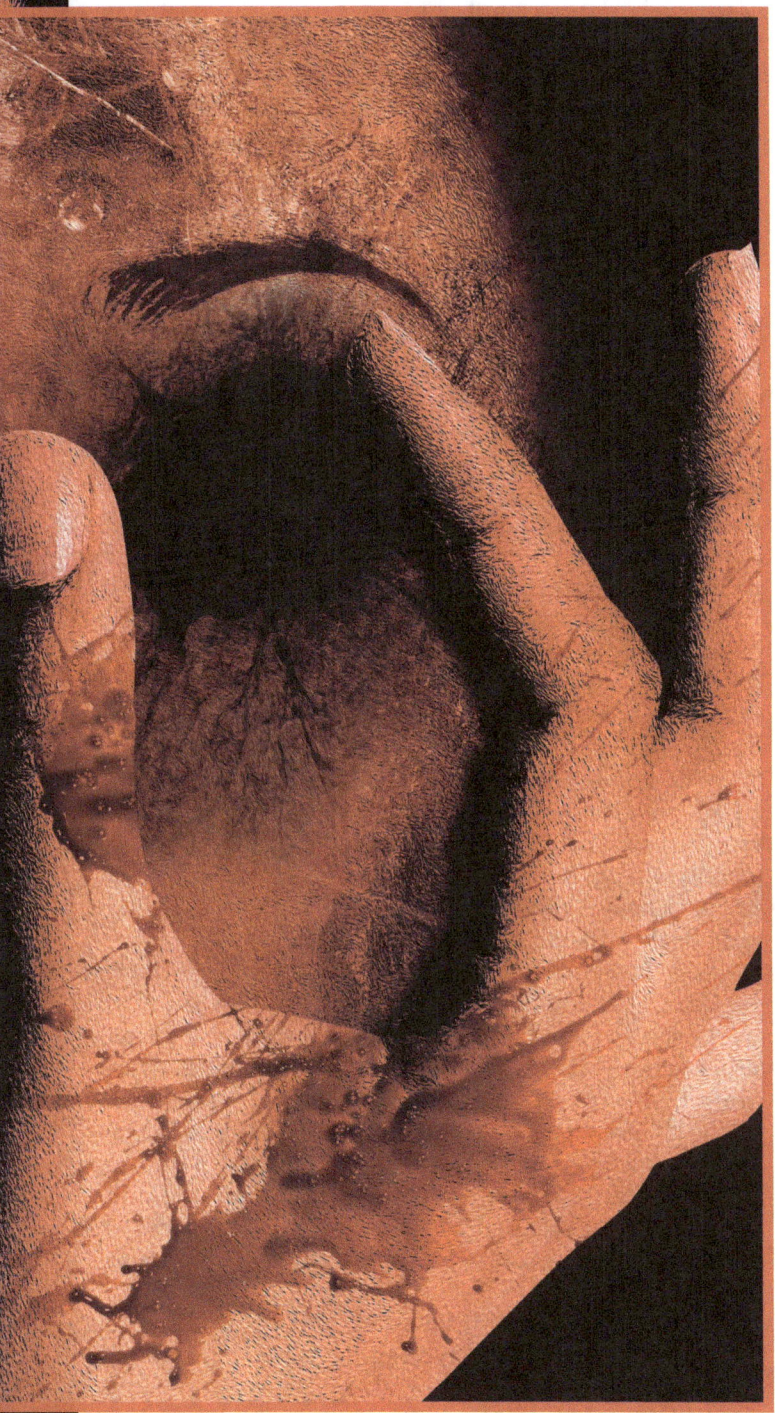

very quiet, she could even hear him speak in a tiny, tinny voice, saying strange obtuse things that took her a while to decipher.

Dr Markham was struggling now, but she'd tied him down well, so he was quite helpless, just like she had been.

She walked over to Dr Markham, keeping her distance, not wanting to get too close for fear of him getting free somehow. His eyes were bloodshot and angry. She knew he would be the type to loathe her now for making him the slave. Powerful guys always hated to lose their power.

"You have to remember that you brought this on yourself," Karla said. "I know what you did to me a week ago, but I don't know what kind of infernal prosthesis you put into my eye to make me see *him*. But it's his show now…"

Karla went over to the leather couch near Dr Markham's desk and sat down. She carefully dug out her iridescent glass eye, crying out in pain as she did so, but it was the only way to free her friend.

Finally, the socket gave up its prize with a slurp and a plop. She held the bloody eye in her hand. It moved gently in the small puddle of gore in her palm until the iris turned and gazed up into her good eye. Karla nodded and then stood up and walked over to a squirming Dr Markham.

She looked down at him like he was a bug on a plate, truly interested in what was going to happen next in an almost clinically detached way. She put the eye up to her ear, listening intently. Then Karla smiled—a big juicy smile that put the fear of God into Dr Markham, because it made her look totally deranged.

Karla showed him her eye, putting it close to his. Dr Markham was startled to see that there seemed to be movement inside the prosthesis. Something was capering and dancing in the pupil—a little golden figure, shaking its fist at him.

Being a happy psychopath Dr Markham was never troubled by guilt, like the other psychos that make up three percent of the population of the United States at any one time. However, he was suddenly troubled by a flashback to a meeting with Dennis Chong, his Chinese genius, a few weeks ago, the man that he had murdered to get his secret stock of exceptional glass eyes. These were the glittering beauties that had paid for his fancy office, car, apartment and willing prostitutes. Dr Markham didn't really need to kill Dennis, but he was squawking about getting paid on time and he had such an enormous stock of eyes that Dr Markham could go on for years without having any new ones made. So he brained Chong with a monkey wrench, carefully packed up his precious eyes and then burned his lab down. Just another arson job in a city plagued by them.

Before he could hypothesize further whether Chong was the ghostly inhabitant of Patient K's new eye, Karla was forcing that very eye into his. Dr Markham shrieked with pain behind the duct tape but the sounds were so muffled that no one heard, no one came.

With brutal enthusiasm, Karla continued to push and finally her eye mercilessly squished Dr Markham's eye into jelly. He blacked out. Karla stepped back to look at her handiwork and was pleased.

Her fake blue eye looked a bit out of place in Dr Markham's face and it would look even worse when he opened his other eye, which was brown, but she was way past aesthetics by now.

***

Dr Markham was out for over an hour. When he finally

did wake up, the pain in his left eye socket was excruciating, beyond anything that he had ever experienced before. He spotted Karla on the couch near his desk, reading one of his surgical manuals. She looked up, smiled and gave a little wave.

Then Dr Markham spotted something in the far left corner of his newly implanted fake eye. It was a little figure, shimmering and dancing, like the one he'd seen in the pupil of Karla's prosthesis. He must be hallucinating with the pain, that was it.

The little being didn't care that he thought it was a hallucination, a fever dream of the mind, no, this glittering creature was alive and mad as hell.

Some minds don't—indeed—won't die. They are so bright, so intelligent, that mere corporeal death does not defeat them. It's as if they refuse to admit that their time on earth is done. Perhaps that's where the idea of ghosts came from. At least that's how Dennis Chong thought of it.

Miraculously reconstituted as a golden entity, Dennis had come back to consciousness in the ocular prosthesis that he'd designed, before it had been inserted into Karla's eye socket. After the procedure, he soon realized what had happened. Although communication was a problem at first, he knew that he needed to get Karla to help him. It soon transpired that she had issues of her own with Dr Markham, so it wasn't very difficult.

Dennis manoeuvred his way to the back of the glass eye and began to pound on the surface, cracking it and squeezing his way through before attacking Dr Markham's retinal wall. With the renewed agony, Dr Markham fought against his bonds, but Karla appeared and injected him with the same concoction of Buscopan, Fentanyl and Midazolam until he calmed down and stopped struggling. However, he still remained conscious.

While Dennis crawled down Dr Markham's optic nerve, through the chiasma and then down the right hand optic nerve to Dr Markham's good eye, Karla walked over to the doctor's artistic collection of ocular prostheses of all ages, types and colours: acrylic, hydroxyapatite, porous polyethylene, bioceramic and some vintage glass eyes that must have dated back to late 16th century Venetian times. There was even one golden eye, perhaps from ancient Sumeria. So many pretty baubles to choose from.

She grabbed as many as she could and popped them in her pocket. She walked over to Dr Markham's medical cabinet. After rummaging around, she was surprised to find a bivalved vaginal speculum, which was normally used to dilate the vagina to enable a medical professional to take a woman's Pap smear. Karla decided that she didn't want to dwell on why Dr Markham would possess such a device. Then she found a McPherson Speculum, which was perfect for her purposes, as it was specially designed for oral examinations.

Karla returned to Dr Markham, who was squirming in his fancy chair. She could hear mysterious sounds coming from within his skull, like a tiny person walking around and banging on the walls.

She sat on Dr Markham's stool, sliced open the duct tape between his lips, and inserted the McPherson Speculum. First she poured some Surgilube lubricant down his throat, then she slowly, methodically, dropped the collection of glass eyes down the speculum, using it like a funnel to fill Dr Markham's belly with glass, acrylic, gold and plastic. He choked a few times, but in the end, he swallowed them all.

In the meantime, Dennis had made his way to the back of Dr Markham's right eye. He vigorously dug through the retinal wall and fought through the gush of vitreous humour gel as it poured into the eye socket of Dr Markham's skull. Then Dennis systematically destroyed his good eye, punching and pulling it from within and scaring Karla, who wasn't expecting Dr Markham's eye to be sucked into what looked like a vortex in his own eye socket. She breathed a sigh of relief when Dennis popped out of what was left of Dr Markham's eye, waving one hand and looking all the world like an old-fashioned steam train driver gesturing at some kids as he chugged past.

Dennis disappeared and made his way back to Karla's false eye. He tapped on the inside of the pupil so she knew that he was safely home. Karla found a surgical instrument that looked like an ice cream scoop (but was actually an evisceration spoon) and pried out her fake eye from Dr Markham's socket. She managed to fix the crack in the back with some surgical tape, so Dennis was secure, then she forced her fake eye back into its socket.

With both eyes now functioning, she turned and looked at Dr Markham. By this point, he was drooling with the pain, the drugs and the blind insanity of it all.

Karla rummaged around the office and found the packed box of Dennis's beautiful ocular creations in the closet. She pushed the box towards the chair and resumed dropping eyes down Dr Markham's throat. Eventually, the sheer volume in his stomach forced the eyes through his abdominal wall, and, like the numbered balls shooting down a Perspex tube in a lottery machine, the ocular prostheses rolled down his colonic passage until he was literally shitting eyes. Then the pressure grew too much and his stomach ruptured. Eyes spilled from the torn flesh and noisily clattered to the floor.

As a final mixed gesture of mercy and rage, Karla cracked Dr Markham's skull open with the crowbar.

As she was leaving his office, she turned and looked at her handiwork. It was truly a gloriously obscene work of art. Eyes were rolling across the floor like marbles in an insane children's game, blood oozed from Dr Markham's eyes, stomach and anus, and for all intents and purposes, the whole scene looked like a painting from the Middle Ages of some tortured saint that had given up the ghost for the love of the good Lord. But Dr Markham was no saint, that's for sure.

Karla, with Dennis riding shotgun in her left eye, departed Dr Markham's office and disappeared into the evening. They would never be alone again. They would always be friends. And now they had a purpose to their lives. To avenge themselves on their enemies, whoever they may be.

Weird Reflections

Weird Reflections

By Brett Talley

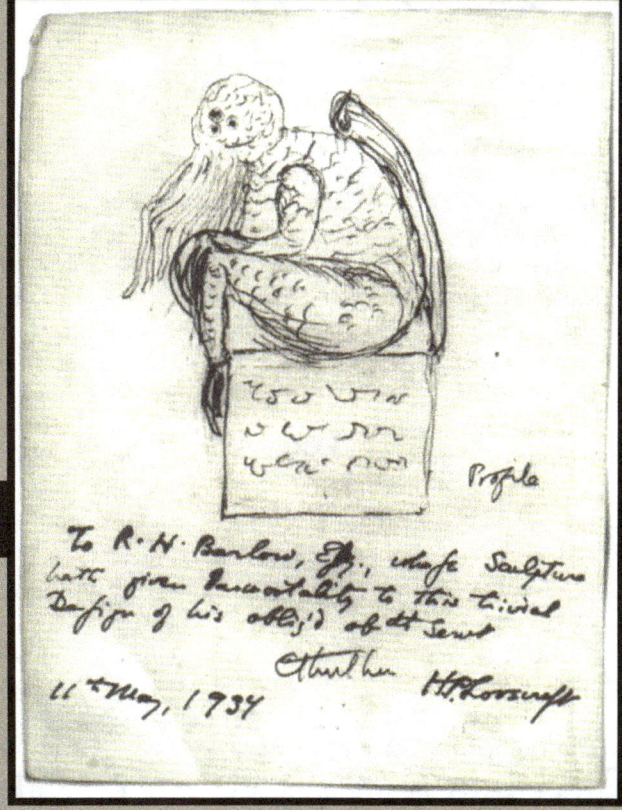

Ask a horror fan to name their favorite purveyor of the supernatural, and H.P. Lovecraft might show up high on their list. And that raises a curious question. Is Lovecraft a writer of supernatural fiction at all?

I can feel your questioning looks. After all, Lovecraft's writing is awash with gods and goddesses, with beings that can live forever, transcend time and space, and bend men's minds to their will. He wrote an essay called "Supernatural Horror in Literature" for Nyarlathotep's sake!

And I'll grant you that. But stick your spades in again and dig deeper. Walk with me down this path a little way, and let's see what we can find. What is the foundation of the cosmic mythology that August Derleth came to call the Cthulhu Mythos? Is it magic? It's certainly something unusual, out of the ordinary. But is it supernatural? Is it mystical? Is it miraculous?

For the most part, the answer to all those questions is no.

Lovecraft, in his seminal essay on supernatural horror, began with a statement that is as profound as it is obviously true: "The oldest and strongest emotion of mankind is fear, and the oldest and strongest kind of fear is fear of the unknown." But the unknown need not be the mystical or the magical. It could just be... the unknown. The empty, darkened alleyway, the black depths of the sea, the empty, long abandoned mansion—they frighten us, whether we believe in ghosts and ghouls and spirits or not, because we simply do not *know* what they might hold. Think of it this way—there's nothing more frightening to college freshmen than a test on a subject they haven't studied.

Take that thought and expand it. Stretch it out and see where it goes. Take it to its farthest limits. They called the stories Lovecraft wrote *cosmic* horror for a reason, and many of his tales represent the first horror science fiction. The great unknown of the wider universe can hold many

secrets. And just as a technology, sufficiently advanced, will appear magic to the uninitiated, the beings that walk in the vastness of space will appear gods to humanity.

Our perspective, after all, is limited to the earth we inhabit and the things within it. We can imagine something beyond that, but most philosophers would tell you that even our imagination cannot escape the natural world and the limits of our experience.

There's a reason most of the aliens on *Star Trek* all look basically the same. There's a reason that every monster is either an amplification or an amalgamation of something we already fear. A giant is just a really big guy. A dragon is a snake or dinosaur with wings that can breathe fire. Even in Cthulhu, we see the combination of a dragon like thing and a cephalopod. Our imaginations simply cannot comprehend of something that is truly *beyond*.

And that's what Lovecraft was reaching for. In his essay, "Notes on Writing Weird Fiction," he wrote this:

> I choose weird stories because they suit my inclination best—one of my strongest and most persistent wishes being to achieve, momentarily, the illusion of some strange suspension or violation of the galling limitations of time, space, and natural law which for ever imprison us and frustrate our curiosity about the infinite cosmic spaces beyond the radius of our sight and analysis. These stories frequently emphasise the element of horror because fear is our deepest and strongest emotion, and the one which best lends itself to the creation of nature-defying illusions. Horror and the unknown or the strange are always closely connected, so that it is hard to create a convincing picture of

shattered natural law or cosmic alienage or "outsideness" without laying stress on the emotion of fear.

Interestingly, from this perspective Lovecraft seems far more intrigued with stretching the bounds of human understanding than he does on writing a good horror yarn. That already puts him in a different stance than your run-of-the-mill writer. Most of us start off wanting to scare, and if we manage to make some deeper statement than that along the way, all the better. Not Lovecraft. His unflinching focus on what causes fear and not the fear itself is one of the reasons few can match his vision.

One wonders if it is also one of the reasons that Lovecraft's writing is decidedly non-supernatural. Lovecraft doesn't need ghosts and ghouls to scare you. He knows that the unknown is good enough. And his interest in the cosmic keeps his feet firmly grounded on earth. So his "gods" aren't really gods at all. Or, I should say, they are only gods to us because we cannot comprehend them. They transcend space and time in a way we cannot comprehend, but their actions need not be seen as magical. They can live so long that death seems impossible, but that doesn't mean they are immortal. They are responsible for the mighty cities of antiquity, but they built them with methods we simply cannot understand.

There's an aside here that's worth exploring, one you may have already caught on to. Does that sound a little bit like the Ancient Alien Theory? In fact, does it sound quite a lot like the Ancient Alien Theory? Before there was Zecharia Sitchin or Erich von Däniken or Giorgio Tsoukalos, there was H.P. Lovecraft. He even had his own Planet X, his own Niburu—Yuggoth. In fact, one noted critic of the Ancient Alien Theory, Jason Colavito, argues convincingly that today's obsession with ancient aliens can be traced directly to H.P. Lovecraft himself. Check out his book, *The Cult of Alien Gods: H.P. Lovecraft And Extraterrestrial Pop Culture*, for the details.

It's perhaps not surprising then that the Ancient Alien Theory itself also denies the supernatural. Stories of gods, angels, and heavenly visitors are explained as simple misunderstandings. The primitive peoples that encountered these beings could not understand them, so they made up stories about gods and goddesses and developed elaborate cults and rituals to worship them and keep the stories alive. Remind you of the Cthulhu Mythos? It should.

It's an open question whether Lovecraft intentionally avoided the supernatural or if it simply sprang from his tendency to embrace scientific theory over religious belief. And it is not the case that supernaturalism is absent entirely from Lovecraft's canon. There are stories where it makes an appearance, sometimes a dominant one—"In The Vault" and "The Hound," for instance. But they are the exception, not the rule.

Take one of these stories that would appear, on the surface at least, to be one of his most supernatural—"The Dreams in the Witch House." The story centers, after all, on a witch—who fears crucifixes no less—and has a human-faced, rat familiar. But the story is actually quite striking for how grounded it is in exotic scientific theory from the very first. Our hero, Gilman, is a mathematician,

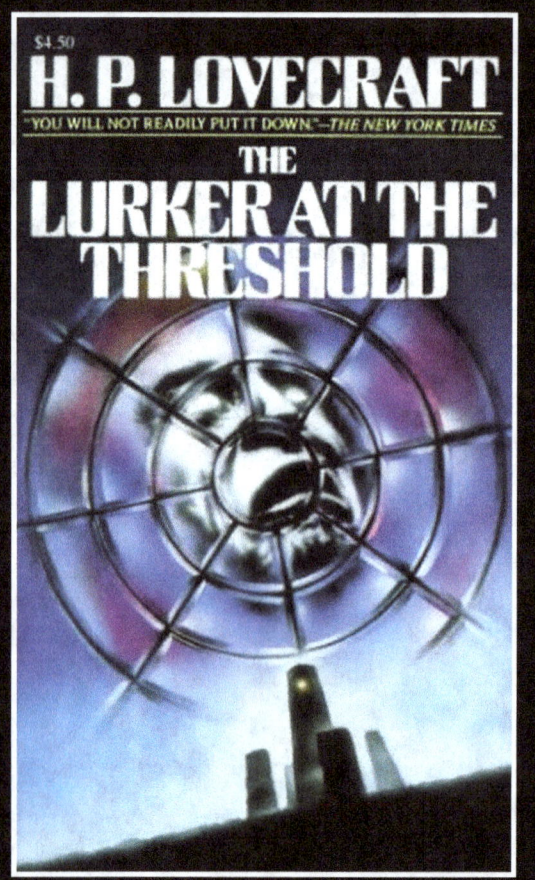

and he has determined that Keziah Mason—noted witch who fled Salem ahead of the hangman's noose—may have possessed knowledge far more important than common spells. Lovecraft writes:

> Non-Euclidean calculus and quantum physics are enough to stretch any brain; and when one mixes them with folklore, and tries to trace a strange background of multi-dimensional reality behind the ghoulish hints of the Gothic tales and the wild whispers of the chimney-corner, one can hardly expect to be wholly free from mental tension… There was much in the Essex County records about Keziah Mason's trial, and what she had admitted under pressure to the Court of Oyer and Terminer had fascinated Gilman beyond all reason. She had told Judge Hathorne of lines and curves that could be made to point out directions leading through the walls of space to other spaces beyond, and had implied that such lines and curves were frequently used at certain midnight meetings in the dark valley of the white stone beyond Meadow Hill and on the unpeopled island in the river. She had spoken also of the Black Man, of her oath, and of her new secret name of Nahab. Then she had drawn those devices on the walls of her cell and vanished.

Now that's some heady stuff. Essentially, Lovecraft is describing Keziah as a member not of a witch-cult, but some black magic mathematician's club that possessed knowledge far beyond our own, knowledge she could use to warp space and time. Her ability to appear and disappear at will was the result of mathematical formulae, not spell books and black cats. Later in the story, Lovecraft discusses the consequences of such a discovery.

> It was also possible that the inhabitants of a given dimensional realm could survive entry to many unknown and incomprehensible realms of additional or indefinitely multiplied dimensions—be they within or outside the given space-time continuum—and that the converse would be likewise true. This was a matter for speculation, though one could be fairly certain that the type of mutation involved in a passage from any given dimensional plane to the next higher plane would not be destructive of biological integrity as we understand it. Gilman could not be very clear about his reasons for this last assumption, but his haziness here was more than overbalanced by his clearness on other complex points. Professor Upham especially liked his demonstration of the

kinship of higher mathematics to certain phases of magical lore transmitted down the ages from an ineffable antiquity—human or pre-human—whose knowledge of the cosmos and its laws was greater than ours.

In that paragraph lies the entire theory behind the Cthulhu Mythos, and it is utterly devoid of supernaturalism. In fact, it explains away "magical lore" as complex mathematics. This is stunning stuff, particularly for the early 1930s when it was written. One could say with confidence that Lovecraft is one of the first writers to take the scientific theories of the day and so convincingly turn them to fiction. And that is a testament to his genius.

In this way, Lovecraft spans a gulf. His stories are fantastic, but many of them can be so thoroughly grounded in plausible scientific theory that it is difficult to call them supernatural. Which is not to say there's nothing of the supernatural in Lovecraft. Of course there is. But that supernaturalism is not at the *heart* of Lovecraft, and that is the key.

Lovecraft proves that the core of the horrific lies not in supernaturalism itself, but in what supernaturalism represents—a break from the reality we expect, and a sightless plunge into the abyss of the unknown.

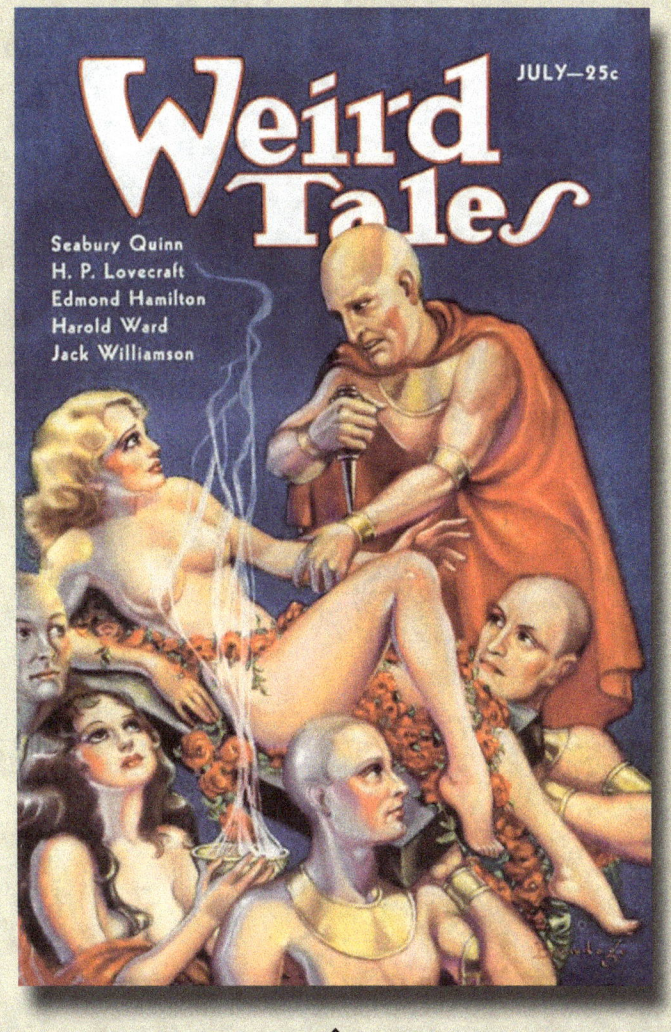

Laird Barron's fourth collection of macabre stories
continues his inquiry into the darkness of the human heart.
Herein, a teen party presages an extinction event;
professional final girl Jessica Mace investigates
a cursed carnival; the wild hunt pursues
a broken-down outdoorsman and his loyal hound.

SWIFT
to
CHASE

LAIRD
BARRON

In Dublin's Fair City

A NECROSCOPE® STORY

BRIAN LUMLEY

Harry Keogh, the Necroscope, had taken the Möbius route to Dublin, Ireland. Still searching for Brenda, the once-beloved wife who had fled him when he suffered his change (for once upon a time Harry had been Alec Kyle; which is to say his current body and mind had belonged to Alec Kyle, where now the mind and soul were Harry's while the body was not… or not quite). Also which, when Kyle's body had first accommodated Harry, the result had seemed such a weird adaptation that Brenda had not been able to accept it as her husband.

Now, however, and however astonishingly, the Necroscope was gradually reforming—or shall we say conforming, transforming, morphing?—into a semblance, avatar or amalgam which Brenda might find more agreeable. For indeed Harry himself had accepted that, however strange the change, he now looked more like *him*, the man he had once been, despite that his initial or original embodiment had "died" in a firefight in a Russian fortress some years ago. So perhaps if Brenda saw him now things might be different between them; perhaps she would more readily accept him as the "real" Harry Keogh.

All of which to explain, however insufficiently, why the Necroscope, the man who could converse with the Great Majority—the grateful dead, who were his friends and would care for him in any way possible—was now in Dublin; for he remembered several occasions when Brenda had mentioned that as a very small child she had been with her parents visiting an elderly relative in Ireland, the single visit she had ever made to Dublin however fondly she recalled it. So even as history is said to repeat, it seemed possible that Dublin was where she had gone, taking their infant boy child with her.

She had mentioned a place on the outskirts of the city, a place of parks, sheltering trees, wooden benches, and winding old streets; part of the ancient Dublin to which Harry had now taken himself. But although he arranged lodgings of only four days at the small hostelry in the antique suburbs, by the third evening Brenda remained unknown and even unheard of by any of the numerous exanimate persons in the well-tended local graveyard. For of course Harry had checked on her whereabouts first with the Great Majority, who would have been aware of the fact if Brenda had come among them.

But that third summer night as the Necroscope lay in his bed in an oak-beamed garret room with a single small window that opened outward on the soft air over a narrow cobbled street, he did hear something. Nothing to do with Brenda, but a female voice and sweet all the same. It reminded him of a refrain he had known from his childhood in a boys' school in the colliery village where he'd been raised from a child to a youth, mainly alone in the land of the living but with a great many friends among those who were no longer living. Part of a sad little song, he'd always thought it, yet a song so strong in its pathos and so easy on the ear and in the mind that it wasn't at all hard to remember. This one small part was simply the cry of a street vendor in the night, which seemed strange in itself until Harry realized that the voice was reaching him on the deadspeak ether, his unique telepathic link with the dead. At which he began to rouse himself a little more fully

from the edge of sleep.

A-live a-live O! A-live a-live O!—sang the voice. And: *cockles and mussels, alive a-live O!*

In his drowsiness and scarcely aware that he did it, Harry began to answer that faint sad cry in the night:

"In Dublin's fair city, where the girls are so pretty
I first set my eyes on sweet Molly Malone,
As she wheeled her wheelbarrow through streets broad and narrow,
Crying cockles and mussels alive a-live O!"

The sweet voice in the night had fallen silent at once, indeed at the very first deadspeak note from the Necroscope's mouth and metaphysical mind. But now she spoke:

Oh? And who be that, then? Just another fool mockin' me? Well if so Oi should warn ye: them that mocks Molly gets cursed by Molly, an' for all that ye're dead it's a very hurtfull curse Oi'll call down on ye! So then, on ye're way now and leave Oi in peace…

More fully awake now, Harry had to smile at her spirit, her threatened malediction, and yet more surely her charming Irish brogue, but he did his best to keep such amusement to himself. "Molly?" he said. "Is it really you, Molly Malone?"

Well o'course it's Oi! she snapped back. *Who else would it be, walkin' the streets an' callin' out me wares, like Oi always did when Oi had a body, an' veins in me body, an' blood in me veins… aye, an' shellfishy wares Oi could sell to the livin', be they good wares or no-so-good wares or not-nearly-so-good wares. So then, that's me an' it's the truth. But Oi'll ask ye again: who be ye? It's strange but ye feel… warm? Now that's somethin' Oi never did feel before, not here in the darkness, anyway! In fact, Oi never felt a thing!*

"No," said Harry, "I don't for a moment suppose you did. But since it's the utter darkness of death of which you're speaking: the darkness of total immobility, inanimation—in short, the cold and darkness of the tomb—that's hardly surprising." His words seemed cold even to Harry himself, but their delivery was soulful and heartfelt.

Oh, it's all o' what ye've said right enough, she replied, her voice hushed to a deadspeak gasp now. *All that an' more! For now Oi also sees a light—a flickerin' like a wee candle's flame! Or Oi think Oi sees it, or Oi fancy Oi sees it. Is it ye, stranger? Is that all ye are? A wee, warm glow an' a kindly voice in the long, long night?*

"No, I'm more than that," said Harry, with a shake of his head that he knew she would sense. "You may have heard of me from others in your darkness; or maybe not, because I've never been this way before. But I'm Harry Keogh, known by the dead as the Necroscope—those of the dead who actually know me, anyway. But word sometimes travels slowly, which is just as well for I can't be everywhere at once!"

Again he heard her deadspeak gasping, a sound strange as strange could be coming from Molly's close-packed crumbling grave in a beggars' cemetery on the far side of the city, for in that grave there was no air to breathe and no lungs to breathe it anyway, just the calcifying bones of the long dead Molly and a few cockle and mussel shells that folks had thrown in with her at the burial. But then:

Harry Keogh, the Necroscope, she said. *Aye, an' Oi have indeed heard o' ye once or twice, but don't ask Oi when for it's hard to tell the time in this place, neither the day, year nor even the decade! But ye're more recent than historic, that much Oi may tell ye; though surely ye know it already.*

"A bit of old Irish, that!" said Harry, smiling. But his smile quickly turned to a frown. And: "Molly," he went on, "you mentioned your wares, the cockles and mussels that you sold from your barrow…"

Aye, an' the occasional crab an' lobster, too, she replied, but warily Harry thought. *What of it?*

"But you said that you sold them 'be they good wares or no-so-good wares or not-nearly-so-good wares.' Now what did you mean by that?"

For a moment Molly was silent, then in a softer, quieter tone said: *Ye may have heard somethin' o' Oi's faether, too. He were also a fishmonger an' sold his wares from a barrow.*

"Indeed, I have heard of him," the Necroscope replied. "And also your Ma. They are in your song too, however briefly."

And he continued:

> "She was a fishmonger, and sure it's no wonder,
> For so were her mother and father before…"

But Molly stopped him right there, with:

First things first, Harry: that's not *Oi's song! It may be about Oi, but Oi don't recognize it. Oi don't accept the truth o' it. Whoever made it up—put it into words—may have thought he were doin' Oi a favour; but the whole truth, good, bad or indifferent would have suited Oi far better. That damned song—excuse Oi's French—leaves far too much to the imagination.*

The Necroscope was taken aback, baffled. "In what way? It all sounds clear enough to me."

No, it gives the wrong impression—or rather, it lacks some very important details, fails to enlarge on certain matters—tends to leave a listener in doubt as to… as to—well, let's just say it leaves a person undecided.

"You think the song fails to represent your true image? Perhaps you'd appreciate it more if it didn't dwell so heavily on your… your sweetness? I mean, how could you be so sweet after all the hard work you must have put into trundling your wares through those streets broad and narrow? Work like that must have been very tough on you. And then there's your death from the fever; I suspect that must mean the plague, or an epidemic of some sort. And I would hazard a guess that it must have taken you at a very young age, and—"

And say no more! she cried. But then, just a moment later, with what was apparently a complete change of heart: *Oh, very well. Why should Oi care after all this time, eh? Go on then, Harry. Sing the next verse an' Oi'll try to explain my problems with it, so Oi will.*

And the Necroscope responded with:

> "She died of a fever and no one could save her,
> And that was the end of sweet Molly Malone,
> Now her ghost wheels her barrow through streets broad

> and narrow
> Crying cockles and mussels alive a-live O!"

An' there ye have it, said Molly, sighing a deadspeak sigh. *Right there in that one verse, tree—er, that'll be three to ye—tree reasons, examples, o' why Oi's not at all happy with it. An' ye're right, that word 'sweet' is one o' them.*

Still baffled, or even more so, Harry said, "You're against the word sweet? But surely that means of a lovely appearance, or a pleasant nature, or both."

Aye, in yere world for sure, she replied. *But in mine it could have another meanin' entirely. As in a juicy piece o' fruit, for example.*

Harry frowned as he pondered the meaning of that last, but she had quickly continued:

As for this 'fever' thing. There was no plague when Oi were taken, neither plague nor epi—er, epi—

"Epidemic?" the Necroscope helped her out. "Which means a terrible contagion that rages across entire regions?"

Nothin' o' the sort. She nodded an uncompromising deadspeak nod. *Not when Oi took ill, anyway. What's more, Oi never even heard o' that word before, even though Oi caught somethin' o' its meanin' from the way ye said it. So then, Epidemic, no… Ah, but there are fevers an' there are fevers, Harry!*

At which the Necroscope believed he was beginning to understand.

An' then there's that other thing, Molly continued. *Oi mean that streets broad an' narrow thing. Well, it's true enough, there were broad streets in Dublin in Oi's day, an' narrow ones, too.*

"Still are," said the Necroscope.

Aye, but now think o' broad as in broad-minded! Molly urged. *An' narrow as in narrow-minded! Did ye not know that in Oi's day many a so-called 'street vendor' was nothin' more than a common tart, a 'sweet'-bodied whore? Sweet, aye—but often as not more than a wee bit sour, too. Never an epidemic, still it killed many a lusty young man—not to mention more than a few o' them street vendors, too. It was their so-called 'wares' that killed 'em—even as much the same thing were what killed Oi!*

"Ah!" Harry gasped, as understanding—as he saw it—suddenly dawned. "That fever you died of was… it was…" But he couldn't say or even think it, not even to himself, let alone to Molly, and so he kept the awful thought—venereal disease—to himself. No matter, for in any case she knew what had given him pause. And:

There now, said Molly with a satisfied nod, her argument justified. *So now ye see why Oi can't trust that song. Why Oi hates it an' them among the dead what tries to sing it to Oi from time to time… because it far too often gives the wrong impression and leaves Oi's reputation in doubt when people misin—er, misint—*

"When they misinterpret it?" said Harry.

Aye, that too… Oi think, Molly agreed, with typically Irish ambiguity. *They misinterpret it—just like you did only a minute ago! Even you, Harry Keogh, mistakin' virtue for vice an' innocence for immorality!*

"But you just said that you too died of—"

No! He sensed the vehement shake of her head. *Oi said it were Oi's* wares *that killed Oi. But where those whores were vendors o' their not-so-sweet bodies, Oi's were the cockles an' mussels in Oi's wheelbarrow!*

Again the Necroscope gasped, as this time he recognized the truth for certain. "You were selling poisoned shellfish!?"

Oh, it's true, so it is! Molly was beginning to sob now, however quietly. *But Oi swear Oi didn't know the harm in it until Oi, too, fell sick o' that killin' mussel fever!*

Harry nodded, frowned and queried: "Your mussels weren't fit for eating, yet you didn't know it? I'm not doubting you, Molly, but that in itself raises a question. I mean, surely you must have had some previous experience of the quality of your wares?"

Oh, Oi did, she replied, as she barely managed to control her sobbing. *But ye see, it was Oi's faether, me Da, what led me astray. An' maybe me poor old Ma too.*

And the Necroscope remembered:

> She was a fishmonger, and sure 'twas no wonder,
> For so were her father and mother before,
> Who both wheeled their barrows through streets broad and narrow,
> Crying cockles and mussels alive a-live O!

"Your parents led you astray?" he said then. "Are you saying that your father sent you out to sell shellfish knowing full well they were unfit for consumption and might poison whoever ate them?"

Let me explain how it were, she said then. And having taken a moment or two to regain a little more control over her emotions:

Those were desperate times, Harry. It was a very cold winter; there was little or no work for the men folk, an' next to nothin' by way o' wages for those few lucky ones who managed to hold on to their jobs. Money? Hah! Precious little o' that in this entire, Godforsaken land! No, none at all, at all. No money to buy warm clothin' for small cold bodies—or decent food for hungry families! So people were starvin'. But enough—that should set the scene for ye.

Oi's parents were good folks, Oi shall always believe that. An' Oi blame me faether's big mistake on the simple fact that he was a good, kindhearted man. He couldn't bear the sight o' skinny little children shiverin' as they begged for scraps o' food. An' so he piled yesterday's shellfish on Oi's barrow and sent Oi out into those streets broad an' narrow. An' he told Oi: 'Sell them if ye can, an' if ye can't then give 'em away. An' meanwhile we'll pray there's no real harm comes o' all this, neither to us nor to them poor 'uns out there in the cold.'

Now, just lookin' at all those shiny black mussels Oi knew there were a big problem here. Because for every half-a-dozen or so o' them bivalves that were clamped tight shut, there was at least one whose shells were open a crack—like it were gaspin' for breath, which o' course it weren't—but which meant that the wee creature inside the shell were either sick or dyin' or already dead o' some sea sickness o' its own! An' as ye've said, Harry, the sick ones weren't fit for eatin', not at all, at all. But because o' the money situ... er, situ—

"Situation," said Harry.

That too, answered the Irish in Molly, as she continued: *Because no one had any money, Oi's Da must have decided that takin' a chance on the mussels were better than lettin' folks waste away an' die o' starvation. An' he probably figured that if there were deaths among Oi's customers, we could always put the blame on hunger or the freezin' weather—though God knows he would have suffered the guilt o' it on his conscience, no less than it were on Ois, forever. Aye, an' Oi still suffers from it, so Oi do!*

"But you did eat of your own wares," said Harry, he hoped in mitigation. "You did run the same grim risk—the same hazard—that you offered your poor customers with every sick mussel. And you did it—what, deliberately? In order to ease your own guilt and maybe something of your folks' too, especially your Da's? But did he—or they—well, get away with it? I mean, were they ever found out, and if so were they shown to be innocent or guilty? Or was the truth never discovered at all? Because in that song we hear very little of them."

There were deaths, o' course there were, she replied. *But it were when Oiself started to suffer that they left Oi with friends*

an' moved on—to London, Oi believe—an' good luck to them. But as far as Oi knows, the truth o' it never did come out, an' by now for sure they're dead an' gone—oh, a hundred years ago an' more, to be sure—Oi's poor old Ma an' Da! Oi did have hopes they might try to contact me some time, but that hasn't happened.

Harry nodded. "It's only recently," he explained, "that the Great Majority have been able to contact one another—which is pretty much down to me, I believe. Because in your time, Molly, there was no Necroscope, and the dead lay quiet in their graves. So I think they must have moved on, your folks, and not just to London."

Moved on? Molly was at once curious. *Oi think Oi may have heard whispers o' such a thing: how sometimes us dead 'uns move on. But... where to?*

"To a better place," Harry replied. "Out of the darkness into the light—from a desert to an oasis—a kind of heaven, if you like, full of the finest dreams you'll ever have, and you'll have them forever. I think that's where you'll find your Ma and Da, Molly. And if so all that you've told me will be proven to be true. Not that I doubted you for a moment."

How, proven to be true?

"Because the dead are only allowed into that better place according to merit, which means the transition takes some of them a long, long time. Only the good and the innocent go there quickly, while the bad linger on in the dark. And the truly evil ones never get there at all."

Ahhh! she sighed… But then said: *Then tell Oi, Harry, how is it Oi's still here? Were Oi as evil as all that?*

He shrugged, but not negligently, and said, "Perhaps you weren't trying hard enough."

Hard enough? But Oi weren't tryin' at all, at all! Oi didn't even know as how Oi had to try!

"Well, now you do," said the Necroscope. "Just dream a good dream, that's all, and try to will yourself into it. Now that you know the better place is there, it should be easier."

But why haven't others o' the Great Majority told Oi the secret o' it? Molly cried. *Why, Oi might have been gone from here long and long ago!*

"But you see," said Harry, "people don't really understand it or accept it until it happens to them. They might sense that it's there, but if they don't strive for it they must simply wait their turn. And they can't be told of it, can't learn of it from those who have gone before, for they are already out of range and there's no contact with them."

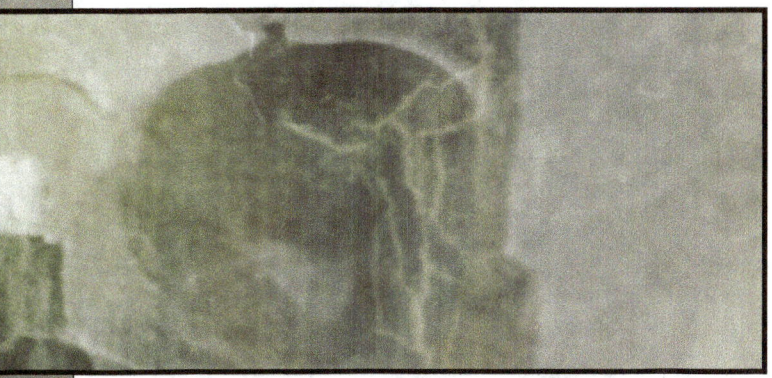

For a moment or two Molly was silent, thoughtful, then said: *No contact with them. Only with ye, eh, Harry?*

"So it would seem," he answered, with another almost apologetic shrug.

But it's really there, this better place, eh?

"Oh, yes."

Then Oi shall strive for it!

"Good!" said Harry.

But for now, she gave a determined nod of her head, *Oi'll finish what Oi started, an' go on trundlin' the old barrow through the dark night streets. If ye'll excuse Oi?*

"Of course," he replied. "For that's the way it is: you'll continue to do in death what you did in life—at least for a little while longer. Goodbye, and good luck, Molly!"

And off she went:

A-live a-live O! A-live a-live O! Cockles an' mussels, alive a-live O!

***

AT THE END OF his fourth evening in Dublin's fair city, when the shadow of night crept like a great soft mantle over streets broad and narrow, Harry Keogh, Necroscope, lay in his bed and thought of tomorrow morning when he would be moving on.

Of course, with the Möbius route at his disposal he could have moved on at any time he desired. "Even

now—*right* now!" he told himself. "At this very minute—if I chose."

As to why he hadn't so chosen: "I *have* enjoyed the break," he muttered to himself. "I've enjoyed Dublin, the accommodation, the food—" And then, with a small shudder—"but no cockles, mussels, or any kind of shellfish! And late last night… I especially enjoyed talking to Molly Malone. But tomorrow morning I'll settle my bill and moments later I'll be back in Edinburgh. And as for Molly—"

At which the real reason he was holding back became obvious… even to Harry himself, who no longer tried to deny it.

It was Molly, of course. She was the reason, and he wondered how she was getting on—wondered if her "striving" had paid off and moved her closer to a transition. And now that it was probably too late, he also wondered how she had looked, sweet Molly Malone, in those long-gone days when she had worked in the city's streets broad and narrow. He could have asked to see her as she remembered herself but hadn't done so in fear of being disappointed. He preferred to "remember" her as he'd always imagined her: a lovely young woman whose sweet slim figure had always seemed oddly incongruous in her fishmonger's, street vendor attire.

But yes, it was definitely too late, for while as always the deadspeak ether was full of the faint and various whispers of the Great Majority, the cries that the Necroscope was straining to hear weren't there—

—Or were they?

For fainter than all the other thoughts, complaints, exclamations of horror and intimations of mortality (these last from the more recently dead, who weren't yet sure of the awful truth), at long last he was rewarded by the distant, scarcely audible murmur of a deadspeak voice he at last recognized as Molly's. But now, instead of her usually clear but somehow mournful echoing cry—*A-live a-live O! A-live a-live O!*—there was joy, great joy however faint and rapidly fading, reaching his metaphysical mind, but barely, as from a million miles away.

It was there for a moment only, and then gone. And the Necroscope smiled to himself, lay his head on his pillow, and at last slept.

And once again as so often before, he knew who and why he was.

But there was one thing more Harry could do, though he made sure no one but himself would ever hear the last verse that he added to Molly's song:

> She died of a fever and no one could save her,
> But that isn't the end of sweet Molly Malone!
> For she's gone far away where the gentle folk play
> Living out better days in that sweetest of homes.
> A-live a-live O! She's a-live, a-live O!
> And there'll ne'er be an end to sweet Molly Malone…

AUTHOR'S NOTE:
Despite exhaustive research, the complete *original* lyrics to Molly Malone have not been found to be copyrighted!

—Brian Lumley

The Limbus saga continues
with five more stories of horror, science fiction, and fantasy
from some of the industry's brightest stars.

JONATHAN MABERRY,
SEANAN McGUIRE, LAIRD BARRON,
DAVID LISS, and KEITH R.A. DeCANDIDO

LIMBUS
INC.

— BOOK III —

EDITED BY BRETT J. TALLEY

How lucky do you feel?

The Horror Writers Association was formed in 1985, and in 1988 the organization began issuing their Bram Stoker Awards. The second book to be awarded the Bram Stoker Award for First Novel, in 1989, was Kelley Wilde's *The Suiting*, published in hardcover by Tor Books. The novel was also well received critically, as evidenced by reviews from *Library Journal*—"A horror first novel with both laughs and chills, this highly readable tale stars Victor Frankl, timid clerk turned body builder, womanizer, and, ultimately, murderer"—and *Publishers Weekly*—"It's an

old adage that 'clothes make the man,' and it would seem to be a stale premise for a story, but first-time novelist Wilde handles the idea with wit and energy."

Wilde went on to publish a second horror novel with Tor, and two more via Dell Abyss, but when the horror market went bust in the 1990s, Wilde was one of many authors caught in the wash, and he wound up not publishing again for almost 20 years. In the following interview, Wilde (a pen name) talks about his early career, where he disappeared to for all those years, and his recent reemergence under the new pen name Reb MacRath.

***

ROBERT MORRISH: Why did you adopt the pen name Kelley Wilde for your early novels?

KELLEY WILDE: Two reasons. Oscar Wilde was one of my literary heroes and I wanted a surname suggesting a witty and literate edge to my work. The first name, initially spelled Kelly, had a bold and just slightly romantic ring to me. But I changed the spelling because I'd grown convinced that women had an easier time getting published than men. My first agent sent me a wonderful letter telling me she heard cash registers ringing when she saw that name. I kept her in the dark about my gender until we had a sale. (One of my reasons for picking an agent out of state.)

RM: Speaking of agents… you changed agents after your first book—why?

KW: Things were never quite the same after my Pennsylvania agent saw a six-foot man get off the bus, not the shy little

Photo courtesy of Kelley Wilde

WHAT THE HELL EVER HAPPENED TO… KELLEY WILDE

BY ROBERT MORRISH

girl she'd imagined. It grew harder to get in touch with her. And that problem was echoed by my editor, who subtly suggested that I find a New York agent. I made the change while working on my second novel… a perilous time for a writer. I made a clean break, though, and changed to Don Maass. But then I got word of a hot new agent who could sell my third and fourth novels on spec. I needed the money… and I paid a steep price for moving on from Don, who never forgave me.

RM: How was your experience with Tor as the publisher for your first two books?

KW: I loved working with Tor and was broken-hearted when they passed on my option clause. I've always suspected that Elpee—a fictional name for that "hot new agent"—said something to cause Tor to break: telling Tor, for instance, that I wanted a crazy advance. No such thing. I'd have taken what was offered. But the break freed Elpee to make an easy sale to her new cash cow, Dell Abyss.

RM: How did you come up with the idea for your first book, *The Suiting*—a suit whose former owner would come to possess the garment's new owner?

KW: I'd lived in Canada for ten years. And in Toronto I couldn't stop passing the gorgeous display windows of Lou Myles Designatore. Back home, I continued to dream of owning a beautiful custom-made suit. It wasn't that big a stretch to imagine a poor nebbish finding a suit in a locker and deciding to keep it. The odds were against the suit being in his size, of course. So the tale began to race when I thought about him bulking up till he looks like the suit's last, dead owner.

RM: Your second novel, *Makoto*, features a Japanese female

protagonist—obviously a challenging endeavor. Did you relish that challenge? And how did the idea for this book develop?

KW: Tor bought this book on spec, on the strength of the first fifty pages. Melissa Singer loved it, partly because she was studying Kendo… and, I think, also because of the female protagonist. Despite the challenges, I had a few strong assets: I was a stranger myself in New York…

I'd studied Japanese and had visited the country twice… plus, I'd studied various martial arts, including Kendo. For a horror novel, the trick had to be a new spin on the beast in the basement. Mo's brought her own demon with her, she learns.

RM: How was it publishing your third and fourth books with Dell, whose Abyss line was viewed as a Very Big Deal when initially launched?

KW: I need to be careful here. It's bad karma to knock publishers. But, on a purely personal note, I'd gone from publishing hardbacks with Tor—a very homey atmosphere—to Dell Abyss—prestigious, yes, but more like an assembly line. They churned their novels out! And Elpee had signed me up for two. But the Dell books proved to be much longer than expected. So meeting the deadlines while work-

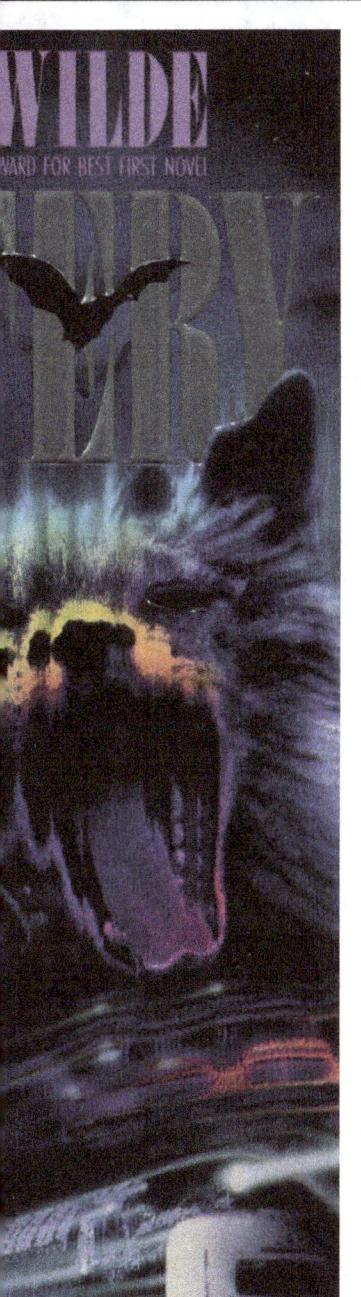

ing full-time nearly did me in. And I ended up not being entirely happy with the two Abyss books.

RM: Your third novel, *Mastery*, featured one of horror's archetypes, the vampire. Did your agent or publisher have any influence on that choice, or was that strictly your choice?

KW: The vampire was my idea—or rather the hyena-vampire. I'd grown bored with traditional vampires and had grown obsessed with doing something different. I doubt that Abyss would have gone for a vampire novel, anyway. But a hyena-vampire on a train speeding back in time to San Francisco in the year of the great quake? On that they were willing to gamble.

RM: When you re-published *Mastery* as an ebook in 2012, you changed the title to *MonsterTime*, and revised the book, cutting its length by 11,000 words. Would you have preferred that title, and that length, in the first place, or did you only decide on those changes when you revisited the book all those years later?

KW: *MonsterTime* had been my original title. But Dell felt that it was too "un-Abyssy." As for the length… The published book was longer than it should have been because I lacked the time to write a shorter version. *Mastery* always remained, in my mind, the one that got away. It would take me years of writing much shorter books to learn how to do it properly. 11,000 words shorter.

RM: A reviewer on goodreads.com said: "MacRath would later reexamine some of the themes and elements presented in [*Mastery*] in his more recent novels: trains, time travel, Alcatraz, and martial arts, all appear and are important to the plot, along with the man on the run, and man out of time/without a country motif." Do you feel that's an accurate/fair assessment?

KW: I do agree. The man without a country motif, in particular, resurfaces over and over again. How could it not? In Canada, I renounced my citizenship and went on to live as a stateless person for ten years. Then, after returning to the States, lived as an 'alien' until I regained my citizenship. By that time, I'd been stateless for nearly half my life.

RM: Your fourth novel, *Angel Kiss*, revisits a theme that was touched upon in *Makoto*, namely that of dating services and mail order brides. Why did that theme resonate with you so strongly that you chose to feature it a second time? Another repeated element was that of a Japanese female protagonist. So… same question: what led you to feature that type of character again?

KW: Oh-oh. True confession time. When I was a lonely wannabe writer, and a renewed American, I tried a correspondence club called Cherry Blossoms. Before I knew it, I had scores of lovely correspondents hoping to move to the States. My first trip to Japan was a wild ride, believe me. I ended up making the very wrong choice… but that's another story. And one I'll never tell. Instead, I told imagined tales of beauties I let go.

RM: *Publishers Weekly* said the following about *Angel Kiss*: "Showing influence from such disparate sources as Kathy Acker, Ian Fleming and comic books, this thriller is bogged down by a confusing, jump-cut narrative." Do you agree with that list of influences? How do you feel about the reviewer's criticism of the jump-cut narrative style?

KW: I disagree with all of the above. I'd read no Kathy Acker, very little Ian Fleming, no comics since my childhood. As far as the jump-cut narrative style, the remark was all wet. I'm reminded of one pop California agent who wrote me a letter complaining that my writing gave him a headache because he had to think too hard. He couldn't play with the dog and watch TV while reading me. Today's readers don't need 19th-century narrative styles with every step spelled out for them. Unless they're watching *Walking Dead* and moving their lips while they read.

RM: After *Angel Kiss* appeared in 1993, you didn't publish again until 2012. I assume you were a victim of the complete bust of the horror market in the 1990s, and of having been typecast as a horror writer, but… why such a long break? When did you and your agent from that period part ways?

KW: I never stopped writing… or submitting. You're quite right about the complete bust of the horror market and my having been typecast. Ironically, I'd wanted to write mysteries from the very start. But I'd been contracted for two horror novels with Tor. I went on to pitch a mystery to Elpee, one that would evolve into *The Alcatraz Correction* many years later. But, she assured me, the choice would be mine if I did just two more horrors. By '93 I was toast, along with so many others.

RM: The following is a quote from your blog: "…I took off to The Desert to learn how to write the sort of books I'd always loved to read: riveting tales of suspense and romance, high on heart and wit and style. I lost count of the time that I spent pounding sand. But one day I found I'd completed twelve books." Why The Desert, and where did you go, exactly? Twelve books! How long were you in The Desert?

KW: Well, The Desert is a state of mind and a way of lifelessness. And one can be there anywhere. My stay lasted twenty years. All through that time I kept working on one novel after another. An upstart agency, since folded, loved my work and made the rounds with my short, edgy Christmas thrillers and with *Southern Scotch*, the first Boss MacTavin mystery. And Tor sat on their submission for almost two years. Over and over, I heard the same words: the books were too short… the Christmas thrillers were too dark… Boss MacTavin was too odd… And yet, compulsively, I kept writing more Boss books and more Christmas thrillers. The Desert became the world's judgment of this award-winning writer's new status as a rebel wannabe.

RM: Since your re-emergence in 2012, you've published five books in your The Fast and The Furies series, and three in your Boss MacTavin Action Mysteries series. You've clearly moved away from the horror genre—have you said all you have to say in that genre? Any unpublished horror novels in a drawer somewhere?

KW: I've published two pieces of flash horror fiction. Other than that, I'm finding fulfillment in the Boss MacTavin mysteries and the short Fast and Furies entries.

RM: These new books all average around 35,000 words, putting them in the novella or very short novel category… do you feel this is an optimal length for fiction, or at least for your fiction?

KW: That's the right length for the Fast and Furies books. The Boss mysteries range from 40,000-45,000. And that is, in my opinion, the optimal length for my fiction. I like sleek, streamlined books that give the impression of fullness within their slender frames. And, as I've contended for twenty-plus years: some mighty slender books are being sold as novels: *The Strange Case of Dr. Jekyll and Mr. Hyde… The Old Man and the Sea… The Color Purple…*

RM: How would you rate/evaluate your success in self-publishing these titles as ebooks?

KW: So far, my success in EbookLandia has been modest in terms of sales and numbers of reviews. There are so many writers out there with far more skill hustling. But I'm in this for the long run and have committed to spreading the word. As Fast Eddy said in *The Color of Money*: "I'm back!"

RM: As I understand it, Reb MacRath was originally intended to be a pen name for the team of you and Brad Strickland. How did you two connect, and did you collaborate for a while before deciding to continue with the MacRath name on your own? How did you decide upon the MacRath pen name?

KW: I'd hoped to collaborate with Brad on the Boss MacTavin mysteries—and, yes, the pen name would have been our team moniker. We went back to 1988, when I published *The Suiting* and he pubbed his *Shadow Show*. The collaboration might have been a doozy, but Brad's enormously prolific... I'm relatively slow... and we would have been reworking a novel I'd written two decades before. The new pen name resulted from my fixation on *Southern Scotch*—a novel and a series that fused the two cultures. The spelling of the last name gave me as much trouble as the ultimate spelling of Kelley!

RM: Did any of the 10 books published so far under the MacRath pen name begin life, in different incarnations, as some of the 12 books you wrote in The Desert? (If not, what is/will be the fate of those 12 books?)

KW: Several of the 10 ebooks are brand new and post-Desert.

Others are completely rewritten versions of books I wrote in The Desert. Two are rewritten Kelley Wilde horror novels. I have two books from The Desert remaining—both dealing with writing: one a how-to book on queries, one a literary thriller about the big publishing crash. I'll start with the first and see if there's any interest in the second.

Fingers crossed—and thanks for your interest in my work.

~~~~~~~~~~~~~~~~~~~~~~~~~~~~~~

Links to Boss MacTavin mysteries:
Southern Scotch: https://www.amazon.com/dp/B008B8H8PS
The Alcatraz Correction: https://www.amazon.com/dp/B009ZZVSVQ
Charlotte Kills: https://www.amazon.com/dp/B00LIBWFZI

FEATURED REVIEWS

BY COLLEEN WANGLUND

Ringu
(1998, Japan)
Director: Hideo Nakata

Based on the 1991 novel of the same title by Koji Suzuki, which is in turn based on an old Japanese folk tale, *Ringu* is widely credited with the rise of the New Wave of Japanese horror in the 1990s. Largely a film of supernatural horror, the film has many themes related to modern-day Japan, taking on cultural and societal advancements in a decidedly critical manner when compared to traditional norms.

Reiko Asakawa (Nanako Matsushima) is a reporter for a television station working on a story about an urban legend currently the hot topic among teenagers at the local high school. The legend centers on a mysterious videotape that, when watched, is followed by a strange phone call telling the recent viewer that they will die in seven days. After the sudden death of her niece Tomoko, Reiko discovers that three of Tomoko's friends also died the same night under unknown circumstances but is also told that they all had watched this strange video together. Tomoko's friend Masami was with Tomoko the night she died and is currently institutionalized, driven insane by what she witnessed.

Reiko finds photographs of the group of friends' recent visit to a resort in Izu, photos that show the four friends faces distorted after having viewed the tape. Reiko goes to the resort, staying in the same cabin the teens rented and finds the tape. After she views it, Reiko gets the same phone call. Returning home, she contacts her ex-husband for help. He takes a photo of Reiko and they see that her face has also been distorted. Watching the videotape, Ryuji (Hiroyuki Sanada) begins looking into the circumstances surrounding the tape and where it may have originated. Ryuji doesn't get a phone call but is visited by a mysterious woman in white who disappears as suddenly as she

approaches him. This convinces Ryuji that the urban legend is real and that he and Reiko are living on borrowed time. The couple learn that the videotape originated on Oshima Island, but not before Reiko discovers her young son Yoichi has watched the tape, supposedly at the direction of his dead cousin Tomoko.

Racing to Oshima Island, Ryuji and Reiko learn about Shizuko Yamamura, a psychic that predicted the deadly eruption of the island's volcano but was subsequently accused of being a fraud and committed suicide. Her husband had determined that Shizuko's daughter Sadako (Rie Ino'o) was even more powerful than her mother, with stronger supernatural powers. Sadako somehow made the videotape with her mind, binding her spirit to it after she was murdered by her father. Reiko and Ryuji go back to the cabin at Izu and find the well where Sadako's body was hidden and find her corpse. Thinking that the curse has been lifted, they both return home. Unfortunately for them, the curse is not so easily lifted. Reiko understands now how the curse works and is determined to save her son.

Ringu is a very good film that ultimately spawned a number of sequels and an American remake. It also led to such memorable Japanese horror films such as *Ju-On* (2000) by Takashi Shimizu, who also directed the American remake *The Grudge* (2004). The acting and directing are quite good (Nataka would go on to direct the Japanese sequel and the American film *The Ring 2*, 2005, as well as films such as *Dark Water*, 2002, and *Kaidan*, 2007), bringing the story to life using atmosphere, creating not just a ghost story but one hell of a psychological thriller. The story itself is quite scary—a curse that once you are exposed to it, you can do nothing to stop it except by putting others in harm's way. This alone brings up issues of morality. Do you save yourself at the expense of others? How do you save your child without dooming another?

The supernatural makes itself known in two ways. The first is in the psychic powers of both Sadako and her mother. Her predictions were made forty years prior to the events of the film and the fear of the unnatural drove people to accuse her of fraud, leading to Shizuko's suicide and ultimately, Sadako's murder. The second is in the curse itself and Sadako's restless spirit taking her revenge out on others. This is common in Japanese horror. The female, who is seen as powerless in life and subservient to the male, dies in a violent manner and all that remains of the spirit is the anger and need for vengeance. It is not necessarily directed at those that caused such a violent end, but at anyone who is unlucky enough to come in contact with the curse. And the curse cannot be stopped because the thirst for revenge can never be satisfied. The female ghost is quite simply blinded by rage.

The female ghost tends to represent the fear of the end of the traditional patriarchal society in Japan. We see this as well with Reiko. She is a modern woman wrestling with a career and single motherhood, though her son is left alone quite frequently. Is this possibly a rebuke against the female becoming equal to the male in Japanese society? This is a theme that can be seen in many modern Japanese horror and exploitation films. Reiko initially is portrayed as neglectful of her child, but ultimately reverts to the traditional role of nurturing mother in her quest to save Yoichi from his possible fate.

Though supernatural, the spirits of the dead are believed to live on in an afterlife, and proper treatment of the body after death and proper reverence of living family members ensures that those spirits will look favorably on their relatives and help them achieve success and good luck. Japanese horror has taken this cultural tradition and turned it into something shockingly scary. And there generally are no happy endings. Historically the female ghost is believed to have much more spiritual power than the male counterpart, which is why she not only has sway in the real world, but can become a most fearsome creature.

Ringu also touches on the fear of modern technology, which is ironic when you consider that Japan has led the world in modern technological advancement. Sadako is able to attach her spirit and her curse to a videotape… she literally comes out of the television screen to take her victims, who all die with their faces frozen in terror. The curse, perhaps, is a foretelling representation of where we have come with our technology—an impersonal *thing* that provides escapism, voyeurism, narcissism, and potential danger being allowed right into our homes with our consent.

Ringu is a classic example of Japanese horror and has not only had some critical acclaim since its initial release by Toho Studios, but has also achieved almost cult status among horror fans everywhere.

~Colleen Wanglund

Ju-On
(2000, Japan)
Director: Takashi Shimizu

Initially a V-Cinema (straight-to-video) release, *Ju-On*, also known as *Ju-On: The Curse*, is a classic example of the New Wave of J-horror that began with the 1998 release of Hideo Nataka's *Ringu*. While not as good a film overall as *Ringu* and others in the genre, writer and director Takashi Shimizu created an entertaining film that would spawn an entire franchise, including two American films directed by Shimizu himself, a few South Korean remakes, as well as multiple novelizations and manga adaptations, and video games. Interestingly, Shimizu's *Ju-On* is a sort-of remake of two short made-for-TV movies. A psychological horror film, *Ju-On* employs the familiar trope of female ghost, which can have societal, cultural, and political meaning in all forms of media dating back centuries. Japan's female ghost is akin to the West's vampire, werewolf, or zombie.

Ju-On is told in six segments, though it is not an anthology film. All of the segments revolve around the same curse, though they are not necessarily in chronological order. The main story of the film revolves around Kayako (Takako Fuji), a housewife and mother who is violently murdered, along with her young son Toshio (Ryota Koyama), by her husband Takeo (Takashi Matsuyama) in a fit of jealousy after finding Kayako's journal detailing her feelings for college friend Shunsuke Kobayashi (Yurei Yanagi). Due to Toshio's absence from school for many days his teacher pays a visit to the home. The teacher happens to be Kayako's secret love Shunsuke Kobayashi. He finds Toshio alone in the messy house and waits for his parents to discuss the absence. While waiting, Kobayashi explores the house due to some unsettling feelings he has. He discovers the journal as well as Kayako's bloody corpse hidden in the attic. Takeo calls the house from Kobayashi's apartment where he has left his pregnant wife. Kayako's corpse then kills Kobayashi while Takeo kills his wife Manami and takes her dead fetus. Kayako ultimately kills Takeo in the street.

From that main story, *Ju-On* moves to the other segments, which tell the stories of various victims of the curse. Another family is living in the house and their teenage daughter Kanna (Asumi Miwa) is being tutored by Yuki (Hitomi Miwa). Kanna leaves suddenly to head back to the school to feed the rabbits kept in the classroom. Yuki is still in the house when she sees a cat (Toshio's dead cat, also killed by Takeo), of which she is terrified. She hears sounds coming from the attic and while investigating is killed by Kayako. Meanwhile Kanna's brother Tsuyoshi (Kazushi Ando) has gone to the school to meet his girlfriend Mizuho (Chiaki Kuriyama). Tsuyoshi never arrives so a teacher checks the school for him. At the same time the police are investigating the discovery of mutilated bodies on school grounds. Are the multiple victims the three teens?

The final segment, which ultimately leads to the film's sequels, is about real estate agent Tatsuya Suzuki (Makoto Ashikawa) trying to sell the house. He calls his sister Kyoko (Yuko Daike) who is somewhat of a spiritualist and can sense ghosts. Kyoko senses the presence of Kayako and knows she is dangerous. Visiting the house after it has been sold, Kyoko senses a possession by Kayako. The stories of the teens Kanna, Tsuyoshi, and Mizuho, Kyoko and the home's new owners, and the police investigating the bodies at the school, all carry over and continue into the sequel.

While *Ju-On* and its subsequent sequels are good films overall, they can be a bit muddled and confusing the way they jump from segment to segment. It is the third film, *Ju-On: The Grudge* (2002), where the story more or less comes together in its entirety and where the viewer learns that the curse extends not just to anyone who comes in even minimal contact with it, but it also survives over years. And this is the core of the horror that is the film— there is no end to the curse. Kayako, as well as her son Toshio, will cause the deaths of many people with no end in sight. This is also the core of most Japanese horror relating to the female ghost.

Traditionally, women throughout Japanese culture have always been viewed as weak while alive but spiritually powerful after death. Funerary practices demand the reverential treatment of the dead to ensure they have an easy journey into the afterlife, and to ensure the dead's blessings on the family. When someone dies a violent death, particularly a woman, she has died in fear and anger. These negative feelings become all that is left of the individual's spirit. The person they were in life no longer exists and their entire spiritual existence becomes unfocused rage. They don't always strike out at the person who harmed them, but the curse they breed will destroy anyone in its path.

This is another example of the fear among Japanese of the collapse of the patriarchal society if women become equal. Shimizu also uses the film to bring domestic violence to light, criticizing society for either ignoring or encouraging it. Women are generally subservient in Japanese culture as Southeast Asia was untouched by the West's sexual revolution of the 1960s. Police turn a blind eye to domestic violence and women suffer. In horror, the women can get their ultimate revenge, but it is at the expense of society as a whole. The supernatural is used to make judgements against current societal, cultural, and political norms and traditions. It is an effective tool in Japan but when the West remakes these films, the cultural significance is usually lost.

For its faults, such as the confusing storytelling and sometimes slow pacing, *Ju-On* is still a scary film. There is some gore but the film relies on atmosphere and the fantastic acting of its cast to build tension, and it works. It does work as a stand-alone movie but viewing the sequels adds to the story as well as the entertainment value. I don't necessarily recommend the American remakes, even though Shimizu directed them himself, but I've never been a fan of remakes.

~Colleen Wanglund

Molly Tanzer

The Language of Flowers

The tree was cold against her back and the earth hard and damp under her bottom but Henry had assessed the lay of the land, and the lee side of *this* tree trunk, and *this* damp patch of earth weren't visible from any vantage point at Moorgate School for Girls. No one would know she was here; no one could see what she was doing. The sensation of having some actual privacy made her frigid hideaway almost as comfortable as a parlor as she tore open the letter and read:

> *Hullo Henry,*
>
> *School still ghastly? Sorry to hear, but at least it'll be Christmas soon, and then we'll be back together again! And after that, it's only a few months until the summer! Hurrah! In the meantime, you must try to bear it, as must we all. School is a good opportunity for us both. We must cram something other than jam tarts into our heads, I suppose.*
>
> *Not much news, save that I threw in my lot with the Fencing Club. I know a club doesn't seem like your sort of thing, but it might not be so bad to join one. Even if you don't make any "friends for life" you might make your days more pleasant. What about asking that Miss Griffiths about starting a horticulture club?*
>
> *I heard from Mother you hacked all your hair off with the Matron's scissors and caused an uproar? Good show, old thing. They can force us to learn what they want us to learn, but they can't force us to be who they want us to be.*
>
> *Keep that chin up. It's our best angle.*
>
> *All my love,*
> *Oliver Wotton*
> *November 8th, 1860*

The wind blew through Henry's ghastly woolen uniform, and her stockings, and her shoes, over the back of her newly bare neck. The leaden sky matched her mood as did the wet rustling of the leaves that yet clung to the desolate branches. She folded the precious missive carefully and placed it in its envelope, but before she tucked it into her pinafore, Henry raised the letter to her nose, and inhaled. She was so lonely for her brother she was desperate for any hint of him that might cling to the damp paper.

"What are you doing?"

Henry jumped and scrambled to her feet, dashing tears from her eyes. Her face burned like a fire. It was humiliating to be caught crying, but she was also furious. She'd worked so hard to secure a private moment to read this letter, and though the girl who had found her was Esther, Henry's only friend at Moorgate, it made her savage to be discovered in such an intimate moment.

"What business is it of yours what I'm doing?" she snarled. "What are *you* doing?"

"Did you just *smell* that letter?"

The sky was gray, and the clouds were gray. The watery sunlight was gray, as were the limbs of the bare trees reaching above them and the earth beneath their feet. Moorgate's pinafores were gray, and the dresses, and socks, while allegedly white, were all gray from too many washings in cold water. Henry felt certain the only color in the world right now was her face, red as a beetroot, obvious and vulgar.

"I thought there was a bug in the envelope," she said, far too quickly.

Esther squinted at her. "Why are you out here anyway? I saw you sneaking out and—"

"You followed me?" Outraged, Henry took a step toward Esther, her fists hard balls at her sides. Esther might be Henry's only friend, but she didn't own Henry; she had no right to Henry when Henry wanted to be alone. "Why would you follow me?"

"To see where you were going," said Esther. "I thought you might like some company."

"I like being alone!"

"Well, I don't," said Esther miserably, and Henry relented. She ought to be more sympathetic. Esther felt the sting of solitude more keenly. "I'd rather do just about anything than sit by some awful tree in the cold by myself."

"Well, no harm done," said Henry, more mildly.

"Was it a letter from a lover?" asked Esther.

Henry almost laughed. "No, of course not."

"Sarah has a lover, she says."

That sort of information, so titillating to the other girls, never much interested Henry. "Mine was from my brother."

"Oh…"

"I just miss him. It's hard, being away from him." Henry felt her face getting red again, so she pushed her loneliness for her twin away.

"I don't think my brother remembers me when I'm at school. But he's only seven." Esther's arms were wrapped around her against the wind.

Henry shivered too. "Shall we go in?" she said. "Tea-time's nearly over; we might still get a cup. Toast's probably all gone though."

Esther nodded eagerly. It hurt Henry's heart how delighted she was to be invited to do something with someone, even attend a daily event like tea-time at Moorgate. Perhaps Oliver was right—maybe she should start some sort of club or organization. Having conversations, even banal ones, made one's day more pleasant.

***

The weather steadily worsened as November wore on. Henry shivered as she dressed in the dark, freezing dormitory; her teeth chattered as she blinked in the weak light, reading improving sermons or practicing her needlework—both awful, infuriating, dull pursuits made worse by the other girls' constant taunts and sniggering. They had never been kind to her, but shearing off her hair had made her a total social outcast.

"Why did you do it?" Esther asked, after Madeline, the leader of the popular girls at Moorgate, entertained the rest by dramatically shrieking "no *boys* in here!" when Henry entered the washroom that morning. "You must have known it would cause a scandal."

Henry considered this as they walked to the greenhouse after lunch, their feet crunching through frost-limned leaves and shallow ice-rimed puddles. She wasn't sure if she could—or should—talk to Esther about something so personal. Outcasts both, they were friends of convenience, not soul mates.

Then again, Esther had confided her share of secrets… like that she had once kissed the butcher's boy; that her father often fought with and even beat her mother when he drank. The latter of those confidences could ruin what little social standing Esther had at Moorgate. Domestic tragedy was just the sort of thing girls like Madeline liked to sniff out to torment the less popular girls. Henry had seen it before, like when Julia had challenged Madeline last year over where they would picnic. Madeline had sighed and said, "I suppose we should do as Julia wishes… we don't want her to run off in a fit of pique to go ruin herself with some low farmhand, like her sister did." Madeline had changed the topic after that, as Julia's eyes welled and her chest heaved with rage, but it had become the talk of the school until the teachers had forbidden another word on the subject. But for weeks after it was whispered about.

Julia was back in Madeline's good graces, but it had taken a long time, perfect obedience, and Madeline finding a new target for her venom-spewing.

Henry decided to trust Esther. "Back at home, I rarely wore dresses… I hate them. They don't feel right. I'd borrow my twin's clothes and wear those. My mother didn't mind—I think she thought I'd grow out of it. But she drew the line at me cutting my hair." As the greenhouse came into sight, Henry ran her hands through her fair mop. "I obeyed, as she was lenient in other ways… but here, with this uniform… the skirt, the petticoat, the pinafore… I had to do *something*. Something that would help me feel like myself."

"I don't think the uniforms here are so bad," said Esther, further confirming for Henry that her friend did not have enough discernment to be a true friend.

Henry missed her brother keenly as they approached the greenhouse. She felt his absence, always, like a backache one could only forget temporarily.

She relaxed a bit when she opened the door to the greenhouse and was greeted by the lush, warm embrace of Moorgate's fragrant jungle in miniature. Here, it was always springtime, it seemed—and summer, and autumn, and winter. Why, the roses were still in bloom, and the laburnum; berries clung to the bushes, some edible, some deadly poison, like the toxic holly. Summer's fruits clung to the vine besides citrus that ought not to ripen until midwinter. Nothing was ever out of season, here.

And yet, most of the girls at Moorgate *hated* their gardening classes. They disliked the hair-frizzing humidity, the dirt under their nails, the long lists of plants they had to memorize. Henry liked it—kneeling among the rose-beds and herbs and shrubs, she didn't have to keep her knees together primly; wasn't admonished for getting sweaty or filthy. And she had a talent for it—it was like she could feel what the plants wanted. It came naturally to her.

Miss Griffiths ruled over the greenhouse, every root and bloom and leaf and shoot her obedient subject. Not only did she have a way with plants—rarely a browning leaf nor withering stalk was seen in Moorgate's greenhouse—she was absolutely Henry's favorite teacher. An older woman, gray-haired and curved like the letter C, Madeline and her friends called her "that old witch" in private, which Henry felt was terribly unfair. Miss Griffiths was one of the kindest teachers at the school; nothing seemed to bother her, not even Henry's chopping off her hair. Rather, she had advocated for Henry when the headmistress had threatened to send her home, permanently, citing Henry's youth, enthusiasm, and independence as markers of a strong personality—not those of an incorrigible troublemaker.

"Miss Wotton, and Miss Earl," she said, as the two girls made their way into the greenhouse. Henry smelled her distinctive rose perfume. "Good afternoon. You're the first to arrive. Come and see what I have here."

Henry left Esther a few steps behind, so eager was she. It turned out to be a pineapple, perfect and tiny, sprouting from a forest of spikes. Henry marveled at it.

"It's not quite ripe yet," said Miss Griffiths, as Esther joined them. "But when it is, I'm going to make a project out of it, for all of us. We'll eat it, then plant the top and see if we can't grow another. Won't that be nice, Miss Gregory?"

Madeline was there, now, with her cabal of sneering, skeptical colleagues.

"Nice?" she asked.

"To share among us one of the most unique fruits in the world, and then grow another, of course," said Miss Griffiths, in her mild way.

Madeline made a show of yawning. "I suppose," she said.

Henry was amazed at how Miss Griffiths took this in stride. "But for today," she said, without acknowledging Madeline's unpleasantness, "we dig."

The girls groaned—even Esther—but Henry did not. In fact, she smiled, though ruefully, remembering her twin's suggestion that she and Miss Griffiths start a horticulture club.

The next several hours ought to have been a short stay in heaven. They didn't do anything particularly exciting, just little tasks like watering or repotting plants, or checking over the tender bulbs to see if any had gone mushy. It was just the sort of thing Henry liked.

Unfortunately, that was not the case for Madeline and her gang. While Madeline encouraged her friends' behavior during their classes in the greenhouse, they were in rare form that day, making quite a bit of fuss over the dullness of their tasks. Henry knew from experience that saying anything would only make them show off more, so she ignored them as she worked. But to her surprise even the usually quiet Esther chimed in a few times. It was not pleasant, and by the end, even the usually imperturbable Miss Griffiths was showing the strain. Her lips were tight with annoyance when she came over to see how Henry was getting on with trimming back the chrysanthemums.

"Very good, Miss Wotton," said Miss Griffiths. Her perfume, while subtle, seemed to replace that of the other flowers, and the earth.

The sound of tittering spoiled the moment. Madeline, who had long before given up on mounding dirt around the roots of the fuchsias, whispered something to Julia and Sarah. Henry blushed.

"Pay them no mind," said Miss Griffiths softly. "Those who take pleasure in cruelty, and in doing things badly, are not worthy of our attention."

Henry went still in surprise. No teacher had ever spoken to her so openly of another student's behavior—much less critiqued the speaker so harshly. She swallowed, or tried to; her throat had gone dry.

It was queer—this brief intimacy made her feel less alone than Esther's constant presence.

"Why don't you stay after," said Miss Griffiths. "Have a cup of tea with me."

"I'd love to," croaked Henry.

After they cleaned up, Esther wandered over to Henry. She was smiling.

"Madeline said I was *too funny*," she reported happily.

"Oh?" said Henry coolly. "I thought you were appallingly rude."

Esther looked shocked, as well she might. Henry had never spoken to her like that before; why, she'd even surprised herself.

"It was only a joke…"

This just made Henry more annoyed at her friend. "I'm sure Madeline thought it was 'only a joke' to shriek and point at me this morning."

There was nothing Esther could really say to that, so she dropped the subject. "Shall we go to tea?"

"I'm staying after to talk to Miss Griffiths."

Esther brightened, excited by the idea. "Oh, really? Can I stay, too?"

Esther was *always* barging in where she wasn't wanted, but the bigger issue, to Henry at least, was that she wanted it both ways. She couldn't torment a teacher and expect to be rewarded with a private audience and special favors. It was outrageous, and Henry felt her annoyance becoming anger.

"No," said Henry, her voice a little louder than strictly appropriate. "It would really just be *too funny*, after the things you said, if I brought you along."

Esther blinked stupidly at Henry, her mouth open. Henry stood her ground until Madeline called "Esther, are you coming?" surprising them both.

"Me?" asked Esther.

Madeline rolled her eyes. "Are there any other girls named Esther here?"

Esther's eyes darted back to Henry, ask if asking her to make the choice. Henry, even angrier now, did not relent—it had been Esther's choice to put her weak personality on display, joining in antics meant to amuse at the expense of others.

With a huffy-sounding sniff, Esther turned and trotted off to join with the others. Henry felt a pang, but didn't call out. If she lost Esther's friendship over this, she'd be lonelier, but the truth was, the split would have happened

eventually. Henry could brook a lot of things, but petty bullying wasn't one of them.

She gave herself time to cool down, walking slowly

along the close lanes of the greenhouse, enjoying the feeling of being alone in a forest. It was so wonderful here;

this realm of perpetual bounty. But she could not wander forever; eventually, when she was calm—or close enough—she knocked on the door of Miss Griffiths' office

in the back. She turned the handle when she heard a quiet, "Come in!"

The room smelled of roses and tea. Miss Griffiths was just pouring a steaming cup, and handing it over, indicated Henry should doctor it as she liked. Henry plopped two sugars in hers and dribbled in a bit of milk as her teacher added a thin slice of lemon to her own cup. The tea was delicious, and even tasted of rose a bit.

"So. Henry." Miss Griffiths took a sip on her tea as Henry grabbed one of the little minced ham sandwiches Miss Griffiths had set out. "Some of the teachers have noticed that you've been having some trouble socializing."

Henry frowned, feeling especially glad she had turned Esther down. She hadn't realized Miss Griffiths wanted to have one of *those* sorts of talks.

"They didn't ask me to talk to you about this," said Miss Griffiths. "I bring it up because I understand what it's like to have trouble at school."

"And yet you chose to return," said Henry, before realizing how rude it sounded. Miss Griffiths just laughed.

"I did. In part because we women have limited options if we need to earn a wage," Henry blushed, but Miss Griffiths smiled kindly at her, "and also because I felt I could do some good, teaching the next generation of girls and reaching out to those who needed it. Which is why, Henry, I've decided to ask if you'd like to become my… assistant. Apprentice. Whatever you'd like to call it is fine with me. You have a natural talent with the plants, and if you'd like to learn more by doing more, I'm inviting you to do so."

Henry didn't even think about it. "Please," she replied eagerly.

"It won't all be easy," said Miss Griffiths. "There's a lot of hard work to be done, and all year too. Some of it in the cold, some of it in the rain…"

"I don't mind hard work," said Henry.

"Well, no time like the present," said Miss Griffiths. "I've let my bookshelves get terribly out of order. Please alphabetize them. I'll be checking over some seed stock, if you have any questions."

There were four tall bookshelves simply loaded down with almanacs, manuals, and books on botany, horticulture, and plant lore. After a few minutes Henry elected to take all the books off the shelves and make piles by author name; it seemed the easiest way to manage the volume of volumes.

Miss Griffiths was a pleasant if quiet working companion; she was happy to let Henry go about her business without questions or interruptions. Which was good, because while Henry was focused on the task at hand, she was also thinking over her interaction with Esther. While Esther had been in the wrong, Henry could understand why she'd been so eager for Madeline's attention. Esther longed to fit in; to have more friends. Henry knew that, and she should have been more understanding. Everyone had their weaknesses. She resolved to apologize that evening.

The question of *how*, however, ate at Henry… until she came across a rather plain-looking book called *The Language of Flowers*. The title rang a bell. Henry had once read that flowers, especially roses, had coded meanings— that knights errant used to tell their lady-loves messages by arranging a bouquet for them. Well, maybe there was a flower that meant "I'm sorry." There were worse ways to begin an apology.

She opened the book and began to look over the table of contents. What she found wasn't quite what she expected. Instead of tables detailing what the various colors of roses might represent, the book instead posited that flowers could actually speak wisdom to man, if one only knew how to listen—that plants in general could convey messages, if cultivated properly. They might tell listeners secrets of medicine, or inspire great art; reveal religious enigmas, or unlock mysteries of nature and the universe. It was intriguing, and Henry actually cleared a bit of space so she could sit more comfortably while she read. The deeper she got into the book, the more she thought there was something the author wasn't saying—even if "F. H. Smith" had quite a bit to say about how best to listen to what plants had to say. It certainly didn't involve putting one's ear to a rose and hoping for the best... no, it was more involved than that. There were various recipes, laid out almost like a cookery book, and while the ingredients were common enough—petals, roots, stems, and leaves— there was a queer, byzantine process to making the food and drink, and if Henry hadn't been such a skeptic, she'd think a lot of it sounded like... witchcraft.

Deeply intrigued, her task neglected, Henry turned the page, and found a new chapter—"Cosmetics and Miscellany." She read:

> One cannot always be eating and drinking things, of course—so if one wishes to never be without the wisdom of flowers, one must find alternate methods of remaining with them. A dab of perfume behind the ear, a pinch of snuff up the nose, will allow for constant, discreet contact with their—

"What are you reading?"

Henry yelped in surprise, astonished that she hadn't smelled Miss Griffiths' rose perfume before her teacher had spoken. Guiltily she shut the tome and glanced about her—the shelves looked worse than when she had begun, and here she was, idly reading.

Miss Griffiths took the book, her expression unreadable. "*The Language of Flowers*," she said softly, so softly. "Interesting choice. What made you pick it up, Miss Wotton?"

"I heard that one could send a message with a flower," she said, telling the truth. "I was harsh to Esther, earlier, and wanted to apologize."

"Hyacinth," said Miss Griffiths lightly. "You may of course cut a sprig." She glanced down at the book. "You read quite a bit without finding your answer—what made you press on?"

"It was so interesting..." Henry's nostrils were filled with the smell of roses—she'd never smelled anything like it, now that she really thought about it. It made her wonder if Miss Griffiths compounded her own perfume... perhaps from a recipe from the book she held in her hands?

Was it possible she, too, had pored over this tome? That she saw it as more than just an oddity or rare collector's piece? Did she listen to the wisdom of flowers? She did have an unusual way with plants. Was it possible they had revealed their secrets to her?

Surely not. Miss Griffiths just had a very green thumb...

"I suggest you put it from your mind. I should never have shelved it with my more reliable books. It *is* interesting, as you said. But, like many interesting books, it is more fascinating than reliable."

"Of course," said Henry, echoing her teacher's words. But neither of them sounded so certain...

Miss Griffiths smiled down at Henry, who was still sitting, surrounded by piles of books. "As it is close to suppertime, I fear I must release you and request you come back tomorrow to tidy up this mess, hmm?"

Her tone was still kindly and gentle, but there was an intensity, a fire behind her eyes that Henry had never seen before. She did not look wholly like herself. It scared Henry, and after saying a few words—Henry scarcely knew what—she ran off, out of the greenhouse, and back to her dormitory as hard as she could pelt. It wasn't until she saw Esther that she remembered she had meant to pluck a sprig of hyacinth for her friend.

It was just as well. Esther did not join her for dinner, electing instead to sit with Madeline and the rest. Henry didn't mind. She had enough to think about.

She dearly wished her brother were with her. It was so hard, being away from him. More often than not they had been of one mind on things. Without him, she felt cleaved, incomplete. Unable to reason things through. She didn't know what to think about the idea that if she were to concoct a tea of this-and-that, and drink it, she might come to understand mysteries obscure to every philosopher, scientist, and priest. She wanted to talk it over with her brother.

She was in her bed, almost asleep, when a thought came to her. If she could but sneak into the greenhouse, and get the book, she could write down one of the simpler recipes and try it for herself. If it didn't work, she would have wasted nothing but a night's sleep. But if it did, the possibilities were endless.

And who was to say... if concocting things from flower petals allowed one to always be in contact with flowers, what was to stop her doing something similar with her hair, or nail clippings—or her brother's? They might come away from the Christmas holidays always able to speak to one another, just by sipping a cup of tea, or dabbing a bit of perfume behind an ear...

Once the idea took hold, Henry couldn't resist it. Silently, she pulled on her uniform and snuck out of the dormitory; out of the school. In the black, freezing night she padded over the frozen earth to the greenhouse. The door was latched, but she also knew from exploring her greenhouse at home, with her brother, that if she jiggled the handle and slid a thin stick along the crack between the door and the frame, it would pop open—and it did.

Once inside, Henry lit the candle she'd stolen and sneaked up to the door to Miss Griffiths' office. That, too, was locked, much to Henry's disappointment. Holding up the weak flame, she considered trying to break in... but not only was it a much stronger lock, it seemed like an excessive invasion of Miss Griffiths' privacy. Plus, she remembered a recipe for one of the teas. At least, she thought she did. Well enough, at least, for a trial run.

She slunk away from the door, toward the dark greenhouse. Roses had figured in this tea, and chrysanthemums—root, stem, leaf, and bloom, compounded into a poultice, and then… then… she'd think about that later. For now, she needed the materials, and while she knew where both should be, skulking around in the dark made the familiar space strange.

When she found the roses she realized she'd also forgotten to bring scissors. True, they were more difficult to come by after she'd cut her hair off, but she should have hunted around a bit. Unwilling to give up the idea as a bad job, Henry turned, intending to hunt down the trowels and clippers they used in class.

That's when she heard the greenhouse door creak open.

Henry blew out her candle and stayed where she was, spending a few moments trying to figure out if she'd really heard the squeal of hinges, or imagined it. Every crunch underfoot or rustle as she passed a plant had made her heart race, seeming louder than it really was. But when she heard the shh-ing and giggling, she knew she wasn't alone.

She ducked down behind the large rosebush, hoping to remain out of their sight, whoever they were. Given the snickering and the carrying on, she assumed it was other girls from Moorgate, not transients. Why they had come, she didn't know—were they having a secret party? Such things weren't unheard of, so she crept closer to see if she could overhear.

"Where is she, do you think?" That was Sarah.

"Somewhere. Hiding somewhere—I'm sure she heard Julia snorting and braying like an ass." And that, of course, was Madeline.

"I didn't—"

"Shut up?" Madeline phrased it as a suggestion, but it wasn't. "Anyway, find her."

They were looking for her. They had followed her. But why?

She heard footsteps along the garden paths—they had fanned out. In the darkness, she couldn't tell if they were close to her or not, so she stayed put. Clearly they weren't hunting her to give her a present; weren't checking in to make sure she was all right. They had some sinister purpose in mind.

The best thing to do would be to get out of there, and quickly. Henry poked her head up. She didn't see anyone between her and the greenhouse door. Dark shapes were moving quietly all around her; she decided to make a break for it. She took a steadying breath—and that's when someone caught her by the neck of her uniform.

She toppled over, as her muscles had been poised for a sprint, and brought down the other with her. They scrabbled in the dark for a moment or two, but then hands pulled them roughly apart. Henry fought like a cat, but was overpowered. When she quieted, she saw that it was Esther who had grabbed her. She opened her mouth, but found she had nothing to say.

"Hello Henrietta. Come out here to sniff more letters from your brother?" asked Madeline. Her smile flashed like lightning in the darkness. Henry's breath caught in her throat, an anguished croak emerging instead of words. She looked at Esther, but her eyes were cold and hard and glittering.

"It's suspicious, you know, sneaking off all the time to read letters from him," Madeline continued. "There's nothing strange about getting letters from your brother, why do you feel the need to hide them? Unless there is something strange going on…"

It was intolerable, having something so private, so pure maligned and spoken of so disgustingly. And what would she say in response? To deny it still gave them power; made it a question deserving of an answer. Henry thrashed impotently, but Julia and Sarah's hands were bony vices.

"It's none of your business what I do, or where, or when," she finally managed.

"Oh, I disagree," said Madeline. "Everything that happens here is my business. While it was your hair you cut off, I have to look at the ugly mess you made. And worse than that, even, it makes this school seem like a refuge for freaks or outcasts when parents or the school governors come to visit. Everyone's behavior here affects everyone else. You always sneaking off to be on your own, or with a teacher," sneered Madeline, "is disruptive to the other girls."

"With a…" Henry once again looked to Esther, who finally looked away. So that was what this was about—her private invitation! Could Esther have really been that jealous of Henry spending a few hours away from her, having tea?

"You think you're so much better than everyone else here," said Esther, as if in answer to Henry's question.

"And you're not," added Madeline, with a sharp look at Esther that made the girl cringe. "It doesn't make you better to be different. Remember, Henrietta—pride goeth before a fall."

Madeline plucked a blossom off the rosebush, and then crushed it in her hands. Petals fell to the ground, fluttering like a flock of wounded birds.

"The thing is," said Madeline, "you need to be taught a lesson… and not in a private meeting with the worst teacher here at Moorgate. You think being special will protect you. Well, it won't—and I'm going to show you tonight. Well… tomorrow." She produced some twine from her pinafore pocket, and handed it to Sarah and Julia, who set to binding Henry's wrists and ankles.

Henry closed her eyes for what came next, for it was too awful to watch. The girls set about digging up various plants, crushing others with their shoes, even breaking panes of glass. They untied Henry after, but left her on the ground, dirty and sobbing. Shivering, when her tears tapered, Henry crammed a rose in her mouth, chewing the bitter blossom, hoping some wisdom would come to her, as the book said it would. Eventually she spit out the pulp. She had learned nothing; heard nothing. She was alone in the greenhouse and was in many ways responsible for its destruction. She had unlocked the door.

It was an impossible situation—there was no good choice between leaving or staying. Regardless, Miss Griffiths would come in, and the story would come out, and Henry had no idea what on earth her teacher would have to say about it all. ◆

20TH ANNIVERSARY EDITION
VAMPIRE
THE MASQUERADE

WORLD OF DARKNESS

BY RICHARD DANSKY

If *Dungeons and Dragons* was solidly a product of the 70s, then the World of Darkness grew just as definitively out of the 90s. A self-described "Gothic-Punk" world, the World of Darkness was the shared setting for a series of horror roleplaying games from Atlanta-based White Wolf Game Studios. [Full disclosure—I started freelancing for WW in 1994 and was a full-time employee from 1995-1999.] Its premise was seductively simple—underneath the "real world" of paychecks and mortgages was a hidden world of monsters, manipulating the course of history, fighting titanic wars of which mere mortals were completely unaware, and occasionally going out and getting their freak on at a local goth club. The first game in the series, *Vampire: The Masquerade*, was also the most popular, spawning sub-lines like *Vampire: The Dark Ages*, video games, a television show, and a partnership with WWE. Other core games in the sequence included *Werewolf: The Apocalypse*, *Mage: The Ascension*, *Wraith: The Oblivion*, and *Changeling: The Dreaming*. Later additions included *Hunter:*

The Vigil, *Orpheus*, and *Mummy: The Resurrection*.

And to say that the World of Darkness struck a chord is an understatement, both with creators and fans. "The idea of 'mood' and 'theme' as something you actively discussed as part of game design" was one of the things that inspired Werewolf line developer Ethan Skemp. "*Vampire* was a mishmash of vampire influences from all over, but its theme was what made it so political when it wasn't a bloody *Near Dark* mess. The need to address theme and mood in every book could get a little repetitive, but it was really engaging to explore how these abstract concepts affected what you were trying to say, and what emotions you were trying to convey." Designer Travis Williams, one of the first members of the WW creative team, agreed. "The most exciting thing about working at White Wolf during those formative years was feeling like we were the tip of the creative spear. The whole concept of you being a mythological monster was new and empowering. A lot of times a WoD chronicle wasn't IF you could do a thing but

SHOULD you do a thing and WHY. It bought a different sort of tabletop gaming atmosphere. Characters had much more influence over the story."

"World of Darkness, for all its fantasy, has a certain connection to everyday life," says editor and writer Jaym Gates, who's worked on multiple anthologies in the setting. The blend of high-powered action gameplay, with massive powers unleashed in familiar settings on one hand, and the need to keep the entire thing hidden from prying mortal eyes on the other led to a tension that hadn't often been expressed in RPGs previously. Best-selling author James A. Moore, who wrote extensively for the World of Darkness, agrees. "Politics in the office is far more interesting when there are lives at stake and the boss really is out to see you crushed."

That connection to the real world also made for an appealing vulnerability. Sure, vampires could control minds, run like the wind, and shape the flesh of the living, depending on which "Clan" they belonged to, but they also had to sleep half the day, and they were always vastly outnumbered by the mortal hordes they moved among. Williams jokes, "You just can't go full Crinos [giant wolf-man form] in the mall because your ATM card wasn't working," but there's truth behind the humor—living "normal" lives when not engaged in supernatural behaviors, protecting loved ones—these were the elements that firmly rooted the setting in a way all the blood and thunder couldn't. And that in turn gave some of the games an emotional weight that resonated deeply with players.

"Playing WoD games gave me a way to tell scary stories with my friends. It being collaborative was a big deal to me, that we could all put something into the game and share it as a group. Our game, our stories, our jokes and nightmares and mix tapes," said Lillian Cohen-Moore, a freelancer who's written for the setting.

Another ingredient that made the World of Darkness stand out was an emphasis on social mechanics in addition to combat ones. The emphasis on persuasion, negotiation and sometimes flat-out blackmail balanced all the blood-letting, and offered players a wide variety of play styles so players could find their own way. This in turn naturally translated into live action roleplaying through the *Mind's Eye Theatre* system, which eventually expanded into a phenomenon featuring hundreds of thousands of players, elaborate costuming and wildly inventive scenarios. Veteran VLARPer and author Ree Soesbee felt there was a reason that *Vampire* and its associated games translated so well to LARP: "In effect, most of LARP is a game without a storyteller. The storytellers move plot and the main thrust of play, but a large percentage of players will interact very little with the LARP storyteller… you want to create pockets of involvement, difficulties that require player-to-player interaction. That style of play is native to *Vampire*."

At its peak, the World of Darkness was generating something close to 70 books of content a year, meaning dozens of creators were involved and the world's continuity got ever more complex. "We had the benefit of dozens, hundreds of people with a passion to create," remembers Skemp. Cohen-Moore, who was a player first and then moved to the writing side, recalls "writing for it felt like adding to an art installation. I was putting a detail into something, and someday other people would see that detail in that bigger picture, and it would add to their experience." And Williams remembers collaborating with "some of the most gifted designers, authors and artists" he's ever worked with. On the other hand, that same increasing complexity became ever harder to keep track of, and intimidated new players. "It was that first edition *Clanbook Malkavian* bit about the blind vampires and the elephant—so many contradictions," Skemp said. And that would eventually pay off explosively. Weighted with keeping track of all of that, Cohen-Moore recalls "this dark voice over my proverbial shoulder whispering 'do not fuck this up.'"

One of the elements baked into all aspects of the setting was an incipient apocalypse, giving the players the feeling that the fate of the world really was at stake. And eventually White Wolf pulled the trigger, starting with *Wraith*, and tumbled the setting into what vampires called Gehenna, a climactic resolution to the entire setting.

Following that, the World of Darkness was reborn. New iterations of the games—*Vampire: The Requiem*, *Changeling: The Lost*, *Werewolf: The Forsaken* and more—and new games—*Scion* and *Promethean* to name two—rose up and built a new World of Darkness with its own flavor. The newer games, now called Chronicles of Darkness, quickly acquired their own devotees and identities. "It was definitely a different approach, even within a given setting," said Skemp, whose tenure bridged the two modes. "Late original WoD was in many ways a reaction to older WoD content, where we were trying to fix some of our doofier mistakes and play on our discovered strengths. Early next-WoD was also a reaction to older WoD content, which is why early games like *Vampire: The Requiem* and *Werewolf: The Forsaken* resemble their predecessors much more than later CoD games like *Changeling: The Lost* did. Once the CoD got rolling, we started building more from scratch."

Eventually, White Wolf was purchased by the Icelandic video game developer CCP, which attempted to produce a World of Darkness MMO. During that time, the publication of new content for the tabletop lines dwindled and finally ended, but the slack was picked up by Onyx Path Publishing. Formed by former White Wolf art director Rich Thomas, Onyx Path licensed many White Wolf properties, including both editions of the World of Darkness, and found there was still rapturous demand for it. When asked why, Gates is matter-of-fact: "That connection to actual human interests and the way the developers have refreshed the line to keep it modern means old fans and new can connect." Moore agrees, saying, "It holds up a mirror to all the things so many of us find fascinating about the human condition. And yes, I said 'human'. They might be monsters, but the struggles they deal with are the very ones we must handle in the real world, merely made richer through the filter of the monstrous."

While the old offices in Atlanta have been shut down, new life has been injected into the World of Darkness recently. Onyx Path continues a robust production schedule, the IP has been purchased by Swedish developers Paradox Interactive, and new interactive audio publisher Earplay is working to bring the setting to an entirely new platform. More than twenty years on, the World of Darkness remains as seductive and vibrant as ever. When asked about its future, Williams is direct: "I feel like I hope it outlives me because I am so proud of my contributions to that setting."

HORROR
WORLD

HELLNOTES

THE HORROR
REVIEW

HORROR, SCIENCE FICTION
& FANTASY REVIEWS

FICTION, MOVIES, AND ART
DEDICATED TO THE HORROR GENRE

JOURNALSTONE
YOUR LINK TO ARTISTIC TALENT

I Can Taste the Blood
Edited by John F. D. Taff and Anthony Rivera
Grey Matter Press
August, 2016
Reviewed by C.M. Saunders

I have the utmost respect for Grey Matter Press. They work with some of the biggest and best names in the business, from writers and editors all the way through to designers and cover artists—everything they do oozes quality. That's one reason why I was so keen to get my hands on this book. That, and the fact that it contains some of my favourite writers. I was also intrigued by the concept; originality is something often sadly lacking in these kinds of anthologies and, it has to be said, in horror fiction in general. To cut a long story short, author John F. D. Taff went out for pizza one night, and decided to use the establishment's washroom. There, he saw the words I CAN TASTE THE BLOOD scrawled on the wall. The statement (or was it an admission?) stirred something in him, and he took a picture on his phone. Fast forward several years, and what we end up with is five different novellas by five different writers, all sharing the same title. Essentially, this book is five unique voices, all riffing off the same idea.

Opening the collection is current darling of the scene, Josh Malerman. That title is no slight, by the way—it is entirely deserved. He first found success as frontman of the rock band the High Strung, but writing was always his calling. Apparently, he wrote forty unpublished novels before 2015's *Bird Box* earned him a Stoker nomination, widespread acclaim, and a (rumoured) movie deal. His effort here is a bleak tale of trickery amongst desert travellers. It seems to be set in the Biblical era, though the time frame, and other details like the location and age of the protagonists, is deliberately left to the reader's discretion. It is written in such a way as these things don't seem important, or even relevant. The fundamental questions are the same, chief among them being if you had a young family to protect and someone knocked on your door in the middle of the night asking for help, would you answer it? This one will live long in the memory.

Next to throw his hat in the ring is twenty-something New Yorker Daniel J. Stone with a story of obsession, addiction, sadomasochism and destructive love. His borderline-poetic prose is often a joy to read but be warned, the graphic depictions of gay sex might add another element of discomfort, apart from all the death and mutilation going on. It's enough to make a straight man squirm. Heck, it's probably enough to make a gay man squirm, too. You keep thinking "surely, he isn't going to go there". Oh, but he does. He does go there, and he takes you along for the bloody ride. In the afterword, which is supplied by every author, Stone describes how painful, even torturous, the writing process is for him, something which certainly comes through on the page. Equal parts unsettling and fascinating.

At first glance, the contribution from Joe Schwartz doesn't really belong in what is essentially a horror collection. His gritty depiction of the seedy underbelly of modern America would perhaps be more at home in a noir crime anthology. But to classify it that way would be doing the author, and his story, a great disservice. There are no ghosts or demons, no witches or werewolves. There aren't even any zombies. Whaat? But this story doesn't need them. Instead, it focuses on the dark side of human nature and rams home the fact that people are capable of far worse horrors than any fictional entity. When all is said and done, this story is one of my favourites in the entire collection.

On we go, and next up is a story by Erik T. Johnson. With the release of his debut collection of fiction imminent, Johnson is a comparative newbie yet displays the range of skills you would expect to find in writers far more experienced and accomplished. He has an impressive turn of phrase, and creates a multi-layered tale full of metaphors and symbolism centered on the weird relationship between a mother and her son. Unfortunately, he lays it on a little thick for my liking and the result is dense, difficult to follow, and never really grips the reader. Not this one, anyway. It's almost as if he's trying too hard, and in my opinion he could benefit a lot from being more direct and honing in more on the crux of what he is trying to say rather than skirting around the edges. Johnson definitely has talent, and his potential could lead him to being a future trailblazer.

The last word goes to Taff himself, one of the leading names in horror and author of over eighty published short stories as well as four novels. His reputation is such that he has earned the moniker 'King of Pain,' and it is entirely justified. If the other contributions to this collection sometimes stray toward the trippy and fantastic, Taff walks up to that line and pisses all over it. Conversely, however, his story also harks back to classic pulp horror in that it is essentially a creature feature which gradually builds to an earth-shattering climax. Like all good stories, there is a message buried deep within the lines.

All in all, *I Can Taste the Blood* is a remarkable offering from one of the finest publishers of dark fiction on the planet. It can either be utilised as an introduction to some of the best new (and old) talent out there or taken it as a whole, in which case you get a load of high weirdness thrown at you with zero fucks given. Which is just how horror should be.

◇◇◇◇◇◇◇◇◇◇◇◇◇◇◇◇◇◇◇◇◇◇◇◇◇◇◇◇◇◇◇◇◇◇◇◇

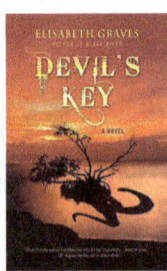

Devil's Key
Elisabeth Graves
Northampton House Press
September 8th, 2016
Reviewed by Stuart Conover

Elisabeth Graves originally published *Devil's Key* in 1999 as Svart Frikt, though this was recently translated into an English release. Without any details it is an interesting tale of a young college student working on her thesis.

First let me say that don't let the synopsis of the novel (which can be found online) fool you, as the writing within the book is quite a bit clearer than the synopsis itself which almost had me not checking it out. If I didn't have a special place in my heart for reading about authors or writers within a horror setting, I might not have read it and I'm honestly glad I decided to give it a try.

The book follows Lucy Fowler, and actually starts off quite dark as Lucy is raped and almost murdered. That isn't the focus on the story though but is there to put her in the mindset we see her in throughout the novel. She is almost done with her thesis but with only one interview left to finish it off, and the midwife she has to interview being on an island in Florida, she felt that getting away might help her move past and be able to finish this chapter of her life. Only, the person she is set to interview is now confined to a psychiatric ward which throws her entire plan into chaos.

Due to a hurricane, Lucy becomes trapped there. During her stay she finds there is a ghost town whose residents all disappeared years before, and when deciding to write about it, things take a turn from the worse. An ancient evil, an ancient curse, and so much more all come into play as Lucy tries to get to the bottom of what happened.

This novel isn't for everyone but some great writing and character development will have you wanting to find out what happens to the woman whose life is turned upside down right from the start. If you are in the mood for a different take on horror without following the same tropes we always see, *Devil's Key* is worth checking out.

Disclaimer: Elisabeth Graves is a sponsor for the JournalStone Network

◇◇◇◇◇◇◇◇◇◇◇◇◇◇◇◇◇◇◇◇◇◇◇◇◇◇◇◇◇◇◇◇◇◇◇◇

The Best Horror of the Year: Volume Eight
Edited by Ellen Datlow
Night Shade Books
June 7, 2016
Reviewed by William Grabowski

Ellen Datlow is one of the hardest-working, iconic figures in Horror, Dark Fantasy, and elsewhere. When she speaks well of a certain author, I—by default—make a point to seek out writing by that person. Datlow won, on August 20, a Hugo Award for Best Editor, Short-Form.

Hence number eight in Night Shade Book's annual compilation, and 20 tales curated from print, online and, perhaps, cobwebbed nowheres isolated in extragalactic gloom. Opening with "Summation 2015," the editor replays that year's incredible fertility. These summations are pure gifts highlighting output both well-known and obscure—notepad opportunities aplenty.

What distinguishes Datlow-edited anthologies from most (not all) others is the mix of newer and not-so-new names tilting toward those less known. Among these are standouts like Gary McMahon, whose "My Boy Builds Coffins" begins as a claustrophobic set-piece and a boy with a fresh hobby as distressing as it is incomprehensible. Dread rises cold behind Mother's and Father's facile dismissals. I was glad having my smug "I know where *this* is going" certainty obliterated by McMahon's sure handling of what feels like inverted folklore howling with phobic panic and loss. A nice setup for Tamsyn Muir's epistolary, "The Woman in the Hill," whose brave and empathetic women search for the missing after crossing an ominous threshold in a Waikopua hillside. Their horrifying encounters evoke awe, an indelible terror and mystery invading emotional control. The darkly mythic gravity reflects that of all ancient, or infrequently explored, landscapes onto which we project fantasies, fears, and despair—or is it the other way around?

"Wilderness remained a place of evil and spiritual catharsis," warns Letitia Trent's "Wilderness." *"Any place in which a person feels stripped, lost, or perplexed, might be called a wilderness"*—which defines the events centering on a lone young woman waiting in a small community airport. In a very few pages, Trent manages a chilly unease as recently jobless Krista surveys the others—family types scarfing pizza, absorbed by cell phones, some casting suspicious glances and—following a break outdoors after the expected flight is announced as late-coming—questions at the single woman's apparent menace. When police wearing gasmasks show up, and assure everything's okay, the collective fear increases. Returning from the bathroom, Krista finds herself victimized by hysteria born of 9/11 and our sense of ever-intrusive surveillance. If you're looking for an example of literary horror as mirror of psychosocial trauma, here it is. A masterful, unsettling work.

Speaking of unsettling, Laird Barron's "In a Cavern, In a Canyon," for me pulled off the exceedingly unlikely "trick" of evoking revulsion simultaneous with existential nausea. Akin to the tales from McMahon, Muir, and Neil Gaiman's novelette "Black Dog," Barron's morphs the potently folkloric into contemporary horror whose elements of deadpan absurdity tear apart our casual assumptions of the universe as a mostly rational "place." We very much like his smart, rough-edged protagonist still struggling in middle-age to unpuzzle her father's strange disappearance, and life itself. She makes a tough decision, and choked my jaded heart. Barron's ability to create a visceral sense of mystery—unfathomable, even anguished—is startling.

Other standouts in a volume of same: Reggie Oliver's "The Rooms Are High," Priya Sharma's "Fabulous Beasts," Stephen Bacon's "Lord of the Sand," Brian Hodge's "This Stagnant Breath of Change," and Carmen Maria Machado's "Descent."

The maturity, craft, and frightening imaginative power so evident in these writers gives me hope for the future of short fiction.

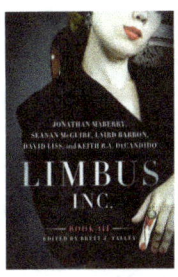

Limbus, Inc., Book III: A Shared World Experience
Edited by Brett Talley
JournalStone
July, 2016
Reviewed by Michael R. Collings

I am a fan of the first two *Limbus, Inc.*, anthologies. I've looked forward to each, read each with particular enjoyment, and written at length about each. When I received a copy of *Limbus, Inc., Book III*, I had two immediate reactions: first, pleasure at seeing a couple of old friends named on the cover; and, second, concern over whether the excellences sustained in the first two volumes would be sustained in a third.

As it turned out, the list of 'friends' increased as I read stories by several writers I was largely unfamiliar with and whose tales intrigued and invited; and any concerns I had about excellences quickly evaporated.

The *Limbus, Inc.*, anthologies are singular in their treatment of narrative. I am reminded, of all things, of Geoffrey Chaucer's splendid *Canterbury Tales*, with its surface story of a pilgrimage to Canterbury, broken at precise intervals by stories related by each of the pilgrims. There is no pilgrimage in the *Limbus, Inc.*, anthologies, but there is a quest—to discover, reveal, and otherwise explore the extent of Limbus, Inc., a mysterious, seemingly all-knowing, virtually all-powerful employment agency that has no apparent limits in time or space.

Brett Talley contributes the connective interludes in the anthology as he follows Malone, a Birmingham detective, who tackles the cryptic and particularly gruesome case of a young woman found murdered at a long-abandoned mine. The only clues: a mysterious image carved into her back, and, as the bottom of the shaft, a zip-lock bag containing papers. All that is legible through the plastic and the blood are the words "Inch by Inch and Row by Row."

Turn the page…and there is Seanan McGuire's "Inch by Inch and Row by Row," an impressive re-imagining of themes from Nathaniel Hawthorne's small horror masterpiece, "Rappaccini's Daughter." Beatrice Walden is perfectly named: "Beatrice" suggests 'bringer of joy,'

and "Walden" echoes Thoreau's pastoral landscape—here inverted to something threatening and death-bringing. Walden has been genetically altered until her body can reproduce toxic substances for her father's research. Even though he is dead, she is still imprisoned by his wishes… until a representative of Limbus, Inc., offers her a way to join human society. As with her father's, however, Limbus's wishes fail to account for Walden as an individual, as a person with her own wishes. As she develops her strengths and abilities, she becomes self-sufficient for the first time in her life, ultimately turning the tables on Limbus, Inc.

In Tally's transitional "First Interlude: Whispers in the City of the Dead," Malone receives a message with an attachment titled "Infamous," sent by 'Jack Rabbit'—a connection backward to Book II and forward to David Liss's aptly named "Infamous." In Liss's story, Chip Dunstan is famous—rather, infamous—for having shot a young black man three years earlier. Now, unemployed, he lives with his mother, binge-eats Doritos, and blames everyone else for his hard times. Limbus, Inc., steps in and offers him a job at a phenomenal salary. All he has to do is live on the premises of a research institute, follow a few non-intrusive rules, and take care of test animals. But Chip isn't satisfied to have his needs fulfilled: he doesn't like his housemates, he doesn't respond well when a co-worker rejects his advances, he just can't keep himself from poking into things—and rooms—that are off limits. But he has excuses for doing so. He always has excuses. Until he discovers the *real* reason behind his aberrant behavior.

Talley's "Second Interlude: It is Written" discloses that Chip Dunstan is more than a character in a story—he is a real person in Malone's world, one who had earned Malone's special hatred. By now, Malone is at a bookstore in Boston tracking another clue to the vicious death of the young woman…which leads him to another story.

Keith R. A. DeCandido's "Right On, Sister!" begins in 1978. Wanda Jackson is barely holding her life together. Her boyfriend was killed during the blackout the year before, and now she lives with her harridan mother, working two jobs to keep herself and her grandmother in food. Life just gets worse, until finally she is contacted by Limbus, Inc., to interview for a job. Her special skill: she can talk people out of—and into—committing crucial actions at the precise moment needed. Unfortunately, that skill takes her into the darkest night of her life.

The "Third Interlude: The Unblinking Eye" aims Malone more directly toward the enigmatic "Jack Rabbit," and into the fourth story, Jonathan Maberry's "The Unlearnable Truths from the Case Files of Sam Hunter." Hunter reprises his role in the first two Limbus volumes as an intrepid, hard-bitten (and hard-biting) detective… and werewolf. He is sitting in his office contemplating sleep when the phone rings. Limbus. With a job. He is to interrupt one of several gangs collecting old books… *dangerous*, old books, with names like *Necronomicon*. Occasionally one of the bad guys utters a phrase beginning with "*Pn'nglui mglw'nafh Cthulhu R'lyeh*," which is itself sufficient to let readers know that nothing less is at stake than the continued existence of humanity in the universe. And only Sam Hunter can ensure that. The longest in the volume, Maberry's novella gives a master storyteller the scope to explore the complexities of tales-within-tales-within-tales, and he manages it effortlessly.

In the "Fourth Interlude: Down the Rabbit Hole," Malone struggles with the fact that if the manuscripts he is discovering are true—and Limbus, Inc., actually exists—then he must make room in his understanding of the world for magical books and werewolves. And in the meantime, he heads to a small Eastern European town where he hopes to find out more about Jack Rabbit.

He does. And receives the manuscript for the most ambitious, and the most difficult, of the stories, Laird Barron's "An Atlatl." Beyond the superficial difficulty of rapidly repeating its title three times, Laird's contribution takes the Limbus tales up a notch by adding a new dimension…literally. Readers have already learned that Limbus encompasses time and space, that it includes the 'real' and the mythical. Now Barron thrusts them into the intricacies of a story told simultaneously (as it were) within the multiverse, in an infinity of nearly identical earths with nearly identical characters moving through nearly identical narratives—emphasis on *nearly*.

The final segment, Talley's "Epilogue: Call Us," wraps up Malone's tale as he finally unravels the mystery of the young woman's death, takes private vengeance upon her killers (and in doing so ensures the end of his career with the police), and receives his own call from Limbus, Inc. After all, he is now unemployed. And they employ.

Individually, the stories are engaging, different enough as stand-alone tales to keep interest high, yet logically linked by Talley's interludes. The volume is a worthy successor to the first two, and raises hopes for a fourth.

Highly recommended.

Disclaimer: This is a JournalStone book, however the views expressed belong solely to the reviewer.

A Feast of Sorrows
Angela Slatter
Prime Books
October, 2016
Reviewed by Mario Guslandi

Here it comes, at last: the first Angela Slatter book published in the USA. An excellent Australian writer whose superb dark stories have appeared in various British anthologies and collections, Slatter is known as the author of a genre of fiction lying somewhere between horror and fantasy, often taking the shape of adult fairy tales.

A Feast of Sorrows assembles fourteen stories, two originals and twelve reprints, which provide a fascinating showcase of Slatter's extraordinary talent as a gifted storyteller and a devoted scholar of the mysteries of human soul.

"Sourdough" is a delightful fable where true love triumphs over evil and witchcraft, while "Dresses, three" is a gentle yarn about love and overwhelming desire, served with a touch of magic.

The delicious "The Badger's Bride" features a girl whose task is to copy a mysterious, ancient book, and the vivid "By My Voice I Shall be Known" depicts a case of cheated love ending with a terrible vengeance.

"Bluebeard's Daughter" nicely revisits the old pirate's tale by elaborating on the deeds of his last wife and her son, while "Light as Mist, Heavy as Hope" provides an enchanting new version of the classic Rumpelstiltskin story. In the powerful fantasy piece "Sister Sister," a former princess is abandoned by her husband and bewitched by her wicked, inhuman sister. The British Fantasy Award-winning "The Coffin-Maker's Daughter" masterfully blends death and lust within the frame of the professional duty of a dismal job. Part of a forthcoming new collection, "The Tallow-Wife" is a remarkable narrative tour de force—it's a dark comedy portraying the downfall of a family, some members of which hide unspeakable secrets. One of the sequels to that novelette, the offbeat "Bearskin," is also included in this volume.

A Feast of Sorrows is a real treat for the reader fond of great storytelling on the dark side of life. Needless to add, it is highly recommended.

A Season with the Witch: The Magic and Mayhem of Halloween in Salem, Massachusetts
J.W. Ocker
The Countryman Press
October 2016
Reviewed by David Goudsward

J.W. Ocker doesn't do things halfway. His previous book, *Poe-Land*, won an Edgar Award for his travels up and down the east coast, visiting locations significant to Edgar Allan Poe, and explaining why they are significant to those associated with the area. This time, Ocker took the opposite approach—he moved his apparently very patient wife and children to Salem, Massachusetts, and stayed for the entire month of October. October is to Salem what Mardi Gras is to New Orleans—a frenetic collection of eclectic people, places, and activities that build momentum and culminate in a concentrated release of weirdness. And instead of going to Salem, the Ockers lived downtown, totally immersed at Halloween's ground zero.

Ocker isn't looking to do a travelogue on which haunted attractions are tourist traps and which bookstores are the creepiest. He is looking for what makes Salem so uniquely Salem by experiencing it firsthand. *A Season with the Witch* does that by chronicling his travels among the shops, sites, and gravestones, carefully interspersed with chats with the denizens, critics, and characters of Salem. From carnies and occultists, to archivists and elected officials, to street preachers and shop owners, Ocker carefully records their often conflicting observations.

Be it ghost tours, cemeteries, historical sites, filming locations, museums, gift shops, street performances, parades, haunted houses, or wax museums—if it happened in Salem, Ocker sampled it, and then wrote about it in his deceptively casual style with the appropriately gentle humor side comments.

Can it be used as a travel guide to Witch City? Absolutely, but you risk missing the sites because you are engrossed in the book. Better to read it first and use a mundane travel guide.

There are not many books that can gracefully segue from Cotton Mather and *The Scarlet Letter* to Elizabeth Montgomery and Laurie Cabot, but this is Salem, where oddness is a lifestyle, and J.W. Ocker is a masterful observer of the foibles, frailties, and fears of the human condition.

〰〰〰〰〰〰〰〰〰〰〰〰〰〰〰〰〰〰〰〰〰〰〰

Arkham Nights: Tales of Mythos Noir
Glynn Owen Barrass & Ron Shiflet
Celaeno Press
2016
Reviewed by Brian M. Sammons

Celaeno Press is a relatively new small press publisher who has been up to bat twice before this latest release. With their first release, *Beyond the Mountains of Madness*, they took a terrifying return trip to one of H.P. Lovecraft's more famous locales of lunacy. They followed that up with a party *In the Court of the Yellow King*, an anthology of tales inspired by Robert W. Chambers' primrose patriarch. This new book, a collection of Cthulhu Mythos collaborations by authors Glynn Owen Barrass and Ron Shiflet, prove that Celaeno Press' third time is also a charm.

Arkham Nights collects seven chunky tales of noir-tinged Cthulhu mythos madness, and I love it for that. I like all flavors of Lovecraftian inspired/infused fiction, from the more traditional tales to the very experimental oddities, and everything in between. One of my favorite subgenres of this subgenre is the hard-boiled tough guy vs. cosmic horror story, and that's where these tales would fall. Yes, the unstoppable forces of the Cthulhu Mythos are usually not vanquished here, so fear not Lovecraftian purists, but these protagonists are not the typical fainting milquetoast academics that populate so many similar tales. They are far more capable, sometimes even badass, and that makes these stories that much more frightening. These are the heroes that in other tales should win, but here, more often than not, the best they can do is survive and live to fight another day. If you like the tough and gritty mixed up with the unnameable and insane, *Arkham Nights* is the book for you.

As for the authors, Glynn Owen Barrass is one of the best authors working in weird fiction today. Full disclosure: I've worked with him on a number of projects over the years, but please don't take this as me pitching for a friend. Take that as more proof of just how good he is at what he does. Do you think I would team up with someone that would make me look bad? With someone I didn't have total and absolute respect for? Hell no. It is because Glynn is such a gifted story teller that I feel blessed and honored to have worked with him.

Ron Shiflet I do not know as well, but every one of his stories I've ever read I have liked. This book has only reminded me of the fact that I need to seek out and read more from this author as soon as possible. That is something I would recommend everyone doing.

In *Arkham Nights*, Shiflet and Barrass blend together seamlessly and deliver seven very good Noir-drenched tales of cosmic horror. It's hard-boiled PIs vs horrors from beyond time and space, what's not to love about that? This might be a little book, topping just over 200 pages, but it is fairly priced and well worth every penny for fans of pulpy horror. You can get it at any of the best online book sellers, or you can visit the home of Celaeno Press at www.celaenopress.com

Arkham Nights is highly recommended.

〰〰〰〰〰〰〰〰〰〰〰〰〰〰〰〰〰〰〰〰〰〰〰

Out of Tune: Book II
Edited by Jonathan Maberry
JournalStone Publishing
May, 2016
Reviewed by Michael R. Collings

When I was first approached about reviewing Jonathan Maberry's anthology of horror and fantasy tales, *Out of Tune*, I was a bit wary. Not from worry about the quality of the work; Maberry has an excellent ear for storytelling, and the list of contributors included a number of authors whose tales I have enjoyed—Eric J. Guignard, James A. Moore, David J. Schow, to list only a few of the fifteen masterful writers.

No, I was concerned more by the theme: folk music. I have loved music all of my life…but mostly classical. And because of my deafness I've not listened to much of anything for a decade. So the idea of stories based on old folk tunes was intimidating.

Then I flipped through the book, just to get a sense of what it contained. The first things I noted were the eerie B/W illustrations by John Coulthart preceding each tale. Without having read the stories, I was impressed by the evocative nature of the drawings, already being drawn into the mood of the anthology. Next came the commentaries at the end of each story, written by Nancy Keim Comley, giving a brief history of the tunes that inspired the authors, quoting lines when relevant, providing a list of artists who have performed them.

And I found my hesitance dissipating. I recognized several of the songs: "Red River Valley," "House of the Rising Sun," and—curiously enough—an old favorite from graduate school, a medieval ballad called "The Twa Corbies."

Okay, this was beginning to get interesting. But still… so many horror writers seem to use snatches of lyrics—often rock or metal, which I've never listened to at all—as a kind of shortcut to characterization, or as chapter headings, leaving me with the sense that I am missing something important by not being able to hum along, as it were.

Maberry answers this final concern in his in his lyrical introduction when he writes:

…on the whole the stories they wrote are independent of the source material. They picked old ballads and songs as inspiration, but none of them sat down to do a straight adaptation. Instead they used some element or feeling within the ballads as a stepping off point. And from there…

Wow.

Magic.

Now *that* I could understand. So I began reading.

Allison Pang's "Respawn, Reboot" seems at first about as far from folk music as possible. It is a complex tale of the current generation's obsession with RPGs and MMOs—with only an occasional touch of banshees and things dark and mysterious. Yet as the story progresses, the two themes draw closer until, in the final paragraphs, they merge into a perfect crescendo of horror, followed by the after-note, which reveals the source poem, W. B. Yeats' "The Stolen Child." And the three parts of the story-experience—introductory illustration, the tale itself, and the information about the song/poem that inspired it—combine to create a whole greater than the sum of its parts. A similar fusion works for all of the stories, which creates a great part of the attractiveness of *Out of Tune, Book 2*.

Cherie M. Priest's "The Knoxville Girl," is a close cousin to Ambrose Bierce's classic horror tale, "An Occurrence at Owl Creek Bridge." In the space of time it takes a young man to shower—and remove any lingering traces of blood—Priest compresses four generations of women suffering abuse at the hands of the men they have chosen, until the final link in the chain must accept it as inevitable or end it forever.

In "The Beams of the Sun," Dan Abnett uses "The Bitter Withy" to create an unnerving story of a dead folk singer; his bitter and vicious wife, Marie; and their thirty-three-year-old son, Jason. Biblical echoes emerge gradually in this tale of near-blasphemous lyrics, a lost book of powerful songs, and a collector's obsession with discovering truth.

David Mack's "Midnight Rider" returns to the nineteenth century for a formidable story of a wealthy rancher, his only daughter, and the man she has chosen for her husband. It incorporates Old West morality, contemporary concerns about racial equality and justice, and the time-honored horror trope of the dead returning to claim its own.

Delilah S. Dawson's "Just Another Black Umbrella" is a weirdly entrancing tale of love and loss, centering around a rigidly correct and controlled funeral-home director and a woman who suddenly appears in his life and just as suddenly disappears.

In Eric Guignard's "The House of the Rising Sun," opium dreams take on a reality that shatters the dreamer, who returns to the house again and again, desperate to fill gaps in his life but able only to find illusion.

Josh Malerman's "Who Is Bringing Milk to Me?" captures the ghostly feeling of Conrad Aiken's "Silent Snow, Secret Snow" in the image of a paralyzed girl whose high point each week is listening to the approach of the milkman, first his footsteps drawing nearer, then his whistle. Aiken's story ends with madness; Malerman's, with something much worse.

"A Tale of Three Deaths," by Rachel Aukes, turns a sordid case of suburban infidelity into a far more threatening story of demonic manipulation and of betrayal for the sake of betrayal; while James A. Moore's "In the Woods, Somewhere" openly embraces the outré and the eldritch as a hard-bitten retired detective recounts his single experience within the perilous realm of færie.

And so they go.

Illustration, story, commentary—all working together to create fifteen unique experiences in visual and aural darkness, building on generations of murder ballads, poems of the uncanny and the inexplicable, songs of love and loss.

The result is an amalgam of the odd and the unexpected that provides shivers, frissons, and delight.

Recommended.

Neil Gaiman's Troll Bridge
Written by Neil Gaiman
Illustrated by Colleen Doran
Dark Horse Books
October 18, 2016
Reviewed by Elaine Pascale

Troll Bridge is Neil Gaiman's anti-*The Giving Tree*—instead of selfishly taking from a loving authority figure, this eerie and melancholy look at aging has a young boy bargaining with a troll at pivotal points in his life. The boy, Jack, prevents the troll from "eating his life," but as he ages, he becomes despondent and loses his shiny wide-eyed niceness. Jack's focus is self-preservation—a goal that becomes less and less honorable as he ages into a sad, unlikeable man.

Author Neil Gaiman is always wonderful, but it is Colleen Doran's treatment of the story that takes it to another level. Her illustrations tell the tale so effectively that words are nearly not needed. When the boy is young and hopeful, she uses quaint greens and yellows. She details the individual pebbles drawn on the train tracks that no longer run, isolating towns from each other and allowing magical thoughts to percolate in the mind of a boy accustomed to playing alone. When he is an adolescent, each petal on the fertile flowers are visible. The plush feathered hair and soft pink bubble gum of the girl he desires highlight the hormone-laden romanticism. When the boy becomes a man, the colors are muted and the images focus on the skeletal trees and claustrophobic row houses that resemble gigantic grave stones.

The positioning of the first person narrator is evocative and leads a reader to the denouement without giving too much away. The young boy will turn his face to woodland creatures and running brooks, drawing the viewer's eyes to Doran's impressive work. The adult man looks down to his shoes, drawing the narrative into his disgruntled detachment from others.

Doran's attention to detail is inspiring. Her artwork flows with a realism that gives the troll gravitas when needed, but also establishes the creature in the realm of magic. At times the troll is scary and threatening, at others, pathetic and needy. The troll's transformation contrasts nicely with Jack's development, and may not have reached the same success if left to a lesser artist.

While *Troll Bridge* is the anti-*The Giving Tree*, both stories speak of the weariness of life. That said, Doran's artwork is the antithesis of weary, its vibrancy breathes new life into an already memorable tale. ◆

Horror, Science Fiction, Fantasy

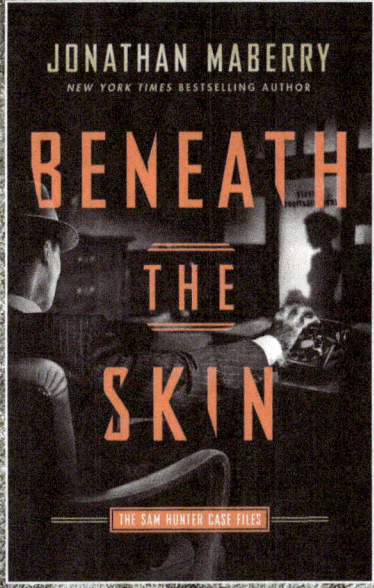

December 2016

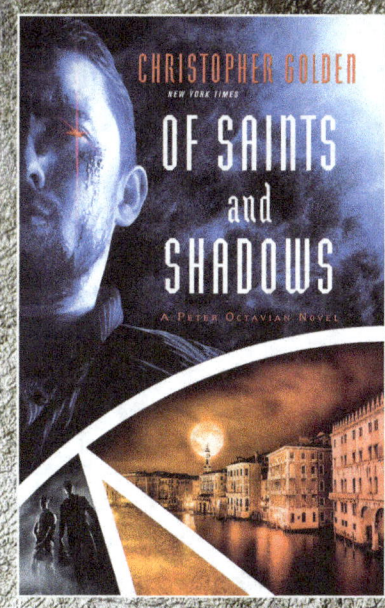

September 2016

November 2016

OCTOBER 2016

SEPTEMBER 2016

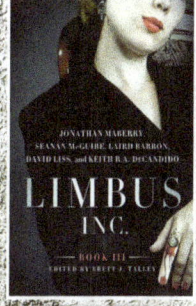

JULY 2016

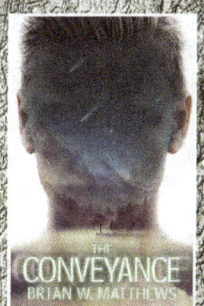

JUNE 2016

MAY 2016

MAY 2016

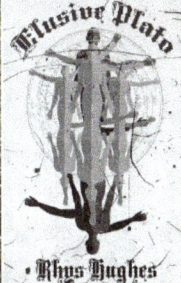

MAY 2016

APRIL 2016

DoubleDown Series, Book VIII
APRIL 2016

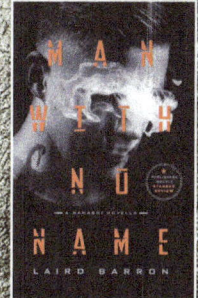

MARCH 2016

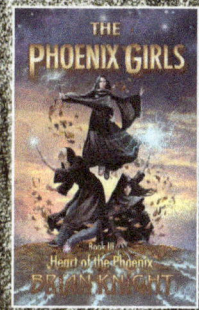

FEBRUARY 2016

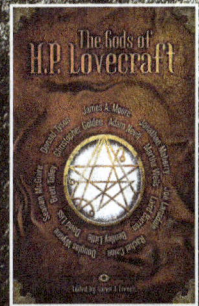

DECEMBER 2015

DECEMBER 2015

JOURNALSTONE
YOUR LINK TO ARTISTIC TALENT

WWW.JOURNALSTONE.COM

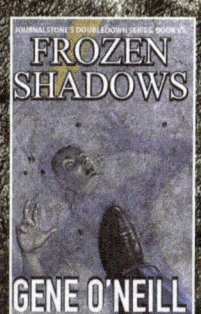

DoubleDown Series, Book VII
SEPTEMBER 2015